these are
my confessions

these are my confessions

Joy King, Electa Rome Parks, Cheryl Robinson, Méta Smith

red

AVON

An Imprint of HarperCollinsPublishers

HarperCollins books may be purchased for educational, business, or sales promotional use. For information please write: Special Markets Department, HarperCollins Publishers, 10 East 53rd Street, New York, NY 10022.

FIRST EDITION

Interior text designed by Diahann Sturge

Library of Congress Cataloging-in-Publication Data

These are my confessions / by Joy King . . . [et al.]—1st ed.
  p. cm.
ISBN: 978-0-06-119311-8
ISBN-10: 0-06-119311-9
1. African Americans—Fiction. 2. Erotic stories, American.   I. King, Joy, 1978-

PS648.E7T475   2007
813'.6080353808996073—dc22   2006037867

07 08 09 10 11   ❖/RRD   10 9 8 7 6 5 4 3 2 1

Contents

Love B-Ball Style

    by Joy King   1

These Are My Confessions

    by Electa Rome Parks   77

Strapped

    by Cheryl Robinson   173

Divas Need Love Too

    by Méta Smith   251

Love B-Ball Style

Joy King

These Are My Confessions is dedicated to all my faithful readers who have shown me so much love in my short span in the literary world. Thank you—your support is greatly appreciated!! Much Love.

First Quarter

Triple Threat

"Once again Glen Goodman has delivered the goods. Like a quiet storm, Goodman came in and stole a pass from an unsuspecting Dexter Jackson, then tiptoed down the sidelines to get loose for a slam dunk," the game's commentator roared. The sound of the crowd put your mind in the state of being at the circus, watching the trapeze artists at work, and watching the greatest show on earth. But instead of being at a Barnum and Bailey production, you were center court for the NBA playoff game between the Chicago Titans and Atlanta Phantoms, with Glen Goodman dominating the scene.

"That's right, baby, work that ball," Sasha screamed, twisting her ample chest to the beat of the team's anthem. All eyes zoomed in on the Beyonce clone because not only did her low-rise skintight jeans and midriff top leave little to the imagination, it was a well known fact that she was Glen's significant other. Sasha had sat in the same courtside seat at every Phantom home game since moving to Atlanta a year ago. Once you got over the pretty face, ten pounds of blond highlighted weave, and the to-die-for body, which included a perfected pair of 34D salines, nobody understood what Glen saw in her. Sasha put the *S* in superficial, with her fake hair, boobs, phony attitude, and, if the rumors were correct, had been an industry groupie before she landed the most sought after bachelor in the NBA.

She blew Glen a kiss as their eyes briefly connected as the crowd stood up and cheered following Glen's slam dunk, the winning shot to seal the deal for the playoff win. Now, only the championship battle was left, and Sasha hoped that not only would her man win the NBA title, but that she in turn would capture the brass ring.

"Girl, let's go," she said to her friend Tracy, who was the girlfriend of one of Glen's teammates. "I want to be right there when Glen exits the locker room. You know all those damn hoochies are going to be swarming him."

"You know it. You better go let those tricks know it's all about you."

"Yeah, that's why I flashed these." Sasha pointed to her bountiful breasts. "To let everybody up in this stadium know what's up." The two ladies clicked their four inch heels on the polished floor as they walked toward the hallway outside the locker room. Some news cameras were waiting for the players to come out, but all hoped to get one of superstar Glen Goodman's classic lines to run with on the eleven o'clock news, ESPN, and tomorrow's newspaper.

"Here he comes now!" one of the reporters yelled.

Glen came out looking like the suave, confident superstar that he was. He paused for a moment and flashed his signature smile, which could brighten even the darkest tunnels.

"Glen, how does it feel to not only hit the winning shot but to score an amazing game high of eighty-five points? You've now beaten Kobe Bryant's record, and are only second to Wilt Chamberlain," the same reporter said.

"Honestly, it's not about the high score it's about my team winning," Glen replied. "I went into overdrive because the Phantoms were lethargic. I had to step it up. I don't believe in losing, especially when I'm on the court," he added in his usual overconfident way.

"Your team—so now the Atlanta Phantoms is your team?" one reporter said sarcastically.

Without missing a beat, Glen countered, "I'm the captain, so yes, it's my team. The players turn to me for leadership, and like the mailman, I always deliver, even on holidays." Then he winked and smiled to his many admirers.

"Okay, no more questions. Mr. Goodman has to go," Glen's personal assistant, Bianca, interceded. Although she'd only been working with Glen for a few weeks, she knew that his arrogance would soon be the centerpiece of every comment he made. No matter how irritating Glen Goodman could be, nobody could deny that he had it all—charisma, talent, and skills that superseded the basketball court. He was definitely a triple threat.

"Glen's new assistant kills me," Sasha snapped as Bianca hurried him away from the thirsty reporters. "She always tries to run everything. You would think she was his agent instead of a lowly assistant. I get so tired of her holding his hand like he's in second grade and she's schoolteacher."

"I feel you," Tracy said. "I'm glad Isaac doesn't have one of those. How did she get that job anyway? I thought he had some older lady as his assistant."

"He did—Ms. Pearl—but the old goose checked out," Sasha said, smacking her lips.

"What? She died? How?"

"Nah, she's not dead. Ms. Pearl had been Glen's father's assistant when he played in the league up until he retired. Then when Glen started playing, she became his assistant. She is damn near sixty years old and had no business being in the hustle and bustle of an on-the-go player like Glen. All those long hours finally got the best of her and she had to take it down. Her niece was a recent college graduate, and I guess couldn't find no job even with her little degree, so Ms. Pearl let her take over the position. It's only supposed to be temporary, but the bitch doesn't seem to be going anywhere."

"That's a trip. You don't mind Glen spending so much time with her?"

"I can't front, it does annoy me. But luckily, she isn't Glen's speed. He's not into those conservative librarian types. He likes sexy divas like myself, so whatever to her."

"Yeah, I feel you," Tracy said, then moved away, to give Sasha some privacy as Bianca led Glen in her direction. Tracy sat on a bench in the corner, watching from the sideline.

A gaggle of cute girls waved at him as he crossed their paths, and Sasha quickly walked forward to claim her property.

"Hi, baby, you played so good tonight," she said before placing a seductive kiss on Glen's lips.

Bianca discreetly rolled her eyes. "Well, Glen," she said, "you seem to be in good hands now, so I'll be heading home."

"Yeah, he is in good hands now, Bianca. Thanks for watching my man for me until I could get to him."

Bianca kept her eyes on Glen, ignoring Sasha's comment, which infuriated her.

"So I'll see you in the morning," Glen said to his assistant. "I want to go over a few things before we start playing the championship games."

"No problem. I'll see you then," Bianca replied, and walked off with Sasha burning a hole in her back.

"Why was miss thing over there playing like she was your publicist or something?" Sasha demanded. "I mean she's only your assistant."

"She's more than my assistant," Glen explained. "Bianca is very skilled. She has a master's degree in marketing, so I feel comfortable giving her more responsibilities. Ms. Pearl was great because she was like a second mother, but Bianca is dope."

"So what, you're thinking of keeping her permanently?"

"That's what I wanted to speak with her about tomorrow. I was hoping she would consider working for me on a long-term basis. I like the way she handles my business, especially with the media. It's hard to find a reliable and proficient assistant. But she has the skills to do multiple jobs."

"She seems a little too boring to work for you."

"I'm looking for someone to handle my business, not go to the clubs with me, I have you for that," Glen said, then kissed Sasha and put his arm around her waist.

"Where's Isaac at?" Tracy inquired, walking up to the couple.

"He should be out any minute. So are we going to celebrate being one step closer to the championship or what?" Glen asked Sasha.

"You know it, baby."

"I'm down, if Isaac would hurry up," Tracy said.

"Cool, let's do this."

When Bianca got home, the first thing she did was pour herself a glass of wine. It was becoming an after-game ritual. The stress of dealing with a high profile athlete was taking a toll on her. She didn't understand how her aunt had survived for so long. She was counting the days down, looking forward to when she would no longer have to play babysitter to an overbearing, egotistical basketball player, but didn't know who was more annoying—Glen, or his bimbo Barbie girlfriend. What she did know was that the sooner she finished her temporary role as Glen's personal assistant, the better.

Bianca kicked off her shoes and sat on the couch, about to unwind, when her phone rang. "Who in the hell could that be, calling me so late?" she mumbled to herself as she picked up the receiver. "Hello."

"Hi, honey, are you sleep?"

Bianca instantly recognized the voice on the other end. "Aunt Pearl, why are you calling so late? It's almost midnight."

"I know, baby, but I need to speak to you."

Bianca eyed the receiver suspiciously. Her aunt sounded so serious, she wondered what was so urgent that she couldn't wait until morning. It made her think about her aunt's health.

"Are you okay?" she asked, worried. "Have you been feeling sick again? Do you need me to come over?"

Bianca's heart was now thumping. Aunt Pearl was like a mother to her, and had been for ten years, since her mother—Pearl's younger sister—had died at the hands of Bianca's abusive father. She'd only been fourteen at the time. After her father was found guilty of murder and sentenced to life in prison, Bianca went to live with her aunt. Both of them were devastated by her mother's death and found comfort in each other. To help ease her grief and not focus on the tragedy, Bianca had thrown all her energy into her schoolwork. When it was time for her to leave for college, her academic skills landed her a full scholarship to a university in Philadelphia. She completed an internship, received a master's degree, then was offered a well-paid marketing position at a top notch advertising firm in New York City. The day she planned to accept the offer, she got the call from her aunt about becoming an assistant to Glen Goodman.

"Calm down," her aunt said. "I'm fine. I just need to speak to you about something very important to me."

"What is it?" Bianca felt a sense of relief as she sat back down, but her curiosity was piquing.

"You know how much I appreciate you taking over my job with Glen. You were truly a lifesaver."

"You don't have to thank me. I would do anything to help you out."

"No, you do deserve a thank-you and so much more. I know you had that great job waiting for you in New York and you turned it down because I needed you. But more important, Glen needed you."

"I understand the Goodmans are like family to you, and I was more than happy to step in and assist you any way I could. Plus, it's only temporary and the job in New York is still waiting for me. They've been great about keeping the position open." There was a long silent pause. "Hello . . . Aunt Pearl, are you there?"

"I'm here." Bianca heard her aunt clearing her throat before continuing. "Bianca, you're like a daughter to me. I never had any kids of my own, but if I did, I would've hoped they all turned out as wonderful as you."

Bianca's gut told her this was a setup for something she wanted no part of. "Umm-hmm."

"So if I ask you for a favor, it's because you're all I have."

"What's the favor?"

"Tomorrow Glen is going to ask you to work for him on a long-term basis, and I want you to say yes." Bianca could hear the subtle pleading in her aunt's voice, but it wasn't enough to garner any sympathy from her.

"You can't be serious? I have one more week to work with that overgrown child and I'm done."

"Bianca, wait. I know Glen can be a bit hard to manage at times, but he means well. You have to understand he's been in the shadow or living the lifestyle of an NBA star all his life. He doesn't know any better."

"Aunt Pearl, not to be rude, but in a week that will no longer be my problem or concern. I've become a borderline alcoholic dealing with him and his slick-with-the-tongue girlfriend. I'm sure there are plenty of hapless souls who would love to be Glen Goodman's assistant, I'm just not one of them."

"But he trusts you. He told me that ever since you started working with him, his professional life has been running smoothly. He said your marketing skills are priceless. He wants you to be more than his assistant. He really does speak highly of you, Bianca. If I thought anyone else could offer him what you can, I wouldn't have agreed to speak to you on his behalf."

"He put you up to this phone call? My goodness, can't he do anything on his own?"

"He simply told me what was on his mind, and I wanted to help him."

"Yeah, that's because everybody wants to save helpless Glen. That's why he's so screwed up now, because everybody kisses his ass, and for the last few weeks I've had to do the exact same thing. I'm sick of it."

"Please, Bianca, reconsider your decision. I've always been there for you and never asked you for much, but I'm begging you to do this for me. Just like you're a daughter to me, Glen is like a son. He has a good heart. If you look past the bravado he throws around, you'll see he's a wonderful young man."

Bianca let out a deep sigh, regretting that she'd ever agreed to take the job in the first place. She felt stuck. There was no way she could refuse a request from her aunt. She had to find another way to get out of her dilemma, one that wouldn't make her the bad guy.

"Okay, Aunt Pearl, if Glen asks me to stay on, then I'll accept his offer."

"I knew you wouldn't let me down. Something wonderful will come out of this for you. You'll see. Now you get some sleep. I know you have to meet Glen early in the morning. Thank you, baby, and good night."

Second Quarter

Position of Power

"Oh Daddy, fuck me harder," Sasha demanded as Glen went deeper inside her with each thrust.

"Damn baby, you feel so good. I'm about to come."

"Come inside of me, Daddy. I want to feel all your warmth."

It was Sasha's way of saying she wanted his baby. She had wanted to get pregnant by Glen from the moment she met him. For the first six months, he wore a condom. When she finally convinced him that she wasn't having sex with anyone else and was on the pill, she maneuvered that condom off his dick. Now, for the last year, she was working to get him to bust off inside of her instead of pulling out. It didn't matter how drunk Glen got, it was as if he was programmed to shoot his seeds in every direction but the inside of her reproductive system.

"Take it in the mouth and swallow it all up for me," Glen directed as he reached his peak and pulled out to explode. Sasha was used to this request, as it was Glen's favorite. She opened her mouth wide and tasted every last drop of his juices. It was getting to the point that she wondered if she should start running to the bathroom, spitting out his come and preserving it so she could have it inserted later on in order to conceive.

"You were wonderful, Daddy."

"So were you," Glen said as he rolled over on his back, feeling exhausted. "Between the game, hitting the club, and the workout you just gave me, I'm tired as hell. I'm going to sleep like a newborn. Good night."

He kissed Sasha on the forehead and fell into a deep sleep within seconds. Sasha glided her gel-tip finger nail up and down Glen's chest, admiring his muscle definition. Out of all the many celebrities she had bedded, none of them had made her feel like Glen. He treated her with respect and made her feel special. She was sure that he had heard some of the rumors that circulated about her, but he didn't seem to either care or believe them, which only made her try harder to get her claws deeper into him. Her past conquests always let it be known that she was nothing more than a great fuck and party girl, but not Glen. That's why she planned on staying with him no matter what.

Beep! Beep! Beep!

Bianca heard the sound of her alarm going off and squeezed the pillow over her head, trying to make the noise fade away. But it didn't help, and she finally dragged herself out of bed to turn it off. The clock said eight-thirty, and she was supposed to meet Glen at ten. It took her forty-five minutes to get to his house because he lived in Buckhead and she lived on the outskirts of Atlanta. That drive alone was enough to make her want to quit.

After a quick breakfast and shower, Bianca threw on her clothes and headed out. She hated to be late, and with morning traffic, there was a very good chance that she would be. She turned up the volume to hear her classical music CD as she thought about what she would say to Glen. Her words had to be executed just right because she had no doubt he would repeat their conversation to her aunt. It was imperative that she seemed cooperative, since her aunt's opinion was extremely important to her. By the time she pulled up to Glen's mansion, it was five after ten.

"I can live with being five minutes late," she said to herself as she approached the front door. She rang the doorbell once, then twice, then three times. By the fifth time, she began banging on the door. She knew Glen was home because the main car he drove was parked in the circular driveway. Just as she was about to pull out her cell phone and dial his house number, the door opened.

"Damn, is somebody attacking you or something?" Sasha spewed as she rubbed her eyes, standing in front of Bianca butt naked.

"No."

"Then what's up with all the banging? People do sleep this time of the morning."

"Your boyfriend and my boss, *soon to be ex-boss*," Bianca said, mumbling the last part under her breath, "asked me to meet him here this morning so we could discuss some things."

"Oh yeah, that's right. Well, he still sleep, we had a lot of excitement last night. You know, celebrating and stuff."

"I remember, Glen told me he planned on going to the club to celebrate the team's win."

"No honey, I don't mean that celebration. I'm talking about part two, after the club, the excitement that took place in our bed when we got home."

"Speaking of bed, you're no longer in it, so can you please put some clothes on?"

"My fault. Glen is so crazy about my body and loves to see me in my birthday suit. I forget that everyone isn't so blessed."

"Is that what you call—"

The tongue-lashing Bianca had been about to put on Sasha abruptly ended when she noticed Glen coming down the wrap-around stairs in his silk boxers. For the first time, she felt a twinge of lust when she eyed her boss. Never had she seen him in the flesh, except for what he showed in his uniform on the basketball court. His smooth butter-pecan-colored skin glistened against the red silk boxers. Seeing each muscle in his arms connected to his bare chiseled chest had a different effect on her than when she got a glimpse of his biceps in his team jersey.

This is what Sasha is waking up to each morning, she thought. Damn she's a lucky bitch.

"Bianca, I apologize," he said to her. "I had a long night, and as you can see, I just got out of bed." He let out a long yawn.

Bianca noticed Sasha, her arms folded, her hip positioned to the side, as if she were irritated. She wondered if Sasha caught the lustful stare in her eyes. But how could Sasha blame her? Bianca had an inkling that Glen's outside package was just the sprinkles, and nothing compared to the tool in his pants. She hoped that Sasha didn't realize she was getting aroused over her man, because that would be one more thing for Sasha to gloat over. Besides, she knew that Glen would never be attracted to someone like her. Not that she was unattractive, but she just wasn't the obvious kind of pretty that a lot of men like Glen would go for.

In fact, Bianca downplayed her looks by wearing no makeup, pulling her hair in a tight bun, and wearing clothes that didn't accentuate one curve. But if anyone were to look closely, they would have seen that she had tons of potential.

"Would you like to reschedule, since you're obviously not ready for our meeting?" she said. Having snapped out of her lustful mind state, she was now furious that she had gotten out of bed early in the morning and driven over an hour, because of traffic, for a meeting he scheduled and wasn't ready for, due to his bumping and grinding with the still very naked Sasha.

"No, what I need to speak to you about is important," Glen said. "Please don't leave."

Hearing the sincerity in his voice, she was surprised. "Okay, I'll stay."

"Thank you. Come in," he said, moving back so Bianca could step inside. "Sasha, you need to put some clothes on," Glen stated, as if just realizing his girlfriend was naked. "Go make yourself at home," he said to Bianca, "and I'll be back downstairs in a few."

She watched intently as Glen went up the stairs and Sasha sashayed behind him, and was horrified when jealousy consumed her. Could she actually be attracted to Glen? she wondered.

Stop, your mind is simply playing tricks on you! It's just physical. Don't take it so seriously. She could never be attracted to a man that would have a bloodsucker like Sasha as a girlfriend.

She told herself all this and more as she walked toward the living room and waited for Glen to return.

"Baby, don't you want to feel inside of me one more time before getting in the shower?" Sasha propositioned Glen in her most seductive voice.

"You know I do, but I can't keep Bianca waiting. I'm late enough as it is."

"Little Miss Do Good will be fine. I'm sure she understands that a man needs to be gratified when he wakes up in the morning."

Before Glen knew it, Sasha had almost all ten inches of him down her throat. She gave him no teeth, just all wet mouth and tongue. Glen leaned his head back, relishing in her professional skills. When she began massaging his manhood with her hand, the combination of that and her mouth sent his mind spinning. He began fucking Sasha's mouth, and seeing Glen so aroused further turned her on. Sasha scooted her body closer to the bed and gently led him forward with her mouth. He was still in a trance of pleasure and just followed her lead as she continued to work his tool as if auditioning for the lead in a porno movie. When she felt his dick throbbing and the jerk of his body, she knew Glen was about to come.

"Oh shit," Glen groaned, ready to release himself.

At that moment, she took his dick out her mouth, quickly lifted her ass on top of the bed and, as the come poured out like a faucet, with a firm grip still on his cock, Sasha rammed it in her pussy, trying to get every drop inside her. Glen was coming so hard his knees buckled and he found himself lying on top of Sasha with his dick fully inserted. A smiled crossed Sasha's face as she felt his sperm swimming inside her, and she prayed just one would make contact and fertilize an egg.

"What the fuck was that about?" Glen said after getting his mind back right.

"What you mean, baby?" Sasha asked innocently.

"You know what the fuck I mean. Why did you make me come inside of you? I know you're not trying to get a baby out of me."

"Of course not, stop being so paranoid, you know I'm on the pill." It was a straight up lie, but it didn't matter to her. She had to find a way to put herself in a position of power, and a baby would be the perfect start. If her trick worked and she did end up pregnant, it would be too late for Glen to do anything about it.

"Fuck all that pill shit, you know I don't like taking those type of chances. I should've never stopped wearing a condom with you."

"Glen, I can't believe you tripping over this shit. I've been living with you for a year and we've been fucking around for two. If I did end up pregnant, would it really be all that bad?"

Glen stared at Sasha for what seemed like forever. He wasn't quite sure if she was running a game on him or if she'd just gotten caught up in the moment of passion. "Sasha," he finally said, "I made it very clear that I don't want any babies right now. I'm twenty-five and I'm not ready to be a father. So yeah, it would be really bad if you tried some slick shit and ended up pregnant when you know that's not what I want."

"Like I said, I'm on the pill. I'm not trying to trap you, if that's what you're suggesting. Your dick was just feeling so good inside my mouth, I wanted to feel it inside my pussy, that's all." Sasha licked her finger and slowly traced it down her stomach until reaching her clit, and she began playing with it. She let out soft *ohs* and *ahs* and watched as Glen became rock hard again. She knew that sex was the perfect way to divert a man from using his brain.

"Don't do this, Sasha, you know I got to get ready."

"One more time won't hurt."

And just like that, Glen found himself soaking up the warmth of Sasha's insides.

What the hell was taking him so long? After sitting patiently on the couch for forty-five minutes, Bianca was now pacing back and forth wondering what the hell Glen was doing. She couldn't believe he'd had her waiting for so long. When he asked her to stay, he seemed sincere, but his actions were saying something entirely different. "I'm out of here," she said then, grabbing her purse off the couch and heading toward the front door.

"Hold up!" she heard Glen yell, and turning around, saw him hurrying downstairs.

"Glen, not only weren't you ready when I got here for a meeting you scheduled, but then you had me waiting nearly an hour. Your priorities are obviously somewhere else."

"It's not like that. My agent called me and we had some really important business to discuss."

"I didn't hear your phone ring."

"He called on my cell phone. I rarely get calls at home."

Something told Bianca that Glen was lying, but it felt useless to start an argument she couldn't win.

"Fine, so what is this meeting about?" She wasn't sure if her aunt had let Glen know that she'd spoken to her, so she thought it was better to pretend she had no idea what he wanted to ask her.

"Do you mind if we go have a seat in the living room? I really don't want to discuss this here, when you almost have one foot out the door," he said, flashing his signature smile. Bianca couldn't deny that he was a charmer without even trying hard.

"Lead the way."

"Once again I apologize for having you wait so long. Can I get you some water, juice, anything?"

"No, I'm fine."

"Let me just get right to it. I think you're incredible. I love Ms. Pearl, but you bring something to the table that I never expected I would find in a personal assistant. I know this was supposed to be a temporary position until I could find someone else to replace you, but I don't want anybody else, I want you."

"What exactly do you want me to do?"

"Of course I want you to continue on with the duties of being my right hand, but I also want to incorporate more of your marketing skills. You're great with the media, and I want your position to reflect all of your skills."

"I don't know, Glen. To take on so many responsibilities will definitely require an increase in my salary. Working for you on a temporary basis and a permanent one are two totally different things."

"I understand that and I have no problem giving you a raise, just name your price."

Bianca thought about it a moment and figured she would ask for more than double what he was paying her now.

"A hundred thousand dollars, not including work-related expenses that may be incurred, and health benefits." She swallowed hard, and felt her heart was going to leap out her chest. She had already decided she would ask Glen for an absurd amount of money hoping he would show her the door, but wasn't sure she would have the balls to ask for it. Now that she had, she was nervous to hear his response.

"Wow, a hundred thousand. That's more than double what I've been paying you. Plus expenses and benefits. You are not playing. But I will be giving you a lot more responsibilities, and being Ms. Pearl's niece, I do have a certain level of trust with you. Yeah, that's a little steep, but I think you're worth it."

"Excuse me?" Bianca blurted involuntarily, surprised he'd agreed to her terms.

Glen gazed at her with a puzzled look. "Excuse you what?"

"I meant to say, excuse me, I'm not finished." She was trying to find a quick way to save face and get out of what she now considered a bigger jam. She had to find a way to make him say no.

"You want more than the hundred plus expenses?" Bianca could hear the shock in his voice. She took a deep breath, preparing for her last demand, which she was sure he would decline.

"As a matter of fact I do. As you know, I live forty-five minutes away from you. With traffic, it can take me an hour and a half to get here. That is very inconvenient, and let's not forget about the ridiculous gas prices. I want to get an apartment closer to you in the Buckhead area, but I feel you should pay the rent since this area is expensive and I'm only moving so you'll have more access to me for work-related purposes."

Bianca had butterflies in her stomach, but after presenting her latest demand, she stood stoically, as if confident with her request.

Glen put his head down for a moment, and she prepared herself mentally for phrases like "You greedy bitch," "What the fuck are you smokin'?" and "Let the door hit you on your way out" to come from his mouth.

Instead, he said, "You drive a hard bargain but your points are valid. Find a one bedroom apartment that you like and I'll make sure the rent is paid. But you'll be responsible for utilities and cable. I think that's only fair. So do we have a deal?"

Bianca didn't know whether to jump for joy with the sweet paycheck and benefits she'd just landed or scream because if she accepted the offer, she would be stuck being Glen's slave, and around the ignorant Sasha. But remembering the promise she'd made to her aunt, both of them were irrelevant.

"Yes, we have a deal," she said, and the two of them shook hands.

From the top of the stairs, Sasha eyed them, cringing at the fact that miss librarian wasn't going anywhere.

The following evening, Bianca and Glen were still working on the final details for a basketball camp he would be launching in the summer. They started early that afternoon but it was taking much longer than either anticipated.

"I need to eat," Glen said, pushing aside some papers he was reading. "How about we go out for dinner?"

"That's okay, we can order in."

"No," he said, putting his hand on Bianca's shoulder. "We need a break, and I want some fresh air. There's a restaurant not too far from here that has banging food. After we eat, we can come back here and finish up."

"Who am I to argue? Some good food always does the body good." Bianca grabbed her purse and the two headed out.

By the time they reached the restaurant, both of them were famished. Wasting no time, they decided to order a family-size seafood platter and share a bottle of wine.

"I've never had seafood this good before. How long has this place been open?" Bianca asked before taking another bite of her crab cake.

"For a minute now, a lot of people aren't hip to this place, and I hope it stays like that."

"Oh, so it's your little secret?" Bianca purred teasingly.

"You make it sound so naughty."

"Do I? That wasn't my intention, it must be the wine. This is our second bottle."

"Rule number one—always blame unusual behavior on the liquor."

"Unusual behavior?" Bianca gave Glen a confused glare.

"Normally you're a little uptight, but you seem relaxed and carefree tonight. It's very attractive." Bianca didn't know if the wine had her mind playing tricks on her, but she was picking up a flirtatious vibe from Glen. "Here, have the rest," he said, pouring what was left of the wine into her glass.

"No, I really shouldn't. I've had way too much already."

"Then one more glass won't hurt."

Bianca didn't argue; she rather enjoyed the warm, tingly sensation engulfing her body. After swallowing the last drop, she looked down at her watch and realized they had been at the restaurant for over three hours.

"Glen, I can't believe what time it is. We haven't even finished all the paperwork. It's time for us to go."

"I've been enjoying your company so much that the time just flew by."

Bianca was taking pleasure in her time with Glen also, but didn't want to admit it. "I know what you mean," she said. "But it's getting late and I'm sure that Sasha must be wondering where you are."

"Actually, one of her girlfriends that she hasn't seen in a long time is in town, so Sasha's spending the night at the hotel with her. I guess so they can do female stuff. You know, stay up all night, gossiping and shit."

"So that's what you think women like to do?"

"Hell if I know, but right now I don't care. I'm more interested in talking about you."

Their eyes locked then, and without speaking a word, a full-fledged conversation was ensuing between the two of them. Bianca felt as if she was becoming sexually hypnotized. It seemed as if Glen's dick was calling her name. The lips on her pussy began to open as if they could hear it too. The very thought of his mouth tasting her moist insides was making her body temperature rise.

"Glen, I'm tired, let's go," she said abruptly. Even in her intoxicated state, Bianca knew she had to put a stop to the lust that was infecting her mind.

After paying the bill, the two left, and remained silent during the ride back to Glen's house. But it didn't lower the heat mounting between them. When Glen pulled up in his driveway, Bianca didn't even give him a chance to turn off the ignition before getting out and heading toward her car.

"Why are you rushing off?" Glen said as he hurried to get out the car and catch up to her. "We still haven't finished up our work for tonight."

"I told you I was tired, I really need to go." Bianca was now standing face-to-face with him. She put her head down, not wanting Glen to see the craving she had for him in her eyes.

"Look at me." Glen lifted her chin. "Are you tired or are you running away from me?"

"I don't know what you're talking about, I have to go." As Bianca broke away from Glen's embrace, he pulled her in, and she was seduced by the passion of his kiss. Her nipples hardened and her knees became weak. "I really need to go," were the last words she remembered saying.

She went from trying to reject Glen's advances to lying on her back with her long legs wrapped around his neck. He held her ass in the palms of his hands as he stroked her wet pussy with his immense cock. She held onto his shoulders for dear life, trying to endure the pleasure and pain he was unleashing on her.

"Damn, baby, your pussy is like that." Right when Bianca was about to come, he pulled out.

"Don't stop, you feel so good," she panted breathlessly.

"I'm not done. I just want to look at you." Glen ran his hands down every curve on Bianca's body and then flipped her over. Then, with his tongue, he licked from the front of her clit to the insides of her ass cheeks.

"Ahhh," Bianca moaned as her body shivered in ecstasy from his touch.

Glen grabbed her hair, pulling her head back before sliding his dick in and pounding in and out of her dripping wet pussy. Bianca's mind and body escaped to a place of elation that she never new existed. By the time he brought her to her third orgasm, she felt completely drained and fell into a deep sleep.

She was the first to awake early the next morning. It took her a second to focus, but she immediately came to when she saw a naked Glen asleep beside her. Then Bianca began reminiscing over everything that had transpired the night before, which led to her waking up in Glen's bed. Feeling a combination of happiness, confusion, and embarrassment, she slithered out of bed and started to get dressed. The sounds of Bianca scrambling to gather her belongings awoke Glen.

"What time is it?" he asked struggling to open his eyes as he gazed at the clock. "It's early, get back in bed."

"I have so much to do today, I need to go." Bianca nervously buttoned her shirt.

"Here you go again. Do I have to come over there and pull you back into bed? Because I will."

"You're not worried that Sasha could come home any minute?"

"Damn, that's a good point," Glen said, shaking his head, and Bianca felt a stab in her heart when she realized he cared about Sasha walking in on them.

"I'm so stupid," she said. "I should've never let myself get caught up."

"What are you talking about?"

"We had sex last night, and the only thing you're worried about is Sasha coming home."

"What the fuck, you're the one who brought her up," Glen retorted.

"Oh, so now it's my fault that you seduced me?"

"You want to play the blame game?"

"Well, you are the one with the girlfriend."

"Yeah, but you knew that already."

For a moment there was complete stillness between them. Bianca's feelings of shame were written all over her face.

"Listen, last night was incredible," Glen said. "I don't want us to argue."

"No, you're absolutely right. I did know you have a girlfriend, yet I chose to give in to temptation instead of using my head. I made a mistake."

"Don't say that." Glen walked over to Bianca and stroked her cheek. "This wasn't a mistake. What happened last night was incredible, and I don't want it to be a onetime thing."

"You still want us to be intimate?"

Glen nodded his head.

"So what about Sasha?"

"She doesn't have to know."

Bianca's eyes widened. "So you want to see me behind Sasha's back. What type of shit is that?" she said, pushing Glen's hand away from her face.

"I don't understand. You want me to just end things with Sasha just like that? Don't you think we need to see what is going to happen between us? We might decide that we have a better business relationship than a personal one."

"Of course, in Glen Goodman's world there is no such thing as putting all your eggs in one basket when it comes to a relationship. You always need a backup plan. Well, excuse me if I don't want to be it. I think you and Sasha are perfect for each other. I want to forget that last night ever happened."

"Are you sure about that?" From the intense look in Glen's eyes Bianca knew his question was a deal breaker.

"Very. I think we should keep our relationship on a business level." That's what her mouth said, but she knew her heart felt totally different.

"That's cool, business it is."

Glen turned away and headed toward the bathroom. leaving

Bianca with a nauseating knot in the pit of her stomach. She desperately wanted to be back in bed with her legs wrapped around Glen's back, feeling every inch of his dick inside of her, but she had way too much pride to carry on a secret affair with him.

Before leaving, she glanced at the bed that she'd had the best sex of her life in, then walked out the door.

Halftime

I Like the Way You Move

You could hear the sound of a pin drop as the entire arena focused on Glen Goodman's next move down the court. With the championship series tied and only fifty seconds left in the final game, everyone was on edge, including Bianca, who wasn't even a basketball fan.

"It's all up to you, Glen, bring it home," Bianca said to herself. Working closer with Glen and feeling all ten inches of him inside of her, she had officially become a basketball fanatic. Although things had been awkward between them since their sexual tryst, she still secretly cheered every time her boss and lover for one night scored. She loved the way Glen moved, on the court and off. The Los Angeles Falcons were up by two, and the clock was quickly ticking away. If a major play wasn't made in the next twenty seconds, there would be no championship celebration in Atlanta.

"Girl, Isaac need to pass Glen the damn ball and stop wasting time," Sasha barked at Tracy, as if she had any control over what her man was doing.

"I'm with you on that," Tracy said.

Then like a horrible clip from a movie trailer, Isaac dropped the ball and everyone dived to try and retrieve it. The home team crowd erupted in a gasp, wondering what would happen next. When the dust cleared, Glen had stolen the ball and made a crossover fake that freed him up at the three-point line. Everyone zoomed in on the clock as Glen released his shot just before the buzzer sounded—and all they saw was net.

The crowd erupted in a deafening cheer. Glen Goodman had once again come through like a soldier and brought the championship home. Sasha and Tracy ran onto the court along with the crowd, wanting to revel in the victory.

"Damn, there is no way we're getting through this crowd," Sasha said.

"Yeah, ain't no way. We should wait outside the locker room like we normally do."

"Fuck that, it's going to be a zoo over there too. Glen gave me the keys to his Rover, we can just wait there."

"Cool," Tracy said, and the two of them bypassed the crowd and headed for Glen's car.

"Is it me, or does it seem like every ball player got a damn Range Rover with some sick rims?" Sasha asked, walking through the garage, feeling as if she'd stepped into a Range Rover dealership. Then, after getting in the front seat and turning on the ignition, she rolled down the windows, with T.I. blaring out of the speakers. "Let me turn this shit down."

"No, it isn't you, every dude in the league is pushing a Range, with the twenty-four-inch rims," Tracy responded from the passenger side. "It must be some sort of initiation requirement. That was like one of the first things Isaac bought when he went pro."

"Oh shit, you been with Isaac since he first got in the league?"

"That's right. We graduated from the same college, and you know this is only his second year in the pros."

"Were you all together in college?"

"All four years," Tracy said, nodding and feeling proud.

Tracy liked Sasha, but she also felt they were in two different categories. She had been trooping it out with Isaac since before he became an NBA player and the money started flowing. When they were in college, Isaac loved playing ball and wanted to get drafted, and he could have easily dropped out of school and went into the league early. But he wanted that degree. Isaac's dedication to getting an education was one of the reasons Tracy loved him so much. If he wasn't practicing or playing a game, then he was with her, studying for a test, or the two of them were just hanging out.

But since he became cool with Glen, Isaac had been changing. Glen liked to go out every night, and when Sasha moved to Atlanta, she was always right there with him. At first Tracy didn't want to be bothered with Sasha because she'd seen her type come and go with just about every player on the team. But somehow Sasha maneuvered her skills to become a permanent fixture. That didn't sit well with Tracy, but instead of making her the enemy, Tracy decided to make her a friend. She knew girls like Sasha had lots of paper chasing friends, and she wasn't about to let one of them come in and steal her man.

"All four years, huh?" Sasha said. "I didn't know that. So you are definitely trying to be his wife."

"Yeah, I would think," Tracy snapped, put off by Sasha's statement.

"You've been in it for a minute, so why hasn't he married you yet?" Sasha asked sarcastically.

"For one, we're only twenty-three and we both feel we have plenty of time for that. Also, we're committed to one another, so when the time is right we'll be walking down the aisle."

"You sound awfully confident. I guess you be working it out in that bedroom," Sasha said with a playful laugh. She made the comment as if she were joking, but not in a good way. Tracy let it go, however, because she didn't want Sasha to think that she felt her relationship with Isaac wasn't solid. She knew that people like Sasha preyed on any sort of vulnerability, and she wasn't about to hand it to her.

"Yeah, girl, something like that. I was telling the dude we need to install a pole in the crib."

"Speaking of poles, we hitting Magic City or what," Glen said, sneaking up on the two ladies, with Bianca and Isaac right behind him.

"Baby, you won!" Sasha shouted. "I'm so proud of you. We can do whatever you like tonight." She stuck her head out the window to plant a passionate kiss on her man. By now, Tracy had jumped out of the Range Rover and was giving Isaac a huge congratulatory hug. Bianca stood to the side, watching the couples grope each other, and decided this was be the perfect time to make her exit.

"Where do you think you're going, Bianca?" Glen screamed, startling her as she was walking away.

"Home. I know you guys want to go out and celebrate, so I won't keep you."

"Keep us, you coming with us." Everybody looked at Glen surprisingly. It was obvious to them that Bianca wasn't exactly the partying type, so they were shocked that Glen was extending the invitation.

Bianca let out an uncomfortable laugh before responding. "I don't think so. I'm really tired. I just want to go home."

"Bianca, you work for me. Remember that great salary I'm paying you with all the perks. That means you agreed to be a willing participant whenever I need you."

"I don't want to go to a strip club."

"It's not about what you want, it's what I want. Come on, I won my first championship ring tonight. You can at least come out and celebrate with me."

She knew how important this night was for Glen, and he was her boss. At the same time, she didn't want to watch as Sasha kept her paws all over Glen for the duration of the night. It amazed Bianca that Glen was able to act as if they hadn't had the most passionate lovemaking session less than a month ago; it also hurt her feelings. Obviously, it had meant much more to her than it to him. Here, he was carrying on with Sasha and inviting her to a strip club like they'd never seen each other naked. But she steeled herself, decided if he could so easily brush it off his shoulders, then so could she.

"Okay, but if I get tired," she said, "I'm taking a taxi home."

"No problem," he replied. "Now get in."

"I'll follow right behind you, man," Isaac said as he and Tracy moved toward his car.

Sasha moved to the passenger seat and Bianca got in the back. She couldn't believe she was hanging out with Glen and Sasha. But she was curious to see the legendary strip club. Magic City had been open and shut down on a few occasions. but its legions of fans were never far behind. Every African American mover and shaker in the entertainment business had been through the infamous doors at one time or another, and now she would be added to the list.

Upon first entering, Bianca noticed the red, white, and pink baby tees in a glass case to her left. The shirts said MAGIC CITY, with rhinestone decorating the silhouette of a woman's sexy body. She was tempted to purchase the pink one, then decided against it since the tee didn't exactly fit into her uptight wardrobe.

Everybody was shaking Glen's and Isaac's hands as they were led to a booth toward the back of the club. The moment they sat down, the DJ gave a shout. "Glen Goodman, who always delivers the goods, and Isaac Johnson from the Atlanta Phantoms are in the house tonight. Coming off their first championship win, they brought the celebration to Magic City. Now, ladies, you always do it right, but I want yah to perform extra nasty for our special guests."

He put on a Young Jeezy club banger, and all you saw was ass popping and tits jiggling, and then came the bottles of bubbly that would be poured all night. Bianca sat back in shocked awe as women did tricks on stage that she had never envisioned in her wildest dreams. A woman who looked all of six feet tall due to the ten-inch platforms she was rocking, had on a black tank top that cut above her breasts with an itsy bitsy thong, and she glided up the steel pole as if she were a slithering snake. Once she reached the top, the Amazon queen began her descent with hips, thighs, and pussy gyrating the pole as if having consensual sex. Then Bianca turned to the two women who were simulating sex with each other. One was standing on top of her head with her legs spread so wide she was basically doing an in the air split. The other woman was between her legs, humping her pussy.

"Is this what it has come to? Cats only dropping paper if chicks fuck each other," Tracy said to Bianca, since Bianca seemed to be the only person besides her who was disgusted with the sex antics going on around them.

"Seems that way, since those are the girls that have stacks of paper in their garter." Bianca and Tracy stared with their mouths wide open as the men showered the strippers with cash. It was raining nothing but money on the showstoppers.

"Isaac, I'm ready to go," Tracy said, with nothing but attitude in her voice.

"We just got here. The party ain't even got started yet."

"The party been started, and I'm ready to go."

"You need to sit back and relax. Enjoy yourself, like Sasha doing." Tracy eyed Sasha, who was sitting next to Glen, and both had a girl dancing for them. "Why don't you get a lap dance or something?" Isaac suggested.

"You can't be serious? I don't want some girl's coochie all up in my face."

"That's your prerogative. But this is my night to celebrate, so you won't mind if I get one." Isaac waved a hundred dollar bill in the air, summoning a buxom girl in a cheerleading outfit to come over. Tracy slapped his arm down.

"Yes, I do mind you getting a lap dance. I told you I was ready to go, and that means let's leave, *now!*"

Due to the loud music, Bianca couldn't hear the exact words being exchanged between Tracy and Isaac, but from the vexed expression on their faces, she knew neither one was happy. Glen and Sasha were a whole other story. Both seemed like two kids in a candy store. They were enjoying the explicit sex show the strippers were giving them. Sasha even poured the dancers champagne, and they broke out in a toast. Bianca had seen enough and decided it was time to break out. She assumed everyone was so caught up in their own scene that nobody would notice that she went missing, especially not Glen.

She reached the exit relieved that no one had stopped her. Watching Glen get lap dances by the buxom beauties had been about to make her ring the alarm.

"Wait!" she heard; it sounded like a female scream, but she was reluctant to turn around, not wanting anyone to keep her from leaving. "I'll share a taxi with you."

Now she did turn back, and saw Tracy approach, out of breath. "You don't want to wait for Isaac?" she asked.

"Fuck Isaac. He so caught up in all this disease infested pussy he can't even think straight."

Bianca didn't know how to respond, so she remained quiet. Tracy's head was down and she was mumbling like a crazy person as they got into the taxi. Bianca was surprised that she had decided to leave Isaac there. She assumed that since Tracy was always with Sasha, she was also a party girl, and that attending strip clubs was the norm for them.

"If you don't mind me asking, why did you leave Isaac in the club?" she asked as the taxi took off.

At first Tracy just shook her head. Then she started smacking her lips like she had so much to say but couldn't get her words to come out. Finally she spoke.

"Girl, I never thought this would happen, but Isaac has got sucked into this whole NBA lifestyle. Slowly but surely I'm losing him." Tears welled up in her eyes as she spoke. It was obvious to Bianca that the situation was very painful for her.

"I didn't mean to upset you, Tracy. We don't have to discuss it any further."

"No, I need somebody to talk to. Sasha trifling ass doesn't care. She loves the life as an NBA player's girl, even if you're constantly being disrespected. But see, I'm not having that bullshit. I was with Isaac before all this, and I'll be damn if I'm going to sit back and let him sling his dick in other bitches like it's all good in our hood. Fuck that, I'll let him go before I sink that low."

Bianca felt sorry for Tracy. She knew that Tracey meant every word she said, but it was killing her to say them. She obviously loved Isaac very much, but he was beginning to relish the perks of being a basketball star, and Tracy wanted their relationship to continue the way it used to be when it was all about them. Isaac was moving forward and Tracy was still living in the past.

After the taxi dropped Tracy off, Bianca sat back and stared out the window. She'd had no words of encouragement for Tracy, and it bothered her. In the brief time she'd worked for Glen, she had a clear understanding of how difficult it was to deal with a man in the NBA, especially if you truly cared about him. If you were a chick looking for a momentary glimpse into fast cars, endless money, and nonstop parties, then dealing with a basketball player was the place to be. But if you were interested in a committed, monogamous relationship with a man who took pleasure in the simple things in life, you had a better chance of success heading to Vegas and winning at the slot machines. She could only take comfort that her encounter with experiencing love b-ball style was brief, though it was one she'd never forget.

Third Quarter

Sweetest Sin

"I know Isaac ass didn't stay out all night," Tracy said, waking up alone in bed. "This motherfucker better stepped out early this morning to get us some breakfast from McDonald's," she vented, breathing hard as she dialed Isaac's cell phone, but it went straight to voice mail. "Isaac, where the fuck are you? It's obvious that you didn't sleep in this bed last night and your phone is off. My female intuition is telling me you up to no good, but for your sake I better be wrong. If you don't call me right back, I'm coming to look for your ass, and if you up to some trifling shit, it's about to be on," Tracy screamed into the phone before slamming it down.

Bianca was in the middle of a dream that she didn't want to wake up from. A beautifully built six feet four man with muscle tone so defined you would think someone crafted it from a sculpture was gently sprinkling kisses around her breasts and down her stomach.

Her back arched as the tip of his tongue seduced her belly button. As she moaned in pleasure and anticipated his next move, he continued his tongue play, entering her gates to heaven. Her hips swiveled to the rhythm of his strokes, and when she looked down to catch a glimpse of the face of the man who was bringing her so much pleasure, it was Glen, and then the alarm went off snapping her out of her sleep.

Bianca hated that she couldn't stop thinking about that one night of forbidden lust she'd shared with Glen. And how could she when it had been the best sex of her life? But she had no choice but to forget about it, she decided, since it had been a mistake and Glen seemed perfectly content with Sasha. To make matters worse, she now had to head over to Glen's house to discuss a ton of media obligations he had lined up, and would have to pretend it didn't crush her seeing him with Sasha. She prayed that she would be able to bury her feelings for Glen somewhere so deep that the pain of not being with him vanished.

"Isaac, open the damn door!" Tracy screamed. She had been banging on Glen's front door for the last fifteen minutes, and wouldn't stop because she was positive Isaac was inside, since his car was parked in front of the garage. She kept calling his cell phone but it was still turned off. Then she started blowing up Sasha's phone, but it was off too. She was pissed because she didn't know Glen's home or cell phone number, so she just continued banging, waiting for someone to show their face. She was at her wits end and began walking toward the back to bust out the glass doors when someone finally came out. But after Tracy saw who it was, she knew it would've been better if the woman had stayed inside. It was the buxom cheerleader who had been entertaining Isaac before she left Magic City.

"Where's Isaac?" she demanded of the chick who seemed like she was still halfway asleep.

"Who?"

"Don't play with me, bitch. Where is my man?"

"Which one is your man?" the girl asked coyly.

Five seconds later Isaac came walking out the door as if he had no clue Tracy was on the front steps waiting for him. "Oh shit, what are you doing here?"

"Oh shit is right. I've been banging on this damn door for fifteen minutes. I guess you was too occupied fucking with this trick that you didn't hear me."

"Look, ho, don't be calling me no trick because your so-called man wanted to stick his dick up in me all night," the stripper said. "You need to check your man and leave me out of it." Tracy stared at her stripper for a moment, and then, without warning, started going upside her head.

"Tracy, chill. Stop acting crazy out here," Isaac barked as he pulled her off the girl.

Tracy was still swinging her arms and kicking as Isaac held her in the air. "Let me go," she demanded.

"Not until you calm down." The stripper was fixing her hair and patting down the clothes that Tracy had practically ripped off.

"I'm fine," Tracy said as Isaac put her down. "After all the shit we've been through, I can't believe you would play me for some two-bit slut. I hope that pussy was worthwhile because I've done enough crying over your sorry ass."

"Tracy, wait. I fucked up, but don't end it over this." Tracy kept walking as Isaac halfheartedly pleaded his case from the front stairs.

When Bianca pulled up at the house for her meeting with Glen, she saw Tracy going at Isaac's Range Rover Terminator style. She had busted out every window except for the front. She was about to do that one too, but Isaac managed to get to her before she could. And then the two of them were battling as Isaac tried to retrieve the brick from Tracy's hand. It seemed that Tracy's anger had given her superhero strength, because Isaac appeared to have difficulty getting the upper hand, though she was much smaller.

The girl who was watching the mayhem looked awfully familiar to Bianca, who ran up to ask her what was going on.

"Well, that crazy bitch tried to kick my ass because I spent the night with her so-called man," the girl said. "I told her not to get mad at me but to check her man for herself. I guess she took my advice and that's why she fucking up his car."

Bianca wondered if she should try to break up their fight or go inside and get Glen. Before she had a chance to make a decision, Glen and Sasha came outside. Luckily, Sasha had enough sense to put on a bathrobe instead of prancing around butt naked.

"Yo, what the fuck is going on out here?" Glen said as he came off his steps. Isaac and Tracy were still going at it, ignoring him as they continued to fight. Glen walked back in the house, and Bianca couldn't believe he wasn't going to do something. But a minute later he reappeared, and all anyone could hear were gunshots ringing in the air. Everybody froze and looked in Glen's direction. "I got to bust off bullets to get you fools' attention. Now what is all this drama about?"

"You know what the fuck is up," Tracy told him. "You let Isaac bring that trick up in your crib so they could fuck. What type of shit is that?"

"Tracy, on the real, Isaac is a grown-ass man. I don't have anything to do with who he lay down with. And for the record, I'm not saying he laid down with anybody," Glen added.

"Tracy, why don't you come inside so you can calm down," Sasha suggested.

"I'm not going anywhere near that damn house after Isaac stayed up all night fucking some bitch."

"I told you—"

Bianca cut the girl off before she could continue. "Honestly, I think you should just stay out of this."

"That's cool, but I need to get the fuck home. I'm tired of watching all this drama," the girl popped as she rolled her eyes.

"Go wait in my car," Bianca said. "I'll call a cab for you." She took out her cell phone and ordered the car service they used frequently to come as soon as possible. Then she walked toward Isaac and Tracy, who was still breathing like a bull.

"Tracy, let's go home," Isaac pleaded. "We need to sit down and talk. I know we can work everything out."

"I'm not going nowhere with you. You made your bed, now lay in it." Tracy tossed the brick on the ground, walked back to her car and drove off. Five minutes later the car service arrived and the stripper jumped in, not saying so much as a good-bye to anybody. Glen went over and said a few words to Isaac before he pulled off in his window-busted-out Range.

Bianca followed Glen and Sasha back into the house, feeling overwhelmed by the events that had occurred there, in the middle of the afternoon.

"Bianca, I'm sorry you had to arrive in the midst of all that chaos," Glen said.

"Well, maybe if you hadn't brought the chaos home there would be no need to apologize."

"What?" he said, taken aback by Bianca's defiance. They were standing in the foyer, with Sasha behind Glen, straining to hear

Bianca's response. Sasha knew that Glen hated for anyone to talk slick to him, and she hoped Bianca's comment would escalate to an argument, which would mean a curtain call for her. "You're blaming me for what went down between Isaac and Tracy?"

"All I'm saying is if you hadn't allowed Isaac to spend the night with his stripper friend at your house, then Tracy wouldn't have been in front of your crib trying to demolish Isaac's car."

"Baby, before you respond to that, I'm going to get ready," Sasha said to Glen. "Don't forget we have to go dress shopping for the official celebration party you're hosting tomorrow night."

"All right, I'll be up there in a little while."

"Oh, and Bianca, I don't know if you're coming to the party, but I understand dressing up isn't really your thing, so if you need some tips on what to wear, feel free to ask." Without even waiting for Bianca to respond, Sasha strutted upstairs.

Bianca was so irritated by Sasha's obvious diss that she was in no mood to even talk to Glen. But she did, saying, "Glen, I know you have things to do, so let's discuss these interviews you have lined up so I can get out of here."

"Before we go over work-related stuff," he replied, "I want to finish discussing what happened earlier."

"I don't think there's anything left to say."

"I disagree. I can't let you blame me for what other grown folks do and not defend myself."

"Look, I feel that you should accept some of the responsibility too. You know that Isaac lives with Tracy and they're supposed to be in a committed relationship. If he didn't come home last night, it would only make sense that she'd come to your crib looking for him since she left him at the strip club with you. So please don't talk to me as if you're surprised the drama ended in the front of your house when you welcomed it to come in."

"Oh, so what? I should have told Isaac that he and his friend couldn't spend the night?"

"Yeah, you could've told grown-ass Isaac to get a room and fuck his stripper friend on his own premises so none of it would've led back to you."

Glen stood thinking about what Bianca was saying. Even though he wasn't about to admit it, he knew that when Isaac told him he wanted to bring the stripper back to his crib, he should have told him to get a hotel room. Tracy had hung out with him and Sasha on numerous occasions, and he even thought of her as being somewhat of a friend. He should have completely stayed out of whatever dirt Isaac was scheming on.

"I feel what you're saying," he said, "I really do, but you don't have to come off as being so judgmental."

"I'm not trying to judge you, Glen. I guess I feel that no one really takes other people's feelings seriously. Tracy was devastated to see her man coming out of your crib with some stripper he was laid up with all night, and she had every right to be. What if things had turned fatal and somebody ended up dead behind that bullshit? In the heat of passion, shit like that happens all the time. Just think if that brick Tracy was bashing around had been a gun, then the police and ambulance could be parked outside your crib right now, and then what?"

"I can't lie. It wasn't that deep for me. I didn't take Tracy's feelings into consideration. I just wanted everybody to have a good time. Damn, I guess that shows what a fucked-up individual I am."

"You're not a fucked-up individual. If a person doesn't take the time to point something out to you, then it can go right over your head."

"Well, I'm glad you did take the time because I definitely learned something today." Glen gazed into Bianca's eyes, and all the feeling he'd been trying to suppress since she'd told him she only wanted them to have a business relationship resurfaced. He felt an emotional connection toward her. It was a strange bond that he'd never felt with another woman. He couldn't resist walking closer to her and placing his right hand gently on her cheek. "Thank you."

"For what?"

"For being you," he answered sincerely.

"It was nothing." Bianca playfully pushed Glen's hand away, and he knew that was her way of not letting him back in. He was hoping she would let her guard down because she couldn't deny their attraction. He could feel the lust brewing inside her. "We really need to go over these interviews," Bianca said, breaking the silence.

Glen was disappointed that she didn't respond the way he hoped, but decided not to push her. "No problem. But before I forget, you are coming to the party tomorrow night?"

"What party?"

"The one Sasha mentioned."

"Oh, that party. I'm not sure. I think I might have plans."

"Plans like what, a date?" Glen asked, unable to contain his jealousy.

"No, not a date, I might have to do something for Aunt Pearl."

He was relieved it wasn't a man she had plans with. "Don't worry about Aunt Pearl. I'll personally put in a call letting her know I need you at the party I'm hosting tomorrow."

"Don't do that."

"Then that means you're coming."

"Yes, I'll be there."

"Great, now let's get to work." Glen was pleased that Bianca would be in attendance. Even though technically she wasn't his girl, he felt territorial when it came to her.

Fourth Quarter

Showstopper

After leaving Glen, Bianca drove straight to her aunt Pearl's house. Pearl lived in a two-story brick house on a quiet cul-de-sac outside of Atlanta. It was the same house Bianca had lived in after her mother died, and it always gave her a warm, secure feeling. It was the only place she truly considered home. Although she still had a key, she decided to ring the doorbell since her aunt wasn't expecting her.

"If it isn't my favorite girl," Aunt Pearl said, greeting her niece in the endearing motherly nature that Bianca loved so much.

"Hi, Auntie, I hope you don't mind me stopping by without notice."

"Don't be silly. Bring your butt in here. I'm surprised you didn't use your key."

"I didn't want to scare you by just walking in."

"I appreciate that. I don't need no surprises. It might cause me to have some sort of relapse," she said jokingly. "So what brings you out to my neck of the woods?"

"Wanted to see how you were doing."

"You could've called me for that." She gave Bianca the eye, letting her know she knew there was much more to her visit.

"You know me so well. I'm going to just come out and say it. I think I'm falling for Glen, and he's hosting this party tomorrow that I don't want to attend because I don't have anything to wear, and then Sasha . . ." Bianca kept rambling on until her aunt cut in.

"Well I'll be. I was wondering how long it would take before you admitted it," she said, sitting down on the couch.

"What are you talking about? I only recently started developing these feelings."

"That's what your mouth says. But I knew something was up when you were determined not to continue working for him. It was as if you were running away from something, which was those feelings you didn't want to have."

"Maybe because I never thought it was possible for him to reciprocate my feelings. I mean, he obviously loves superficial women like Sasha, and how can I compete with that? The two of us are polar opposites."

"Men go through phases of being attracted to certain types of women. Some of them never outgrow it and others just need the right woman to show them that different can be better. If you really care about Glen, then don't let him slip away."

"If you mean make a total fool out of myself, I'll pass."

"You never know. Glen is like a sweet little boy who just needs guidance in the right direction. He's dated plenty of women and they've all been like Sasha, a tempting piece of candy on the outside with absolutely nothing in the center."

"So obviously that's what he likes, which I'm not."

"Now, who doesn't like candy? Everybody is attracted to something that looks delicious to devour, that's part of being human. But you're the one who chooses not to use what God gave you to further lure Glen in."

"What do you mean by that?"

"You know exactly what I mean. Walking around all the time in ultraconservative clothes, not putting so much as some lip gloss on those luscious lips. I'm not saying you have to be done up all the time, but damn, honey, you got to let your hair down sometimes so a man knows you have a pulse."

"Aunt Pearl, you are so crazy."

"I'm so serious. You have enough assets to give any woman a run for her money. Instead of hiding them under those layers of clothes, flaunt what you were blessed with."

"I know, but it's hard. I always remember how beautiful and vibrant mother was, and out of jealousy my dad just took that away from her in one split second. It seems that in love and life, it leads to nothing but pain and heartache."

"My dear child, I know how deeply your mother's death affected you. My heart hasn't been the same either, but you can't stop living because your mother stopped breathing. Trust me, she would want you to find love and be happy, not to close yourself off and wither away."

"I know, but then falling in love with a man like Glen, I feel I'm destined for a broken heart."

"Nothing in love or life is guaranteed. But I will tell you it's better to have truly loved with all your heart at least once then to never have loved at all."

"You're absolutely right. So what advice would you give me?"

"Well, first you need to attend that party tomorrow, but not just go, go looking so damn good that you erase Sasha out of Glen's mind once and for all. Leave it to your aunt Pearl. When I'm done with you, you'll outshine every female in that entire party, including Sasha."

When Sasha woke up, the first thing she did was take out the dress she was wearing to the party that night. She couldn't help but admire the ocean blue Stella McCartney creation, which guaranteed that she would be the baddest chick at the entire affair. The plunging neckline highlighted her surgically enhanced bodice, and with the blinged-out hello kitty necklace dangling down her chest, all eyes would be on her. As she continued to look over her ensemble, she couldn't believe how far she'd come. A few years ago she had been waiting tables at a diner in a two-bit town in Indiana, and now she was luxuriating in Glen Goodman's mansion and escorting him to an NBA championship party, wearing a dress by a top notch designer, with diamonds decorating her body. Nobody would believe her success. Hitchhiking out of Indiana was the best move she'd ever made.

Once Sasha had arrived in Michigan, she immediately hooked up at Platinum, one of the ritziest strip clubs in Detroit. Soon, she was the most sought after exotic dancer in the club, especially after she got her breast enlargement. The fast cash, and parlaying with the city's biggest ballers, introduced her to the lifestyle she'd always wanted to live. But it wasn't until she met Glen Goodman that things really started looking up for her. While on vacation with another dancer in Miami, she ran into Glen because they were staying at the same hotel when he was in town for a game. In her juicy couture jogging suit and bouncy ponytail, Glen thought Sasha was a sweet girl in town for some fun, and she played that role to a hilt. She told Glen she was a college student, and never mentioned her full-time position as the reigning queen of the stripper pole. With Sasha playing the good girl role, they had been dating ever since.

"Baby, what time are we leaving tonight?" she asked when Glen came out the shower.

"Around eight."

"Is it just going to be me and you or are some of your teammates riding with us too?"

"Nobody else is coming with us, except for maybe Bianca. I have to call her to find out," Glen said while putting on his clothes.

"Bianca's coming to the party?" Sasha asked with astonishment in her voice.

"Of course, she does work with me."

"I don't know why you keep her around, she is so annoying. I just knew you were going to fire her ass after she tried to get fly with you."

"You talking about that discussion we had yesterday about Isaac and Tracy?"

"Hello, yes."

"That was nothing. Bianca has the right to express her opinion, and I actually appreciated her keeping it real with me. She had some very valid points."

Sasha couldn't believe what she was hearing. Glen could be such a hothead, and never liked anyone to step out of line with him, but he was standing there defending little miss goody two shoes. She wanted to vomit. "If you say so," she said.

"I have to run some errands. I'll be back a little later, and then we can head to the party." Glen kissed Sasha good-bye as he walked out, then she sat down on the bed and thought about how miserable she would be if Bianca rode with them to the party that night. The idea of hanging with Bianca made her think about Tracy, and she wondered if Tracy had made up with Isaac yet. She'd tried calling her a few times yesterday, but Tracy didn't pick up. She decided to try again.

Ring ring ring . . .

"Hello."

"Hey girl," Sasha said, trying to sound upbeat.

"What do you want, Sasha?"

"Why you say it like that? I know you not mad at me because of that shit that went down with Isaac."

"Answer this question and I'll let you know. If I hadn't caught Isaac with that stripper bitch, would you have told me he spent the night with her?"

Sasha thought for a moment about what she should say before answering the question. "You my girl, of course I would've let you know. I even told Glen that night it was fucked up he was letting Isaac bring that trick up in our crib. I didn't want that bitch nowhere around me, but you know how these dudes are, they always stick together."

It was a lie. In fact, she'd played a subtle role in what transpired. She'd noticed the cheerleader stripper giving Isaac a lap dance, and afterward became chummy with her, and actually told the girl if she wanted to make some real money she should try and spend the night with Isaac. The stripper took the suggestion to heart and flirted with Isaac for the duration of the night. She promised him a sexual experience of a lifetime if he took her home. Three bottles of bubbly later, they were off to Glen's house, twisting each other out. Sasha never thought Tracy would bust Isaac. She'd only played a role in orchestrating the sexual tryst for her own self-pleasure, since earlier that evening Tracy had acted as if she had Isaac securely in her back pocket, and Sasha wanted to prove that she didn't.

"I appreciate that, Sasha," Tracy said. "I can't even believe Glen let that bullshit go down in his crib. He could've at least told Isaac to get his own damn hotel room. But he don't give a fuck about me. All he cares about is trifling ass Isaac."

"I guess that means you and Isaac haven't made up?"

"Hell no. I'm done with him."

"So where are you staying?"

"Thank goodness my cousin lives in Atlanta. She has a two bedroom, so I'm staying in the guest room."

"So what are you going to do, stay in your cousin's crib forever?"

"What the fuck am I supposed to do? Take Isaac no good ass back so he can continue to cheat on me and think I'll sit around and take it?"

Sasha thought Tracy should do just that. She didn't think Tracy was the flyest chick, and it would be damn near impossible for her to land somebody better than Isaac. Tracy had put mad years in with him. Why let some other girl slide in and reap all the benefits, because they would be flocking to him like bees to honey.

"It's up to you what you want to do," she said. "But all I'm saying is that you been dealing with the cat for a long time. How are you going to go from living with this dude to bunking at your cousin's crib? I guess the next thing you're going to tell me is that you're going to apply for a job and work for a living."

"I do have a degree, Sasha, so I can get a job and take care of myself."

"If you say so, booboo. But listen, I have some errands to run before going to this party tonight."

"What party?"

"You know, the NBA championship party that Glen is hosting."

"Oh yeah, I forgot about that. I'm sure Isaac will be there."

"I'm sure he will be too. If he brings a date, would you like me to tell you?"

"No thanks, because if he does have a date, she must not be keeping him too entertained since he's been blowing up my phone."

"Oh, so you've talked to Isaac?" Sasha was itching to know.

"Nope. I said he called, doesn't mean I answered."

"Whatever works for you. But yeah, like I was saying, I must be going. I'll definitely be in touch, though."

"Okay, have fun," Tracy said dryly before hanging up.

It was two hours before the party, and Bianca was completely nervous. She and Aunt Pearl had spent all day yesterday preparing for the evening's gala, and she'd just gotten back from having her hair and makeup done. When Bianca looked in the mirror, she couldn't believe the reflection staring back at her. It was a transformation she wasn't prepared for. She was gently touching her face, in awe of her newfound beauty, and was jolted out of her trance when the phone rang.

"Hello."

"Hi, there."

"Glen, how are you," Bianca chimed, pleasantly surprised to hear his voice.

"I'm good. So what time do you want me to pick you up?"

"Excuse me?"

"For the party tonight, I know you didn't change your mind?"

"Oh no, I'm definitely coming, but I don't need a ride, I'll meet you there."

"Are you sure? I have no problem picking you up. As a matter of fact, I would prefer it so I would know for sure you were showing up."

"No, I don't need a ride, and yes, I'm showing up."

"You promise?"

"I promise."

"Wonderful, I look forward to seeing you. Oh, and don't forget to save me a dance."

"I will."

Glen looked down at his cell after hanging up with Bianca. He felt excited about seeing her. He wished that Bianca was his date instead of Sasha. Although he cared about Sasha, being with her on an everyday basis made him realize that though her outer package was appealing, there was not a lot to be desired on the inside. He recalled that when he met her she'd said she was a college student, but since moving in with him, he had never even seen her with a book, let alone studying. He'd offered to pay her college tuition, but she said she had grown tired of school and was trying to figure out what she wanted to do with her life. Glen had all the money in the world, but he still wanted his woman to have a life outside of his, and Sasha showed no interest in that. Lately, he'd begun to realize that there was more to a relationship than beauty. Without mutual goals and things in common, how could it last?

When he arrived home, he headed straight to the bedroom. Sasha was stepping out of the shower, still dripping wet.

"Hi, Daddy, I've been missing you all day," she confessed as she dropped her towel. Glen couldn't lie; Sasha's body was flawless. She didn't even have any scars from her breast implants, which were remarkable, but he wasn't interested in having sex with her before leaving for the party. He still had Bianca on his mind, and that erased the temptation dangling before him.

"I really need to get in the shower," he said. "I don't want us to be late for the party."

"Baby, we have time. Lie down and let me give you something to think about until we get back home tonight," Sasha said, licking her lips seductively. Normally, that would be enough for Glen to step out of his pants and give Sasha what she wanted, but things felt different now, and he knew it was his newfound feelings for Bianca.

"Not now, Sasha. Get dressed, we have plenty of time later on for that," he said as he marched passed her.

"Good idea. I need to preserve my sexy for tonight's event," Sasha said, walking into the bedroom-sized closet.

By the time Glen and Sasha arrived at the Ritz-Carlton, the gala was in full swing. To Sasha, it seemed that every rapper, athlete, bigwig politician, and entertainment celebrity was blessing the spot. She did a precise inspection of every chick in the ballroom, and none of them came close to taking her shine away. Her Stella dress was emphasizing every curve just right, so she didn't understand why Glen had been so standoffish in the car. Normally his hands would have been preying on every part of her body, but tonight he seemed to be in another world.

"What's up?" Isaac said, walking up behind Sasha and Glen. When they turned around, Sasha was stunned to see that Isaac had brought the cheerleader stripper as his date.

"Damn, that bitch must let him bust off in her mouth and swallow too," Sasha reasoned, wondering what other reason Isaac would have for keeping her around like she was an official chick.

"Good to see you man," Glen said, giving Isaac a pound.

"Hi," Sasha said in a chipper voice to Isaac's date. "I'm sorry I never got the name you use outside of Magic City. I only know you as Passion, but that couldn't possibly be your government name."

"No problem, it's Penelope. Nice to see you again, but thank goodness under different circumstances."

Sasha replied by giving Penelope a stiff smile. Then out of the blue the whole room transfixed their stares in one direction, and Sasha looked that way too, dying to know what had everybody's undivided attention.

"Who in the world is that?" Isaac asked, being the first in their crew to zoom in on the woman who had mesmerized the room. The gorgeous goddess in a champagne-colored dress glided down the long staircase leading to the center of the ballroom, her long black tousled hair bouncing with each step she took. Her skin was luminous against the silk that draped her statuette body. Sasha studied the woman from the drop emeralds that sparkled in her ears to the diamond-studded Jimmy Choo heels that adorned her feet and had to admit that the lovely specimen was hands down the fiercest chick in the entire room. She hoped that at any moment her date would be at her side, so her man and every other one could stop drooling.

"I think I'm in love," Glen said under his breath, but Isaac heard him.

"You and me both. Who do you think she's here with?"

"I have no idea, but whoever he is, I take my hat off to him."

When the unknown woman reached the bottom stair and made her way through the crowd, every man turned to say hello. Sasha became jittery when it seemed the woman was making a beeline in their direction. It wasn't until the lady got within touching distance that she realized who the dream girl was, and her stomach instantly tightened up in knots.

"Hi, Glen."

"Bianca?" Glen said, as more of a question than a greeting.

"Of course it's me silly."

"Bianca, your assistant?" Isaac asked, not believing his eyes.

"You can't be the same girl that put me in the taxi the other day," Penelope said.

"To answer both of your questions, yes, I'm that girl. It's amazing what a dress and some makeup can do right. I can't believe all the glares and stares I'm getting." She giggled.

"You look absolutely incredible. I didn't even recognize you," Glen admitted.

"I don't know if I should take that as a compliment or be offended," Bianca said with a smile.

"Hi, Bianca. You look lovely tonight," Sasha said, stepping forward and standing between Bianca and Glen.

"Thanks, I guess I didn't need to take you up on your offer for styling tips."

Sasha felt her face turn red after the stinging remark. She didn't know how to respond, so she remained mute. Just when she believed her tension level had reached its limit, one of Glen's teammates approached and asked Bianca to dance.

"She'd love to," Sasha answered quickly, trying to get rid of the woman she never thought she'd consider competition.

The teammate took Bianca's hand and led her to the dance floor, as Glen watched with fire in his eyes.

"Why the fuck did you do that?" Glen asked.

"Do what?"

"Put Bianca off on some stranger?"

"Excuse me, Charlie isn't a stranger, he's your teammate, remember?"

"Still, Bianca doesn't know Charlie. How do you know she wanted to dance with him?"

"I didn't see her putting up a fight. The only person that seems to have a problem with it is you. Why is that?"

"I don't have a problem with it. I'm fine. Excuse me for a minute, I need to go speak to the coach." Sasha turned to where Bianca and Charlie were dancing and was once again astonished that the woman who'd been in their foyer yesterday was the same show-stopper who was here tonight. She'd always known that Bianca had potential under those baggy clothes and the plain Jane face, but never did she imagine that Bianca had all that going on.

"Isaac and I are going to dance, you should find Glen and join us," Penelope suggested.

"You two go ahead, we'll join you shortly."

Sasha turned her attention back to Bianca and decided she'd take Penelope's advice. She tracked Glen down at a table, talking to his coach, and lured him to the floor. They slow jammed to an oldie but goody by Jodeci, and as they did, Glen sneaked looks at Bianca and Charlie. It incensed him that his teammate had his arms around Bianca's waist as if they were a couple.

Midway through the song, Sasha couldn't hold her bladder any longer. "Baby, I'll be right back. I have to use the restroom."

"Go ahead. I'll be sitting down at our table waiting for you."

"Okay," Sasha said, and gave Glen a kiss on the lips. Then she hurried away, not wanting to leave him by himself for too long.

Once she disappeared, Glen wasted no time getting to Bianca. "Excuse me, Charlie, but I need to speak to my assistant."

Charlie eyed Bianca, hoping to catch some resistance and not wanting to leave the woman's side, but when she didn't object, he bowed out gracefully.

The second Glen's hands touched her skin, Bianca felt butterflies in her stomach. "So what is it you need to talk to me about?"

"I don't have time to engage in word games since Sasha will be coming back any minute, but I had to tell you that I think I'm falling in love with you."

Bianca's heart felt like it leaped out her chest. That was one confession she didn't expect Glen to make. She was speechless.

"You've been so heavy on my mind, and then when you showed up here tonight, I could no longer deny how strong my feelings are for you."

"What about Sasha?"

"It's hard to let someone go when you allow them to get so close. But I do know I don't want to be with Sasha, I want to be with you."

"Are you sure you're not just overwhelmed from seeing me in a decent outfit?" Bianca joked.

"I've already seen you at your best, naked." Bianca couldn't help but blush. "I want to sit down and really talk to you about how I feel. Do you mind making an early exit?"

"Not at all."

"Then let's go," Glen said as he took Bianca's hand and led the way.

"Are you okay?" Isaac asked, startling Sasha. "Sorry, I didn't mean to scare you, but I noticed that you seemed a little out of it."

"It's that obvious?" Sasha replied angrily, fidgeting with her hair. "I went to the bathroom and when I came out I spotted Glen dancing up close and personal with Bianca. By the time I torpedoed through this crowd, the two of them were ghosts. Have you seen Glen?"

"No, not since earlier with you, but if he is with Bianca, I'm sure it's nothing. They're probably somewhere discussing work-related stuff," he added, trying in vain to ease Sasha's mind.

"Isaac, we're at a party and it's after ten. What type of business would the two of them be discussing?" Sasha shouted.

"Calm down. There's no sense in getting upset."

"I need to stop him." Sasha was now frantic. Isaac firmly put his hand on her shoulder, wanting to make sure he had her attention.

"Listen to me. Chasing Glen down like a madwoman is a waste of time. You can never stop a man from doing what he wants to do. I'm not trying to hurt you, Sasha, but that's the truth. My advice is for you to go home, and if and when Glen's ready, he'll come back."

Glen and Bianca escaped upstairs to a penthouse suite at the Ritz-Carlton. Anticipation filled the air when Bianca stepped into the over 1,400-plus-square-foot suite. The marble entry and panoramic bay windows welcomed her with open arms. "This place is bigger than my apartment," she stated, moving smoothly toward the window as if floating on air. "The view is incredible."

"You're right, it is." Bianca turned back and gazed at Glen, knowing that view he was speaking of was her. "Can I get you something to drink?"

"No thank you." Bianca once again turned her head to absorb the moonlit skyline.

"I guess what's out there is more interesting than me."

"I'm sorry. It's not that at all. I feel like I'm in some incredible dream. I'm so scared I'll wake up and it'll all be gone that staring off into the sky gives me something to hold on to."

"You can hold on to me."

"Glen, the next time I hold on to you, I don't want to ever let go."

"Who said you would have to?"

"I don't want to share you, not with Sasha or any other woman," Bianca stated solemnly.

"You won't have to. After we made love that first time, I knew you were the one, but for a couple of reasons I wasn't ready to take a chance on real love. I want to explain some things to you. Come have a seat."

Bianca sat down on a chair next to the mahogany table.

"Since I can remember, the scrutiny that comes with being a celebrity is all I've been exposed to. My father was a huge NBA star, and by the time I was ten it was expected that I would follow in his footsteps. I know I come off as arrogant and cocky a lot of times, but it's only because I've been living in my father's shadow since the day I was born. The comparisons never stop, and they never will, no matter how much I accomplish. It's made me build this wall to protect myself because there is always that chance that I might fail, and all eyes will be on me if I do. That's difficult for me to deal with, but it's my reality. The people in my life only care about how I play the game. They've never shown any interest on what moves me in my personal relationships."

"Not even your parents?"

"My dad likes to critique my game on the court but not off. The only advice he's ever given me about personal relationships is that if possible, never have a baby with a woman you don't want to be with, and if you do, take care of your responsibilities so you don't have to hear her mouth.

"Growing up, I adored my mother, but she didn't have any backbone when it came to my father. I hate to say it, but she was no more than a trophy wife, and so when I got older, that's all I thought a woman was worth. The idea of falling in love and having a real relationship with a woman was not even something I put much thought into. But when I met you, I knew right away you were unlike any other woman I had ever met. You didn't pretend to be something you weren't because you had an ulterior motive. You told me the truth, whether I wanted to hear it or not, and I respected you for that. I was drawn to your intelligence and how genuine you are. It wasn't about being physical. But when we did make love, it just intensified my feelings even more. Then seeing you tonight, bringing the beauty and sexy back, was an added bonus because you had already captured my heart."

Bianca walked toward Glen and put her finger over his mouth. "Stop talking and make love to me."

He was more than happy to oblige. From the throbbing of his dick, his impulse was to throw Bianca across the table, rip off her clothes, and thrust himself inside of her. Instead, he opted to take his time and make love to her nice and slow. With Bianca's hair sweeping against his face, her fragrance intoxicated him. He gently gripped the nape of her neck and began from the tip of her chin, peppering kisses down her slender neck until he reached her succulent breasts. As the straps on Bianca's dress fell off her shoulders, he cupped her golden brown rounds, letting his tongue rotate back and forth, licking the tip of her sugary nipples. He caressed her voluptuous ass until his hand slid up Bianca's silky smooth inner thigh, touching her sweet, pulsating vagina. His fingers glided with ease on Bianca's clitoris, sending her body into a minor tremor.

"Baby, don't you think I've waited long enough?" she whispered in his ear. "Please give me what my body's been craving since the last time I felt your dick inside of me."

"You'll never have to wait for this dick again. It belongs to you now."

"You promise?" Bianca asked demurely.

"Promise." Glen lifted Bianca up and carried her to the king-size bed. He laid her down with each angle curving to resemble the letter S, and with her long hair spreading out like flowing feathers, she put him in the mind of an exotic black mermaid. He took off his tuxedo, savoring the thought of tasting all of her.

Bianca's eyes widened as she admired the rippling muscles ornamenting Glen's flawless physique. She rose off the bed, yearning to stroke the body that was calling her name. Glen placed his hand on the back of her dress and unzipped it completely down to the arch in her back. He pulled the dress from her body and slipped off her Jimmy Choos, then used her long legs as a map to her inner sanctuary. Bianca pulled him in tight, ready to take all of him, but then he paused.

"Can I taste you first?" His request seemed as innocent as asking for a bite of a delicious piece of cherry pie. He stood still waiting for her to respond.

"Yes," she managed to say under a breathless murmur.

Then all she could do to keep from screaming out in ecstasy was to clench tightly to the bed sheets as Glen's tongue made love to her. He took his erotic pleasuring of her to the next level by tasting her clit and finger fucking her simultaneously. Just as she was about to reach her climax, he stopped his tongue action and replaced it with his rock hard dick. Bianca's juices swallowed his manhood like a sweet coating over an ice cream sundae. She clutched his firm buttocks, pulling him farther in, until she felt as if his manhood was in the pit of her stomach. His width and length filled her up completely. Glen pinned her legs back as he kept each thrust steady, while heightening her arousal by massaging her breast with his mouth. Both were in complete sexual bliss as their bodies became one.

"Baby, I'm about to come," Bianca sighed, holding on tighter to Glen.

"Me too."

"Ahhhhh, ohhhh, I love you, Glen."

"I love you too," he moaned as they reached their climax in unison.

The lovers remained intertwined in each other's rapture all night, the sun shining across their sleeping faces the following morning.

Overtime

I Surrender

Sasha awoke from a nightmare, drenched in sweat. In her dream, Glen and Bianca were married with two kids, living happily ever after, and she was back in Indiana waiting tables at the diner she had escaped from years ago. She turned to the side of the bed Glen slept on, but of course he wasn't there.

"That motherfucker spent the night with that bitch!" she screamed, picking up the lamp on the nightstand and throwing it across the room, crashing it against the plasma television. Then she picked up the phone and dialed both Glen's cell phones and his car phone, but got no answer. She tried to calm herself down but was overtaken by rage. Bianca had come along and stolen her man without even brandishing a weapon.

She prayed that it would end up being a one-night stand, and that afterward, Glen would see the pussy wasn't that great and come crawling back to her.

* * *

"Rise and shine, my beautiful princess," Glen said, kissing Bianca on her forehead.

"What time is it?"

"Two in the afternoon."

"Are you serious? I never sleep this late. It must be because I was lying in your arms."

"Lying next to you did feel so right. I've never been so mentally and physically connected to a woman before. You have to be the person I was meant to spend the rest of my life with."

"Do you really mean that?"

"Yes, I put that on everything I love."

"Glen, I'm scared," she admitted.

"Why?"

"Because you represent everything I thought could never work in a relationship. Superstar athlete with fame, money, an endless choice of women, plus the one you already have."

"I know. I can't front that seriously settling down seemed way off for me. But being with you makes me ready for the wedding, kids, white picket fence—okay, make that gated mansion," he chuckled.

"Are you sure you want that life with me?"

"That, and so much more."

"How are you going to explain that to Sasha?"

"I'll handle it. I know she's been feeling that the vibe is off, but I'll let her know you're the one I want to be with."

"You know she's going to lose it."

"Yeah, at first, but Sasha is a survivor, she'll bounce back. I'd rather tell her the truth now then lead her on. She can move on with her life and find happiness the way I have with you." Glen bent down and kissed Bianca, and the two began making love once again.

* * *

Isaac woke up for the third morning in a row with Penelope by his side. After trying every sexual position known to mankind with the cheerleader stripper, he'd become increasingly bored with her. He realized just how much he missed Tracy, and decided he would do anything possible to get her back. "Penelope, wake up," he said, shaking the still sleeping girl.

She slowly started coming out of her sex and liquor induced coma. "What is it?"

"I need you to get up, get dressed, and leave."

"Huh, I don't understand."

"I'll call you a cab, but I'm ready for you to go now."

Isaac's demand woke Penelope right up. "What happened? I thought it was all good between us."

"It was, but we've had enough fun. It's time for me to get back to reality."

Penelope wasn't stupid, she'd played this game many times. She knew exactly what Isaac meant. "So you're going back to your girl-friend?"

"Yeah, if she'll have me."

"She'd be crazy not to. I can tell you're a really great guy, even if you did fuck around on her."

"I hope she's as understanding."

After Penelope got dressed, Isaac walked her downstairs to the waiting taxi. He handed her a fist-sized knot of one hundred dollar bills totaling ten thousand dollars. He felt it was the least he could do for her services.

"You have real class, Isaac," she told him. "If you ever need to talk, you know where to find me."

Back in his apartment, Isaac sat down and called Tracy. For the first time since all the drama went down, she answered the phone.

"Baby, I want you to come home," were the first words out of Isaac's mouth.

Sasha ran to the top of the stairs when she heard the front door opening. "Glen, I was so worried about you. I'm glad you're home." After going through every emotion, from crying to screaming to contemplating murder, she had decided to use a different approach. Instead of flipping out and calling Glen every name in the book, she pretended that Bianca wasn't even part of the equation, hoping that after today she wouldn't be.

"No, I'm fine. I was with—" Sasha cut him off.

"You don't have to explain. We don't need to discuss what happened last night. It's the past, and we should focus on the present. What we have is so much stronger than whatever meaningless dalliance you had last night."

Glen stared up at Sasha and started feeling guilty. He'd expected her to come at him with all sorts of four letter words and maybe even objects to go upside his head with, but her demeanor and attitude were surprisingly calm. Sasha walked down the stairs wearing a subtle terry-cloth sundress, another surprise. He figured she would be sashaying down the stairs with tits and ass jiggling, trying to seduce him into bed.

"How about we go in the kitchen and I make you something to eat?"

Glen started to wonder if he had walked into the right house. It damn sure looked like his crib, and the woman in front of him was an excellent replica of Sasha, but her actions were those of a stranger. "Okay, I am hungry." More than that, he was curious as to what Sasha planned in the way of food. He didn't even know she could cook. In their whole time of dating she had never served him so much as a drink of water. He sat down at the table and watched as she began whipping up a meal.

"Would you like a snack while I'm preparing your food?"

"I'll just take a glass of juice."

As he requested, Sasha poured him a glass of juice, and set it down on the table with a smile on her face. Glen started getting antsy about the discussion he was about to have with her, but knew he had to get it over with.

"Sasha, as I was saying when I got home, I have to talk to you about something."

"I told you it wasn't necessary."

"But it is because I'm in love with Bianca and I want to be with her." As soon as the words were out of his mouth, he felt relieved. He waited to hear the tongue lashing Sasha would give him.

"Glen, because you fell up in some new, untouched pussy, now you're in love," she said coolly.

"It's more than sex. I've been developing feelings for Bianca for some time now."

"During the same time you were falling asleep and waking up making love to me, during that time?" Glen felt a lump in his throat as he struggled to answer Sasha's questions. He hadn't planned on the conversation going like this. Somehow, Sasha had managed to turn the tables and make him question himself.

"I'll admit that I care about you, Sasha, and we shared some good times together, but what I have with Bianca is different. I want to spend the rest of my life with her."

"You mean like marriage, family—that type of life?"

"Yes," he answered, not wanting to crush Sasha, but since she'd asked, he wanted to be honest.

"I see. Well, how do you think Bianca will take being a step-mother?" Sasha said, continuing to cook Glen's meal as if she hadn't just dropped a bombshell.

"What are you talking about?"

"I'm talking about the child I'm carrying, your child." Glen stood up and then sat back down, getting a migraine as if a hammer was knocking on his head.

"You're on the pill and I always pull out."

"Not a little over a month ago when I gave you the best head of your life and then we had sex before you got in the shower, I unfortunately misplaced my pills and didn't take them that month."

Glen wasn't sure what had him reeling more, remembering the one time he got so caught up in Sasha's dick-sucking that when she pulled him in, he did in fact explode inside of her, or how confident her declaration of being pregnant was.

Sasha knew she had Glen by the balls, and she planned on squeezing them until he couldn't breathe. "And don't even think about asking me to have an abortion. Even though you're leaving me for Bianca, I still love you very much, and the child I'm carrying is a reflection of that." As if nothing had changed, she added, "Your food is ready, so relax and enjoy your meal."

Bianca was still on cloud nine, relishing her time with Glen. She never knew love would feel this good. She'd only been with one other man her whole life, and that ended up being a summer fling that left her with a broken heart. It was after her first year of college, and instead of going home, she opted to stay and take extra courses during the summer break. She met a handsome football player who was taking courses to get caught up so he would be able to play for the upcoming season.

First, he asked Bianca to tutor him, which she agreed to do. But then he showed a romantic interest, which totally surprised her.

Bianca was a bookworm, not the kind of girl she'd seen the football player on campus with. They soon began a passionate love affair that lasted throughout the summer. With Bianca doing all his schoolwork and studying with him for his tests, her lover aced his summer classes. Meanwhile, during their time together, he confessed his undying love and promised to remain committed to her. Being young and naive, Bianca believed every word. She had given her virginity to the football stud, and in her heart wanted to marry him. It wasn't until a week before school was about to start and he stopped answering her calls that she became alarmed. When she finally ran into him in the student lounge the first week of school, holding hands with a beautiful sorority sister, she realized he had just used her for the summer and then tossed her away like a dirty napkin. He gave her no explanation as to why he stopped seeing her, just simply stated that their relationship was over.

From that day on Bianca had never trusted men and refused to date any of them. She continued to study hard and focus on doing great in school, but that experience made her petrified to ever take a chance on love again—until now. Glen gave her the self-assurance she needed to open her heart and fall in love. A smile crept across her face, knowing that at that moment Glen was ending his relationship with Sasha and they would soon enjoy exploring their newfound love.

Glen hadn't moved from the kitchen table. The plate of Cuban cuisine Sasha had prepared was still sitting in front of him, untouched. The sun had gone down hours ago, but he couldn't tear himself away from his chair. Sasha's pregnancy bombshell was tearing him up. It threw a monkey wrench into his plans with Bianca. They were in the beginning of their love affair, and he wasn't sure if they could endure the unexpected arrival of a baby he was having with another woman. In his heart, he knew that he wanted to give their love a try, but he wasn't confident that Bianca would come to the same conclusion. Of course, the only way to know for sure was to give her the choice, so he grabbed his car keys and headed for the door.

"Where are you going?" Sasha had been sitting in the living room patiently waiting for feedback from Glen after she gave given him her news. He'd been speechless.

"I'm going to see Bianca."

"Do you plan on telling her about the baby?"

"Of course, she has the right to decide whether she wants to continue things knowing that you're pregnant with my child."

"What if she doesn't, then what?"

"I don't know, Sasha. I don't even want to think about that. I'm hoping she'll decide we can get past this."

"So what, you all can continue on your love affair and then you just throw me out in the streets and forget about your child?"

"Of course not. I'm going to be a father to my child. You don't ever have to second-guess that."

"What about me?"

"Sasha, I'll make sure you're provided for throughout your pregnancy and after. Honestly, I don't want you stressing right now. You need to take care of yourself for the baby's sake."

"I appreciate that. Good luck with Bianca."

Sasha sat in the dark preparing her next move as if playing a game of chess. Ideally, as far as she was concerned, Bianca would bow out, not wanting to be bothered with a baby mama, especially one as treacherous as her. But landing a man like Glen was incredibly tempting, and Bianca might decide the battle was worthwhile. If Bianca decided to ride it out, Sasha knew she would have to find another way to lure Glen back. For now, Sasha could tell that the calm, cool, collective approach was pushing the right buttons with him. As badly as he wanted to be mad and flip out on her because she wasn't pulling the normal card, "If you're not with me I'll make your life a living hell attitude," her calm approach had caused Glen to be cordial, which was exactly what she wanted. That meant all she would have to do was catch him at the right time, when he was vulnerable, and she'd be back in his bed.

As Glen drove to Bianca's apartment, he struggled with how he would break the news to her about Sasha. This was no way to start a new relationship, but he hoped it would make their bond stronger instead of ripping them apart. He got out of his car and slowly walked to Bianca's front door. He never thought he would come to a place in his life when he would fear losing a woman, and realized now that's what happened when you fell in love. He rang the doorbell, and within seconds Bianca answered.

"Hi, baby," she said. "I've been missing you since the moment I left you."

Glen wrapped his arms tightly around Bianca, never wanting to let go. "I missed you too. I've been waiting to hold you again all day. You feel so good," he said, hoping it wouldn't be the last time he would hold her in his arms like this.

"Would you like me to get you anything?"

"No, you're all I need." Glen's words sounded sweet, but his body language was saying something else.

"What's wrong? You seem a little edgy. I guess things didn't go so well with Sasha?"

"It's a little more complicated than that."

"What's so complicated? I'm sure Sasha got extra dramatic and probably threatened to ruin your life and mine, but that was her anger talking. She'll cool down."

"Actually, she was extremely calm."

Bianca did a double take. "Calm. That isn't a word I thought I'd ever hear used to describe Sasha."

"Me neither. But she was. And she shared some interesting news with me."

"What news?"

Glen was building up the courage to spill his guts as he paced back and forth.

"Glen, what's wrong? You're scaring me."

"I'm not trying to. The news is still fresh in my mind, and finding the right words is difficult."

"Stop trying to figure out the right words and just say it." Bianca was becoming frustrated, trying to read Glen's mind. She wanted to know what had him walking on eggshells.

"Sasha is pregnant with my child."

Bianca's heart dropped. When she finally found true love, once again the beautiful sorority sister was coming along and taking away her happiness. She stood up and held her stomach as the pain of rejection captured her. "And of course she's going to have it, and what you've decided is to leave me and go back to her?"

"Yes, I mean no. I mean yes, she's going to have the baby, but no, I'm not going to leave you. I love you. I want to spend the rest of my life with you, Bianca."

Bianca wanted to believe Glen, but a baby put a whole new spin on things. "But she's carrying your child. I can't compete with that."

"I'm not asking you to. I want you to be a part of my life and my child's. This baby doesn't change the love I have for you. I just hope it doesn't change how you feel about me."

"Nothing can change how I feel about you, and of course I would love your child. But what about Sasha? She'll use that baby to try to get you back every chance she gets. Every time you go visit your child, I know Sasha will be plotting and scheming to make her move on you." Glen reached out and held Bianca's face in the palm of his hands. "Do you love me?" he asked, staring into her eyes.

"Of course I love you. Why would you even ask something like that?"

"Because I need to know that for better or worse you'll stand by my side no matter what."

"Always."

"Then not Sasha or anyone one else will be able to come between us. No matter how many tricks she may try to pull out her bag, our unity will keep our love intact. You have to truly believe that. You can't allow your insecurities to destroy what we have. The only people that can ruin what we have are us."

"You make it sound so simple. But love is far from simple, Glen. My heart was broken once before, and I never thought I would be able to trust another man with my love until you. If you hurt me, it would be too devastating." Tears began falling down Bianca's face, and Glen kissed each of them away. He wanted her to be secure with the feelings they shared. It was imperative for her to believe his love would never waver.

"Baby, your heart is safe in my hands. I will protect it because now it belongs to me. The only tears I want you to cry are those of happiness, not pain. Now let me make love to you so we can create and bring our own child into this world."

"You're ready for us to have a baby together?"

"Nothing would make me happier, except for you being my wife, but we can discuss that at a later time. But, Bianca it's okay to surrender your love to me," Glen said, flashing his signature smile.

Looking into his eyes, Bianca finally believed that Glen wasn't like the football player who had stolen her heart and then broke it. She was no longer the young girl who didn't understand the difference between love and infatuation. Glen was all man, and she was now a mature woman who could follow her heart. Yes, with love you'd always be taking a chance that the other person might hurt or disappoint you. But what was the sense in living if you weren't willing to take the biggest gamble of all, experiencing love b-ball style?

JOY KING was born in Toledo, Ohio, and raised in California, Maryland, and North Carolina. She represents a new genre of young, hip, sexy novels that take readers behind the velvet rope of the glamorous but often shady relationships in the entertainment industry.

Joy attended North Carolina Central University and Pace University, where she majored in journalism. Emerging onto the entertainment scene in the late nineties, Joy accepted an internship position, and immediately began to work her way up the ranks, at the Terrie Williams Agency. She worked hands-on with Johnnie Cochran, the Essence Awards, The NBA Players' Association, Moët & Chandon, and other entertainment executives and celebrities.

In 1999, Joy attended the Lee Strasburg Theater Institute before accepting a job as Director of Hip Hop Relations at Click Radio, where she developed segments featuring the biggest names in hip hop. Joy pushed her department to new levels by creating an outlet that placed hip hop in the forefront of the cyber world.

Joy made her debut in the literary world with *Dirty Little Secrets*, a novel that is loosely based on her life. The sequel, *Hooker to Housewife*, will be in released in April 2007.

A prolific writer, Ms. King also writes street novels under the pseudonym Deja King. With the debut of *Bitch*, Ms. King garnered a loyal urban following who are eagerly anticipating the sequel, *Bitch Reloaded*, which will be released in 2007.

These Are My Confessions

Electa Rome Parks

This is dedicated to all the keepers of secrets . . . know that the truth heals.

The Beginning . . .

"Oooh yeah, baby! That's right! Don't stop doing what you're doing!" Drake was in heaven.

"Okay, babe. Anything you say. You sure you can handle this?" I teased in between licks.

Starting in small circles, I twirled my tongue up and down his shaft, and with each flick reached farther and farther down. When I placed all of him inside my warm mouth, I thought Drake was going to collapse in a heap in the middle of the floor.

"Damn, Kennedy. You do that shit too good," he exclaimed as his eyes rolled back in his head like he was going into convulsions.

"Who do you love?" I asked, momentarily pausing to look up at Drake. I needed to hear him say it, again.

"Don't stop now! Put it back in. I was almost there. Put it in," Drake moaned, trying to place his stiff, massive organ back in the comfort, wetness, and warmth of my eager, accommodating mouth.

"Not until you answer my question," I stated, shyly looking up at him from beside the sofa in my living room.

"Damn, Kennedy, you can't tease a man like this," he exclaimed, pushing my long hair back out of my flushed face. Unsuccessfully, he tried to force my head back down with his other hand.

"Who do you love?"

I took the opportunity to suck down on his tip, just like he had taught me. Not too hard, but with enough pressure to cause him to involuntarily shudder and close his eyes. Drake had patiently and expertly instructed me on everything he liked for me to do to him in bed. The things I didn't care for, I did them anyway. Just to please him. *Cosmopolitan* magazine articles revealed what you wouldn't do for your man, another woman would. Women should learn to be accommodating in the bedroom. I went above and beyond for Drake.

Tonight was costume night. Sometimes Drake and I played games where I'd dress up in costumes and live out his fantasies. It kept the sex exciting and interesting, is what Drake said. I had no complaints. Tonight, I had on a red and blue cheerleading uniform minus my panties and bra. I even sported long socks and tennis shoes to complete the look. As I squatted on the floor with my open, bent legs, Drake manually stimulated me and squeezed my breasts through the thin fabric while I pleased him. My wetness was all over his fingers. I think I was addicted to his dick; it was beautiful, just like him, and I could suck him for hours.

"Kennedy, baby. You know I love you. From the first day I saw you, I've loved you," he exclaimed, rubbing some more on my spot. I felt my knees getting weak.

I let out a slow, sensual moan, closed my eyes and bit down on my bottom lip. "Yeah, right there." I opened my legs even wider, granting Drake full access.

He reached to push my head back down, and I searched his face for the truth. I knew Drake sometimes told me what he thought I wanted to hear. His confessions, sometimes, didn't hold an ounce of truth.

"Come on, baby. Work my dick. Do it like I taught you. Suck that lollipop."

"Hmm, you taste sweet," I cooed, licking my lips.

"It was love at first sight when you walked through my door. I knew you were the one."

Drake had told me all I needed to hear. His words were music to my soul. I went to work, harder and faster than before. How many licks does it take to get to the center of the tootsie roll pop? Slurping, wet sounds echoed throughout the stillness of the moment. We never made love with any background music or noise. Drake was turned on by the sensual, raw sounds and smells of our lovemaking.

"Ohhh yeah! That's it! That's my girl! Damn!" he screamed out in ecstasy as I moved just in time before he spewed all over me. With his eyes still closed and a big smile on his gorgeous face, Drake collapsed against my sofa, pulled me to him, and caressed my hair and face over and over. He loved to run his hands through my long, wavy locks. Drake despised when I wore my hair pulled up in a ponytail, and he expected me to take it down when I was with him. I obliged. Always accommodating.

"You're getting better. Go get a warm washcloth for your man," he said, pulling up my skirt and smacking me on the ass two times, leaving a light red mark.

I stared at him from my spot on the floor. Getting better? I thought he'd enjoyed that. I knew he did. I was on point with all he had taught me. I made a mental note to do better the next time. I had finally gotten my gag reflex under control. Maybe, next time I'd surprise him by swallowing.

"Go on, baby. Hurry up," he demanded, bending down and taking one of my throbbing nipples in his mouth like he possessed it and absently playing between my quivering legs. "I'm ready to eat some honey because your pussy always tastes sweet."

I quickly jumped up to retrieve a towel because I knew what was in store for me. My kitty twitched. Twitched again. Drake was off the chain when it came to sexing me. He had turned me out; inside and out.

Ring. Ring. Ring.

In my daze, I glanced around and surveyed my surroundings. In my bed, safe and sound in my tiny apartment. The ringing telephone woke me from my flashback of events that had transpired several months earlier, during happier times. The tingling between my legs was present day and very real. My coochie was having some serious dick withdrawals and feeling like an addict for a piece of Drake. However, that would happen only over my dead body.

Drake.

Drake, I never want to set my eyes on him for the rest of my life. If I never, ever see him, that would be too soon. I don't know what led me to believe that I'd make a difference in his life and he'd fall hopelessly and helplessly in love with me. What made me think that I'd possess him someday? Drake could never be possessed by a mere woman. I think he secretly hates the female population and only tolerates and uses us for his enjoyment and pleasure.

Snuggling deeper under my comforter and adjusting my pillows, I glanced at the digital clock that sat on my nightstand. It read 7:35 A.M. I had tossed and turned for most of the night with fretful dreams when I did dose off for a few restless minutes. There was definitely no sleeping now; I was wide-awake and antsy. For a second I had forgotten it was a Saturday morning, no work. I reached down beside my bed, retrieved, and once again examined my brand-new leather journal and thought, Why not? It had tons of blank, lined pages to write on. Maybe if I wrote some of my jumbled thoughts down, I could make some sense of the turn my life had taken. But where to begin?

I remember a college professor telling his creative writing class that every story has a beginning, middle, and ending. Simple enough. I'll start at the beginning. Maybe in the process I'd answer the million-dollar question: What makes a woman want to end her life over a man? These are my confessions:

Dear Journal,

I guess I should start by telling you something about myself. Let's see. There's really not much to tell, that's interesting anyway. I'm pretty average in most ways and live a relatively tame lifestyle. That is until recently. I'm twenty-eight years old. Work as a customer service representative for a telecommunications company in Midtown. By the way, it's a job I don't particularly care for, but I do my best nevertheless. It could be a cool job, but there is always so much drama going on with the women there. Trivia stuff at that. Why can't women just get along?

Oh, I'm adopted. Mother and Daddy adopted me when I was two months old. I was born to a teenage, crack-addicted biological mother who gave me up at birth. Signed over her maternal rights. Just like that. With the snap of two fingers. In the blink of an eye. She signed over her maternal rights, and I became a ward of the state of Georgia. She wasn't even sure who my biological father was. That line on my birth certificate was left blank.

I don't get it. And believe me, I've tried. How can a

mother, any mother, give birth to a child that she has carried for nine months, felt her moving around inside her, bonded with, and then, then . . . just give her up like she's dumping the trash? Me, I could never do that in a million years. It's actually ironic, my life didn't mean anything to my biological mother and I guess it didn't mean anything to me either since I tried to take it over a month ago. Thirty days ago.

Luckily for me, Mother and Daddy came into my life when I was two months old. Mother said she took one look at me lying all alone in the hospital crib, underweight because I was born premature, and knew she had to have me to love, shield, and nurture. Mother said she'd never forget how small, fragile, and vulnerable I appeared. Like I was calling out for her to love and protect me. And she did and hasn't stopped loving me in all my twenty-eight years.

What else? I guess you could say I'm a loner. I don't have very many friends, male or female. That's fine with me. I've halfway attempted to be friends with women at work, but in the end, there are always too many jealousies, insecurities, and backstabbing going on for me. Mother said I shouldn't stress or worry about it. She claims these women are jealous of my good looks. I don't know, I think I have average looks. I'm about five-seven. Very fair skinned, long, naturally wavy brownish-red hair, hazel eyes, and a slim frame. Strangers are always saying I could easily be a model with my long legs, slim waist, and exotic looks.

Anyhow, whatever the reason, I choose to go to work, perform my job duties, and leave. My coworkers assume I'm a snob since I won't get involved in their gossip, after-work activities, and petty ways. Until a year ago, most weekends found me at home curled up with a good book. Occasionally, Taylor, a college friend, would convince me to hit a local night spot. I'd tag along, to please her, even though the club scene wasn't really me. Clubbing wasn't my thing. Typically, I'd sit in a corner for most of the night, nurse one drink and turn down dances left and right. Taylor, on the other hand, lived on the dance floor and loved the attention men showered her with.

I've never been good with men either. I can count on one hand the number of boyfriends I've had. I've never had problems attracting men, only attracting the right ones. I honestly think I have an invisible sign posted on my forehead that reads: Use and Abuse Me. Please. The wrong ones flock to me like bees to honey.

After I met Drake, I thought all that had changed. Was all in my past. I felt like I had won the lottery and I had the chance for love, marriage, and a family. How wrong I was. Love is so blind, it feels right even when it's wrong.

Life After the Incident . . .

Gloomy and bleak, just like me, most of Monday morning found me answering and returning client calls, researching existing problems, and completing follow-up items. This was my first week back at work—after my incident. I had made it halfway down my "to do" list when the phone rang again.

"Hello, Kennedy Logan speaking."

"Yeah. Yeah. Yeah. Save it, save it. Sweetie, what's going on? You got a minute? I'm seriously stressing on my end. What are you doing?"

It was Taylor. As usual, she was talking a mile a minute, showed no signs of stalling, and I couldn't get a word in edgewise.

"Working," I replied sarcastically.

"I'm so glad you're back at work, because your mother wouldn't let me within one hundred feet of you. I think she set up guard duty next to your phone. I get the impression she thinks I'm a bad influence on you or something."

"Taylor, be for real. You know Mother loves you like a second daughter. She's always asking about you and how you're doing."

"Well, I wouldn't have known it the way she has treated me the last couple of weeks. Every time I called, you were always busy or resting, according to her. I didn't feel the love. Not at all."

"Taylor, you know how Mother is, and I didn't know she was screening my calls. I thought I hadn't heard from you because you were out of town on business."

"Well, now you know. Plus, when has being out of town ever stopped me from calling you?"

"True. Well, I apologize."

"Plus, I'm so mad at you. I had to go to the club by myself that night you promised you'd hang out."

"Oh, I'm sorry. I've had so much on my mind that I completely forgot all about that," I lied.

"I know you forgot. Of course, when I called to remind you, your mother wouldn't put me through. Said you were resting and still not feeling well."

"Did she?"

"Yes, K."

"Ump."

"Kennedy, what's going on? For real."

"What do you mean?"

"I mean just what I asked, what's really going on? Why did you stay out from work this long? A month? And why had Mrs. Logan moved in with you and was acting like your personal bodyguard? Who or what does she have to protect you from?"

"Taylor, I've already told you what happened. Mother was nursing me back from the flu. Even now, my body hasn't fully recovered. I'm always tired and I've lost weight. Mother's back at her house now." I wondered silently, how did you inform your best friend that you almost overdosed on prescription pills because of a man? And Mother found me.

"Kennedy, come on now. This is me you're talking to. I've known you for a minute. I know how you act when you try to lie."

Silence.

"You are not very good at it."

To calm down, I breathed deeply through my nose. "Taylor, I don't feel like talking about this right now. Okay?" I felt a headache coming on.

"Knowing what a private person you are, I'm going to respect your request, but soon you gotta let me know what's really going on."

"Yeah, soon."

"I'm going to hold you to that," Taylor quirked with determination in her voice.

"Yeah, whatever."

"Whatever, my ass. I am. I'm always in your corner and don't you forget that."

"I know."

"Anyway, I'm supposed to be on a self-imposed twenty minute break. My coworkers have gotten on my last nerve; everybody is tripping, so I had to take a breather. I'm gonna have to go, but I have to know one thing," Taylor said in a near whisper.

"What?"

"Have you seen him yet?"

"Seen who?"

"K, what is wrong with you today? Who do you think? Drake."

"You know we broke up. I wish you'd stop worrying about me and Drake with your nosy self. No, I haven't seen him, and I'm not looking for him either."

"I'm not nosy!"

"Yes, you are. You are the nosiest person I know besides Mother."

"Well, I'm in good company," she laughed.

"Whatever."

"K, you'll have to see him sooner or later. For God's sake, you work for the same company. I still can't believe, you of all people, got caught up in an office romance."

"That's right. Pour more salt on my wounds."

"I'm sorry, but you're usually so practical about everything. This office romance was so uncharacteristic of you."

"I guess Drake was very persuasive."

"Just don't let him sweet-talk you, change your mind, and draw you back into his life and his bed. His dick is not gold."

"I won't, Mother. Now stop bugging me," I laughed, but the laugher never reached my eyes.

"Kennedy, I know you, and you didn't stop loving that man overnight. You don't give your love away frivolously. You're vulnerable right now and Drake knows that. So, be weary of that slimy snake in the grass."

"Okay, I will. I promise. Now, enough."

"Drake doesn't deserve you."

"That's what you and Mother keep telling me," I cited, playing with the phone cord, wrapping it around my thin fingers.

"Well, it's true. You're too good for him. Always was."

Deadly silence.

"Hello?"

"I'm here."

"I have to run; we have our weekly meeting in a few minutes. I'll talk to you later. Maybe we can do lunch one day this week and play catch-up."

"Cool. Let me know," I answered as we said our good-byes and hung up the phone. My mind was reeling back to what Taylor had said, the exact same thing Drake had stated in what seemed like eons ago. I would have to see him sooner or later. Hopefully, it would be later, much later. Like when hell froze over.

First Encounter . . .

Dear Journal,

The first time I laid eyes on Drake was a year, two months, and a day ago. I can break it down to the hours, minutes, even seconds if you asked me to because I recall it just like it was yesterday. If only I had known or sensed in some way that he'd be trouble. Trouble with a capital T. It's true, if it's too good to be true, then it probably is. All that glitters isn't gold. Drake was more like fool's gold.

I was hand delivering business reports and correspondence, up on the sixth floor, to one of the managers, Bill Walker. Mr. Walker managed some of the top tier clients that I serviced. We were engaged in the usual, cordial, how's the weather chitchat in his spacious office. Not much of anything was really being said. Just polite conversation. Then

Mr. Walker asked me the question that changed my entire life—for the worse.

"Kennedy, have you met our new manager, Drake Collins? He came to us by way of California roughly two weeks ago."

"No, I haven't."

"Well, come and let me introduce the two of you. You'll probably work with him periodically on accounts and assist in getting him up to speed."

We walked out of Mr. Walker's corner office and strolled four doors over. I envied management. They all had large, stately offices that had floor-to-ceiling windows and were privileged to a spectacular view of Atlanta and could see as far away as Stone Mountain. Me, I had a tiny cubicle that didn't have a door I could conveniently close for privacy, and I definitely didn't have a view of the city. My view was the grayish walls of my cubbyhole.

With my degree in business administration, I could be in management within a few years, but I didn't have the desire to work my way up the ladder. Sometimes I felt that corporate America was not for me. I didn't know what I wanted to do. Whenever I complained to Mother, she encouraged me to go back to school for my MBA. Sometimes I thought it was a good idea, but other times I wasn't feeling like another two or more years of professors, studying, and exams. With a full-time job, when would I have the time or energy?

As we walked into Mr. Collins's office, sitting with his back to us and talking on the phone was an African-American male who I hadn't seen before. He signaled with his finger that he'd be just a moment. We patiently waited

for him to end his phone call, and I quickly checked out
his office space with curiosity. Everything was neat, in
place, and very efficient-looking. There weren't a lot of
personal items such as photos or anything of that nature.
So I wasn't sure if he was married or had any children.
This new manager had a few colorful framed prints and
affirmations on his wall and credenza. I still hadn't gotten
a good look at this Mr. Collins yet. I was secretly thinking
about all the work piled up on my desk.

Finally, he turned around and stood up to address us and
I stumbled head first into his soulful eyes. Standing before
me was the absolute most gorgeous man I had ever seen
in my entire life. My breath caught in my throat. He was
almost flawless; almost too perfect. Drake was the perfect
specimen of a strong, black man, on the outside anyway.
The only imperfection I saw was a small scar, barely notice-
able, right below his perfect bottom lip. I wanted to reach
out, touch his cheek and see if he was real because the man
standing before me had to be an illusion.

With close-cropped, slightly wavy hair, light brown eyes
with specks of green, a thin mustache, and smooth dark
brown skin, he was a god. And to top it all off, he had a
beautiful smile to match his six feet, two inch frame. Even
through his business jacket, I could make out the six-pack
that was beneath his blue dress shirt. It was obvious he
worked out at a gym because he was too tight. I figured he
was around thirty, no older than thirty-three. Yes, this was
all man because just his presence was affecting me.

I was truly shocked I hadn't heard the women on my floor
talking, gossiping, and placing claims on this manly specimen. You couldn't miss Drake. When he walked in a room,

he was the kind of man who made you pause in whatever you were doing and just drool. He commanded attention. I had simply blocked out my coworkers' comments regarding him, or maybe they didn't bother to inform me about him. I know they didn't consider me competition, not because of my looks, but because they knew I didn't date on the job.

I didn't believe in office romances. I had witnessed what messing with the boss could do for you—give you your walking papers when the relationship went south, or just an internal black ball followed you out the door. The termination of office affairs had ended some promising careers at my company.

"Kennedy, Kennedy?" Mr. Walker repeated, giving me an odd look with a slight smile on his pale face. Mr. Walker was forever in need of a few hours of sun, but he was pretty decent. He always treated me with respect and valued my opinion regarding clients. Recently, he personally called and asked me why I hadn't interviewed for one of the management positions that was open. Internal associates always received first priority over external candidates. Mr. Walker thought I was a perfect candidate to interview for the position.

"Oh, I'm sorry," I said, swallowing the lump that had suddenly formed in my throat. "I spaced out for a moment. I guess I was thinking about the workload waiting on my desk downstairs."

"Well, yes. You guys have been swamped with a high volume of calls lately, since we installed the new software. Don't worry, Drake and I won't keep you long."

Drake and I awkwardly stared at each other. I longed to hear what his voice would sound like directed toward me. I *thought it would be rich, deep and sexy. Suddenly, images of him whispering sweet nothings in my ear clouded my brain. What was going on?*

"As I was saying, Kennedy, I'd like for you to meet Drake Collins. Drake, this is Kennedy Logan. She's one of our best customer service representatives. Kennedy has helped me out on numerous occasions and has an excellent rapport with many of our top tier clients. She's a great asset to the company."

As I tried unsuccessfully to stop the huge blush that had assaulted my face, I held out my slightly shaky right hand. I was pretty light-skinned, so I knew that Drake and Mr. Walker noticed the redness that flushed my cheeks, neck and face.

"Nice to meet you, Mr. Collins. Welcome aboard."

"Same here, nice to meet you too," he stated as his huge hand swallowed mine. I couldn't help but notice the contrast of our skin tones as they meshed in a handshake. I observed that Drake had perfectly manicured nails. And his hands were smooth and soft to the touch. I knew then that this man took care of himself and hadn't done any hard labor a day in his life. He had been pampered and catered to.

Even though we were in a professional setting, I saw Drake quickly take me in from head to toe. Starting at my feet, he swiftly admired my long legs, paused at my hips, made his way up to my chest, and finally took in my glowing face. All in a matter of seconds. When I went out with Taylor, this was the same look that I typically received from the men in the clubs. In the clubs, it turned me off because I always felt like I was being sized up like a piece of raw meat by the hungry lions. For some reason, with Drake, my heart gave a quick flutter. This completely caught me off guard.

"Kennedy. What a lovely name." My name just flowed off his tongue like a fine wine poured into expensive crystal glassware.

"Thank you."

"Are you originally from Atlanta, Kennedy?"

"Yes, born and raised here. A Georgia peach."

"I can't believe it. I'm finding it's rare to find a true Atlanta native. Everyone here seems to be a transplant from New York, Florida, or someplace up North."

"Well, you've found me."

"Indeed I did."

He smiled.

I smiled.

"Maybe you can suggest some good restaurants for lunch and dinner, for that matter. I just relocated here from Los Angeles, and I'm still learning my way around and finding the hot spots in the city."

"I'm afraid I'm the wrong one to ask. I usually eat lunch at my desk, I'm a diehard brown bagger," I explained, Drake's eyes never left mine. I could get lost in them. Drown. When the sunlight from his open window blinds hit them just right, the specks of green in his eyes danced around in merry circles.

When we heard Mr. Walker politely clear his throat, we came back to reality. As I brushed my wild hair out of my face, I quickly blushed again and looked down at the floor. Suddenly, I wished I had worn my nice black Donna Karan suit and put on some makeup. Plus, I was in dire need of a manicure. I quickly balled my fingers into tight fists at my sides and hoped he hadn't noticed.

"Well, Miss Kennedy . . . it is Miss, isn't it?"

"Yes." I wanted to scream out, Yes, I'm single. Single and available. It had been a while since I'd been in a long-term relationship. Any relationship.

"It's a pleasure to meet you, and I may have to call you so you can explain some of these reports you guys generate in your department. And if Bill recommended you, then you must be great," he said, holding my hand again—a bit too long. I shuddered. Felt a moistness that surprised me.

"Nice meeting you too. And sure, I'll be glad to explain the client reports. They can be a bit confusing to someone not used to reviewing them. Just give me a call. I'm in the directory, extension 3–5123."

"I may certainly do that," he said, finally releasing his hand and eyes from mine. My heart stopped fluttering then, slowly returned to near normal.

As Mr. Walker and I walked out, I felt Drake's eyes as they seductively caressed my butt. When I discreetly glanced back, our eyes meshed, I was lost, and he smiled. I offered a weak one in return and kept walking, faster. Somebody was a lucky woman because I knew that man had a woman. And if she was smart, she was a woman who kept a close eye on him. Drake could almost make a woman go back on her promise to never date someone she worked with. As Taylor would say, "Don't shit where you eat."

Approximately a week after I was introduced to Drake at work, I picked up my ringing phone to find him on line two.

"Miss Logan?"

"Yes. Speaking."

"This is Drake Collins."

"Hi. How are you?"

"Good. And yourself?"

"I'm great. How are you adjusting to the company and your new role?"

"I can't complain. Everything is going well both on and off the job. Everybody that I've met in Atlanta has extended true southern hospitality to me. Strangers actually speak to you in the streets and everyone is super friendly and laid back. I really think I'm going to enjoy living here."

"That's good."

"Listen, I don't know what your schedule looks like today, but would you have a few minutes, maybe an hour, to walk me through some of these reports? I know you service most of the clients on this list."

I looked around at the pile of paperwork on my desk, but found myself agreeing to come up to his office in twenty minutes.

"Sure, I can squeeze you in."

"It won't be a problem?" Drake questioned in that deep voice of his.

"No, not at all. See you in twenty."

"Great. You're a sweetheart, Miss Logan. I owe you one."

Exactly twenty minutes later, after making a quick trip to the restroom, brushing my teeth, and combing through my thick mane of hair, I was softly knocking at Mr. Collins's closed door.

"Come in."

I slowly opened the door and strolled in. Drake was working with an Excel spreadsheet on his PC. He looked *up and smiled in my direction. Perfect white teeth. Again, I couldn't get over how utterly gorgeous he was. I simply stared. And he was all man. Solid. Drake carried himself like a man definitely in charge of any situation. I admired that.*

"Hi, Kennedy. You're right on time," he stated, looking down at his gold wristwatch.

I still stood near the open door.

"Come on in and close the door because it's been pretty hectic and noisy on the floor today. I don't want us to be disturbed."

"Okay. Sure." I shut the door and was enveloped into his space.

Standing up, he said, "You can take my chair. I'm going to be walking back and forth and pulling files, et cetera. It'll be easier for you to sit and for me to stand."

"Sounds like a plan." I smiled.

I took a seat in his black, soft leather, swivel chair and felt his alluring fragrance and aura completely overtake me. As I made myself comfortable, Drake pulled out a stack of computer printouts and laid them in the center of his elegant cherrywood desk and deposited himself on the edge of the desk, right next to me. With his suit jacket off and the sleeves to his white starched shirt rolled up, it was obvious that he was ready to get down to some serious business.

"Miss Kennedy, what is this mess? I can't make heads or tales out of most of it. There are all these acronyms for everything. Where is a list that explains all the codes?"

I picked up a stack of the paperwork that he was referring to, reviewed them briefly, and started to explain what we were looking at in reference to our clients, their demograph-

ics, bundles, etc. The entire time, I was very aware of Drake being very near me. So close. I could feel the heat rising from his body. I could see the tiny hairs standing up on his arms. Too close for comfort. Definitely.

When he was reviewing the printouts, I used that time to secretly check him out, closer. He had the smoothest brown skin, and his hands were so large, yet smooth. His haircut was perfect, like he had just stepped out of a barber's chair, and the way his eyelashes swooshed over his eyelids was super sexy.

At one point, he stopped looking at the printouts and glanced over at me. For a moment I thought he had caught me staring. I panicked. Coughing, I quickly looked down at the report in front of me.

"What is that delicious perfume you're wearing? It smells wonderful."

"Ellen Tracy."

"Smells nice on you," he said, and went back to examining the trail of paperwork he had laid out in neat stacks on his desk and credenza.

"Thank you."

A couple of times I thought I felt him staring down the low-cut silk blouse that I wore with a straight black skirt and black pumps. From Drake's point of view, he could clearly see my black lace bra and probably could see the swell of my breasts as they rose and fell in his presence with a desire and mind of their own.

"Where is that list of codes?" he asked, looking around at the stacks of reports on his desk.

"There they are, third stack from your right," I explained as we reached for the code sheet at the same time. When his *hand touched my fingers, I experienced cool chills run up and down my arms. I quickly placed my hands back in my lap to steady them.*

"Good. This is exactly what I need. Thank you."

"You're welcome."

Running his hand across his head, Drake absently glanced down at his wristwatch.

"You know what? I've kept you long enough today. I didn't realize it was so late, and you haven't even eaten lunch."

"No, but I'm glad to help out any way I can."

"Miss Logan, you've been an incredible help. Unfortunately, we only made it through a quarter of the reports. Can we meet again next week? Say, next Friday at ten o'clock?" he asked, looking at me expectantly. "Is that asking too much?"

"No. That shouldn't be a problem."

"How about penciling in two hours on your calendar?"

"I'll see what I can do."

"If you'd like, I can check with your manager to make sure she's cool with it. Your manager is Peggy Hunt, isn't she?"

"Yes."

"Good. That'll give me the chance to put in a good word for you as well. Let her know what a great asset you've been to me."

"You don't have to do that."

"I know, but I want to," Drake volunteered, with that smile shining bright.

"Thanks, that'll be wonderful."

"Okay then, next week it is. Take care, Miss Logan."

"You too," I said, retrieving my belongings, then opening

the door and heading out with a warm tingling coursing between my legs.

Wednesday of the following week I ran into Drake in the lobby, down by the security desk. He was talking with someone that I vaguely recalled meeting at an interdepartmental business meeting. Drake abruptly ended their conversation, came up behind me and fell in pace with me. The fluttering began again.

"Hi, Miss Logan." He smiled. I loved that smile.

"Hi, Mr. Collins." I grinned back, looking up at him.

"Please. Call me Drake."

"Well, in that case, please call me Kennedy." We grinned at each other again.

"Where are you headed?"

I held up my lunch bag. "Since the women on my floor are seriously tripping today, I decided to sit in the cafeteria with my leftovers from last night and read."

Drake reached to check out the cover of the book I held in my other hand. "Is it good?"

"So far it's excellent. It's by a local Atlanta author."

"Cool, maybe I'll check her out. I love supporting our own local talent."

I nodded.

"I'm headed to lunch as well, but I hate eating alone. Could you do me the honor of joining me?"

"I don't know. I was—"

"I'll even buy. Come on. Say yes. I owe you for all your hard work last week."

"Really, it's not necessary. I was just doing my job."

"I'm not taking no for an answer."

"Okay, sure. Since you put it that way. Why not?" I said as

I left my bagged lunch at the security desk for safekeeping.

"Where would you like to eat, Kennedy?"

"I've overheard my coworkers talking about this recently opened Italian restaurant that's not far from here; it's within walking distance and has delicious lunch specials."

"Excellent. Lead the way," he said, opening the door that led to the busy street.

As we walked the couple of blocks, I noticed the women checking Drake out. He walked with a confident stride.

An hour later, an hour that flew by, I couldn't believe I had laughed, talked, and had such a wonderful time. The food was mouth-watering and the conversation even better. Our conversation wasn't forced; it came natural and easy. As I ate my seafood pasta and Greek salad, Drake had me in stitches over some of his tales of growing up in Los Angeles. His descriptions were so vivid; I felt like I was right there with him. I found myself opening up in ways I never expected. I surprised myself by confiding in him about my dissatisfaction with my current position. He really seemed to understand, and even offered suggestions and advice. A few times I'd look up and find him staring at me. I'd look down and play with a strand of my hair in order to avoid his eyes, which appeared to reach within my soul and seek out my deepest desires.

"May I ask you a personal question?" he asked, suddenly serious.

"Sure, why not? Ask away."

"Are you seeing or dating anyone in particular?"

I paused for only a moment. "No and no."

"That's hard to believe. A beautiful lady like yourself. I'd think you'd have men beating down your front door."

"I'm afraid not," I said, twirling another strand of my hair around and through my middle fingers.

"Why is that?"

"I'm afraid I'm too picky and selective."

"What are you saying? There aren't any good men in Atlanta?"

"If there are, I'm not meeting them."

"Is it true that there's a large and growing gay and lesbian population?"

"That's what I've been told. Atlanta isn't called the new San Francisco for no reason."

"Interesting. You know, you remind me so much of my first love. She was kinda quiet, with your smothering, alluring beauty and innocent sexiness."

I blushed. "Really?" I asked, breaking our eye contact.

"I'm sorry. I shouldn't have said that. That was inappropriate. I apologize if I made you uncomfortable in any way."

"No. I'm fine."

Drake glanced down at his watch. "Man, look at the time. I guess we'd better be getting back before they come looking for us and while we still have jobs." He signaled for the waiter and the check.

"You're absolutely right. My manager demands promptness from our team. I wouldn't want to get on her black list because of tardiness."

He winked conspiratorially. "Don't worry. I'll handle her. If she asks, I'll say we were on a boring business lunch that dragged on."

Drake and I made it back to the building and waited at the first bank of elevators to go up to our floors. The elevator doors opened and a stream of people rushed out. As we stepped in, surprisingly, he and I were the only two people in the elevator. I stood to one side and Drake on the other. There was a comfortable silence that only we could truly appreciate.

"Drake, thanks for the lunch. I see what I'm missing by eating at my desk all the time. I have to get out more and enjoy the Midtown restaurants."

"I definitely enjoyed the meal and the company. See you Friday, Kennedy," he said as we arrived at my floor and I stepped off. "Kennedy?" he called, holding the elevator door open.

"Yes?" I stopped walking and turned around.

"Don't worry. You'll meet that special man soon."

"If you say so."

"I know so." The door shut with me still staring at it and trying to figure out his hidden message.

On Friday, I was back in Drake's office, behind closed doors again. Since Fridays were casual, I was dressed down in a cotton, long-sleeve, button-down shirt and dark navy blue slacks, with my hair pulled back in a ponytail. I was looking more like a college student than a professional businesswoman. But at least I didn't overdo it, like some of the women on my floor who obviously thought Casual Friday meant Nightclub Friday.

Drake had on a tennis shirt embossed with our corporate logo and khaki pants. Even dressed down, the man was all that. He probably looked sexy wearing a sweaty T-shirt and holey shorts while he scratched his butt. Now that I had gotten a better view of those abs, I had an overwhelming urge to reach out and squeeze them. I couldn't deny it—the man was making me crazy.

"Let me get up so you can claim your seat," he laughed, showing those straight white teeth that reminded me of the sexy actor Taye Diggs.

I smiled, somewhat shyly. "Thank you, sir. Good afternoon."

"Oh, let's not go back to that formality. We had a great lunch the other day and I thought all those barriers came down with the meal. Deal?"

"Deal."

As I moved into my assigned seat, we briefly brushed against each other, and my nipples instantly hardened like never before. Drake smelled divine.

"Excuse me," I said, catching my breath.

"Sure. You look nice today. But you always look good."

"Thanks. Are you ready to get started?"

"Yes. But first I want to ask you something."

"Okay." I looked up at him expectantly.

"This is totally not business related, but I feel comfortable around you. I hope you feel the same about me."

I stared at him and searched his face, unsure of what he was going to ask me. I guess he saw uncertainty reflected in my eyes.

"Really, my question is nothing major. I went to Vision nightclub the other night and almost got mobbed by the women there. Are Atlanta women always that aggressive?"

I laughed and exhaled. "I don't know, I guess so, from what I've heard. I don't do the club scene much, but the women in Atlanta are pretty bold. The women-to-men ratio is pretty high, so the competition is fierce and no holds barred."

"I see. Well, curious minds wanted to know. That's all. It's cool. I had women asking me to dance. Wanting to buy me drinks and take me home."

"Welcome to Atlanta."

He didn't say anything, just stared at me.

"What?"

"Nothing. I probably shouldn't say this again, but you are a beautiful woman."

"And thank you again," I said, looking off before Drake saw how flustered he was making me.

"No really, you are gorgeous. Are my comments making you uncomfortable?" he asked, searching my face for answers.

"Of course not. I love being told I'm beautiful by a handsome man," I said, laughing my nervous giggle. I found myself searching for strands of my hair to twist between my fingers. I forgot it was up in a ponytail. So my hand clung and lingered in the air, making me feel foolish.

"You should be used to it by now, Kennedy." His eyes never left my face. Was he still searching for a reaction?

There was an awkward, uncomfortable silence as I felt my face heat up. I shuffled the paperwork on his desktop.

"Well, I guess we need to get to work and earn our paychecks. I only have two of your precious hours, and we still have a lot to cover."

"Let's dig in," I stated, eager to get back to business-related matters. I was more comfortable discussing clients and their needs.

Drake and I worked steadily for over an hour. I typed codes into his PC, and my neck was getting stiff, so I found myself massaging it with my free hand. Without expecting it, Drake came up behind me.

"Got a kink?"

I nodded my head and kept typing.

"Here, let me fix that." He proceeded to firmly but gently knead the muscles of my neck with his large hands. It felt so good that I found myself closing my eyes and reclining back against his expert hand.

"How's that? Better?"

"Much better." I didn't want him to stop.

"Good," he said as his hand inched farther down. I could feel the heat of his fingertips through my thin cotton shirt. He hesitated.

I froze too, stiff as a board. I didn't breathe. Didn't dare to.

"Kennedy, I know this sounds crazy, but I have this overwhelming urge to touch you."

I didn't say anything. I didn't know what to say or do. This man was my superior. With my back to him, I kept staring at the computer screen like it held all the answers. The secret to life. My mind was screaming, Yes, yes, yes, touch me, but my tongue wouldn't verbalize it. I was in conflict because I would be going against my self-imposed work policy. Yet, I'd never had such a strong sexual attraction to any man before. Drake was the complete package: handsome, professional, financially secure, from the looks of it, well-rounded, and sexy. Drake had it all; he was every woman's dream. Even Mother would approve.

"Kennedy?" he said, pressing his hand firmly against my shoulder.

I didn't utter a word. I couldn't. By now my chest was heaving up and down. My mind was screaming for me to stop this madness before it went too far. However, *for once in my life I wasn't thinking with my brain.*

"Kennedy?" Every time Drake spoke my name, his right hand went down a little farther. Almost there.

"Kennedy, talk to me. Do you want this?" This time his hand made contact. I tensed up and immediately found myself relaxing as his fingers skillfully began caressing my breasts and hard, throbbing nipples. Without realizing it, I leaned into his hand. I embraced his touch.

"Hmmm. You feel so good. Just like I imagined. I dreamed about you the other night." His fingers were kneading firmly, but gently. When he tweaked a nipple between his thumb and forefinger, I swooned.

"Turn around, let me see you." He proceeded to swirl my chair around, and I was flushed. I looked down at the floor.

Drake slowly, gently, lifted my chin back up. "Look at me." His eyes never left mine as he proceeded to unbutton the tiny buttons on my shirt. He took his time. Drawing the anticipation out. I was breathing so deeply, I thought I would hyperventilate and need a brown paper bag to breathe into.

"Drake? I'm not sure about this."

"Sssh. It's okay," he softly whispered, rubbing his index finger sensually across my lips. So light, it felt like a feather.

"Somebody might walk in."

"Kennedy, take a chance. Trust me. They are all at lunch now. Besides, my associates know not to disturb me when my door is closed.

"Beautiful," he said, proceeding to lift up my lacy bra and push it out of the way. My breasts were fully exposed, sitting high, and my nipples were already proudly erect. On display. Beckoning him.

There wasn't any more talking. Drake bent down in

front of me, without my permission, and proceeded to suck my breasts like a starving man. He was definitely a breast man because this went on for about thirty minutes with him sucking, touching, licking, and squeezing them until I moaned out loud several times. Perfect care was given to each breast.

Drake made me feel so good. I held onto the side of my chair and gave into the wonderful sensations as he pulled me near. The only sounds were our breathing, moaning, and his sucking. My nipples were as hard as they had ever been, and every time he tweaked them, I moaned out loud. He didn't touch me anywhere else. Drake didn't even kiss me, only my neck. Showered me with light, delicate kisses. Whispered in my ear. Sucked my breasts some more and tenderly bit down on my nipples. He was on a mission. Finally, he stopped abruptly and stood back up. I couldn't read the blank expression on his face.

"Kennedy, you're a sweet lady. So sweet," he stated, gently cupping my face.

I didn't respond.

He leaned back down and stroked my nipples between his fingers one more time. Had a nipple in each hand, pulling. Again, an involuntary moan of pleasure escaped me as I saw a small smile of victory grace his face.

"That should take the edge off," he said with a sparkle in his eyes. "Listen, why don't we knock off for today. We've accomplished a lot. Let's meet again next week."

"I don't know," I said, swiftly attempting to button up my shirt. Awkward. Tense.

"I've already talked with your manager, and she said I could have you for as long as I need you."

"Did she?" I questioned.

"So, it's settled. Same time next week," he said, sitting on the edge of his desk and intensely watching me as I clumsily fastened the last button on my shirt. My breasts were straining to be free again. To be handled by him.

"Same time, then."

"Sure."

"How you feeling?" he asked, teasing my breasts through the fabric of my blouse and making me light-headed.

"Okay."

"Just okay? Well, I haven't done my job effectively."

"I'm feeling great," I volunteered too eagerly.

"That sounds better. Much better."

Drake was still caressing. Probing. Feeling me up.

"Well, I'd better go." I stood up on weak knees.

"Are you sure?" he asked, towering over me. Still touching me. Hand underneath my shirt. Squeezing. Fondling. Tweaking.

"I'd better get back; I only allocated two hours for this project," I barely managed to get the words out.

Drake had sat back on the edge of his desk, and he stared at me with lust-filled eyes as he gently pulled me to him, within his open legs. I clearly saw the outline of his hard, thick dick. He saw me looking and grinned. I quickly looked away, feeling like I'd been caught by the teacher doing something naughty.

Pressing my hand against his erection, he lowered his head and bit down on each nipple through my shirt, then stated, "If you're sure."

"I'm sure," I managed to mutter. "I have to go." A lump had formed in my throat.

Palming my butt cheeks and pulling me into him, he said, "You have pretty breasts."

"I really have to go."

"Take care, then," he said, pulling down and smoothing out my shirt.

I proceeded to gather my pen, purse, and other belongings. I was totally confused as to what had just happened. I knew what had occurred, but Drake was now acting like nothing was out of the ordinary. He was seated at his desk and writing something on a Post-it note. Oblivious to my departure.

"See you next week," I said, for lack of anything better to say. My trembling hand was on the doorknob.

"And Kennedy?" Drake stated right before I opened the door. He didn't even look up.

"Yes?"

"Next Friday, wear a skirt."

The Seduction Continues . . .

Dear Journal,

After what transpired in Drake's office, I should have run
for the high hills. I've never, ever, done anything like that
in my life. I can't believe I let it happen. Maybe it was
the thrill and excitement, perhaps it was doing things that
were not in my character, maybe it was because Drake was
my superior, or perhaps it was because Drake brought out a
level of sexuality in me that I didn't know existed.

To my credit, I will admit that during the preceding week,
I debated back and forth whether I'd show up at the ap-
pointed time. To be honest, I could have easily gotten out of
it by telling my manager that my workload was too heavy.
I purposely avoided Drake by not venturing into our lobby
area during lunch, not even to take care of personal mat-

ters. I literally camped out in my cubicle and hoped that he wouldn't call. Every time an internal call came through, I prayed it wasn't Drake.

I was totally confused over what happened. My feelings flip-flopped back and forth. One minute I was flattered that he liked me, the next I wondered did he really like me or did he think I was some sort of whore for what I let him do to me. One thing I was sure of, I was very attracted to Drake. Probably more attracted to him than any other man I had ever met. It didn't help that word had gotten out about him on my floor and my coworkers were constantly making comments about the sexy new manager upstairs and what he could do for them.

Basically, for seven days my mind was in a total state of chaos. My emotions bounced back and forth like a tennis match. When Friday finally arrived, I still wasn't sure what my final decision would be. I had picked up the phone several times to cancel our appointment and make up some excuse as to why I needed to. However, there was just something about Drake that drew me to him. I couldn't stay away until I learned and experienced more.

At my designated time, I found myself taking the elevator up to his floor. As requested, I was dressed in a casual skirt and top. I don't know why Drake made that particular request, but I obliged him. As usual, I knocked on the closed door, heard Drake's sexy voice requesting that I come in. I took two deep breaths, because it was now or never, and stepped into the office of the man who, in the months that followed, I'd blindly love and follow.

"Hi." I smiled timidly. Being in Drake's presence brought out all my insecurities. I always wondered if I looked pretty *enough or was intelligent enough. After all, he could have his pick of women. Why choose me?*

"Hey, Kennedy. Give me a minute," he stated in a direct, professional tone. He hadn't even looked up from his paperwork.

"Take your time." In my nervousness, I found myself playing with a strand of my hair and biting down on my bottom lip.

Drake, dressed in a pair of linen pants and button-down shirt, looked very serious today. There was no indication of what had gone down only a week earlier. This day, he was Mr. Professional. I was beginning to think that I'd imagined the entire incident; maybe it was an erotic dream.

He proceeded to pull out the final stack of reports and place it next to me on the desk. We were in our usual position: me sitting at his desk, in his chair, and Drake sitting on the edge of his desk or standing up behind me.

"Looks like we can finally see the light at the end of the tunnel," he said.

"Looks that way."

"Kennedy, you've been a great help."

"Really, I'm just doing my job."

"I must say I'm going to miss your company. Where have you been keeping yourself this week?" Finally. He was giving me his undivided attention.

"What do you mean?" I asked as he walked up behind me and glanced out his window, overlooking the city. Without turning around in my chair, I sensed him checking me out.

"I usually see you in the elevator or catch a glimpse of you in the lobby, but this week I didn't run into you. I looked for

you. Hoped to see you. Seeing you, even for a few seconds, always makes my day. You're a breath of fresh air."

I blushed. "Oh, I've had a lot of paperwork to catch up on and not to mention my growing to-do list."

"Well, I hope I haven't put you behind schedule."

"No, we are unusually busy for this time of the year; this is not the norm."

"This makes me appreciate you helping me out all the more." There was that perfect smile again. I shivered when I thought of those lips nibbling on my neck.

"You're welcome."

By now he had moved and was sitting in the chair across from his desk. The one usually reserved for visitors. For a moment the only sound in the room was our breathing. Self-conscious, I looked down. Drake continued to stare intensely at me.

"I really like you Kennedy Logan. You know that? I could get into you."

I didn't comment; didn't know what to say.

"I know this could be complicated for both of us, but I'd love to see you outside the office. I don't typically mix business and pleasure, but there's something about you that's different, worth breaking the rules for. I can't get you off my mind. I'm seriously feeling you."

"Me either . . . I don't mix business with pleasure."

"Well, we are adults. We can handle this. There are exceptions to everything. Right? Rules are made to be broken."

I didn't respond. My thoughts were racing, bumping, colliding into each other at rapid speed.

"And I'm sure we could be discreet. No one has to know."

I glanced down at my Fossil watch. "We'd better get started. Don't you think?"

Drake glared at me for a few seconds and then he smiled that fabulous, one hundred watt smile. The one that made my heartbeat speed up, my pulse race, and my legs quiver.

"Don't say another word. I understand. Lets get started . . . on this paperwork."

Drake and I worked diligently for the next forty-five minutes or so. I didn't want to see another stack of printouts for a long, long time. We had accomplished quite a bit in a short span. Now, he was joking around and telling me about some of his encounters since coming to work for our company. He had the diction and movements of some of the senior managers down to a science. He had me in stitches with his imitations. I'd never laughed so hard. I told him he missed his calling, he should have been a stand-up comedian on BET. Our mood had quickly switched from business to playful in a matter of minutes. He took me totally off guard when he asked, "Why haven't you mentioned what happened between us?"

I hesitated and crossed my legs. "I don't know, I thought maybe I had imagined the entire thing."

"No, it definitely was real," he stated, looking at me from his spot back on the edge of the desk.

"Oh," was all I could say.

"You are too funny, Kennedy. You've never done anything like that before, have you?" he asked, amused.

"No, I can't say that I have, not in a professional setting anyway."

"See, that's what so refreshing about you. There is so much you haven't experienced. You've lived a sheltered life, Kennedy Logan."

"Well, I don't know if that's good or bad."

"It's not bad. You just need to loosen up and let go sometimes. Don't freak out over everything. Life is too short not
to try to experience all it has to offer."

"That's funny, you sound just like my friend, Taylor."

"Well, she's right. We're right," Drake proclaimed proudly.

"I'm not sure I know how to let loose. I'm pretty boring."

"Don't worry. Stick with me. I can show you things, Miss
Logan, that you wouldn't believe or couldn't perceive before."

"I bet you can, Mr. Collins," I stated, boldly flirting with
him now.

"How old are you?"

"I'm twenty-eight, with a June birthday."

"Oh, so that makes you a Gemini. Y'all love hard—give
your all in relationships. See, I'm up to par on astrology."

"You are crazy," I laughed, forgetting where we were.

"Am I? I think I'm a thirty-year-old man who speaks his
mind and goes after what he wants. And I want you," he
stated, only inches from my face now. I smelled the mint he
had only a few minutes earlier popped into his mouth. "I
typically get what I want."

"Really?"

"Yes. Really."

With that, Drake came and kneeled down in front of
my chair. I noticed the muscles of his thighs expand and
bulge against the fabric of his pants. Seconds later, while he
cupped my chin and looked deep into my eyes, he moved his
other hand from my ankles up to my thighs, taking my skirt
with him in one swift swoosh. I instantly closed my eyes
and let out a surrendering sigh. I couldn't fight this. When I

opened them again, he had my skirt pulled up, showing off my silky red panties as his large hand rubbed and massaged between my open thighs. Already I experienced a warmness spreading and radiating within.

"Pull those off," Drake demanded.

"Pardon me?"

He laughed and repeated himself, "You heard me. Pull those off." Whispering now. "Take off your panties."

"I don't know, Drake, somebody might walk in." I could barely think with him opening my legs and touching me.

"They won't. Trust me. You do trust me, don't you?" His middle finger found my spot, as it slid underneath my panties. Dove in deep. Pulled out and pushed in with two fingers.

I nodded my head. With my eyes never leaving his face, I took a deep breath, stood up and slipped my panties off and dropped them to the floor, then just stood there, not knowing what to do next. With his hands on my shoulders, Drake slowly pushed me back down into his chair. He spread my legs as wide as they'd go and went to work. I allowed him to do whatever with me. I didn't fight him. I didn't protest. I didn't say no. I . . . simply . . . surrendered.

First, he placed his gorgeous face down there and gently rubbed it around. Then his tongue proceeded to do things to me that my mind had only imagined. At one point he had to put his free hand over my mouth to muffle my intense moans. Drake was relentless with his mouth and fingers. He knew exactly what to do to get my body to respond. I was putty in his hands. Mere molding clay. I couldn't move. I couldn't think. I couldn't breathe. I couldn't do anything but come.

For thirty minutes, yes thirty minutes, Drake took me to heaven with his oral pleasure. When he added his fingers to the equation, I thought I'd go out of my freaking mind. Added to the surrealness and excitement was the fact that there was an entire floor of associates and managers, just on the other side of that door, just beyond his closed door, and they had no idea what was going on.

Later, Drake had me wide open, sprawled across his desk, on my back, with my private parts and breasts exposed, in full view for the world to see. At one point I thought I'd die of fright and embarrassment. There was a soft knock at his door, his secretary. I froze. Drake was cool and actually kept pushing his three fingers in and out of my womanhood. Ever so slowly. In and out. Deeper. Slowly.

"Yes?" He pushed in.

"Mr. Collins, I wanted to remind you that I'm leaving early today."

"See you Monday. Have a great weekend, Brenda." He pulled out. His fingers were glistering with my wetness.

"You too."

"I will," he said, inserting another finger, now four. He had me moving up and down to his finger motion as he took me to yet another orgasm while he coaxed me through.

"Yeah. That's it. Let yourself go. That's my girl," he whispered. "Tell me you love the way I make your pussy feel."

I lay back against the desktop, half on, half off, totally exhausted. Waiting for my breathing to return to normal. My chest rapidly heaving up and down.

"Tell me," he whispered near my ear. "It feels good, doesn't it?" His warm breath tickled my ear. I shivered in anticipation over his skillful fingers.

"I love the way you make me feel," I said in a monotone voice.

Drake laughed and said, "I know you do. You are so wet right now. Dripping. You enjoy me eating your pussy? Don't you?"

I remained silent. His fingers were still inside me, moving, teasing me.

"Let me hear you say pussy."

"Nooo," I squeeched.

"Come on," he said, moving his fingers around a bit, exploring. Opening me up.

As another spasm shook my body, I closed my eyes and shook my head.

"Just say, 'I want you to eat my pussy again, Drake,' and I'll leave you alone."

He leaned in closer. Whispered in my ear, "Say, 'Shove your tongue up my wet pussy and make me come.'"

I couldn't say it. He laughed and pulled out his fingers. He held up his index finger, showing it to me, which was drenched with my wetness.

"I bet you've never tasted yourself either, have you?"

He didn't wait for an answer. "Come here," he stated, guiding his finger into my mouth before I could protest. "Lick it off." His eyes held mine. Waiting on me to comply.

I didn't move.

Drake pushed his fingers back inside me and pulled out. "Lick it off, Kennedy."

He gently opened my mouth with his fingers, and I did what he told me. I proceeded to taste myself.

"That's right. Get it all," he demanded, using his free hand to play with my pussy some more, gently squeezing my clit.

"I'm going to enjoy turning you out," he whispered as he caressed my face.

"What?"

"Nothing, baby. Nothing."

With a big smile on my face, I left his office fifteen minutes later. Drake had my phone number, home address, and confirmation for a date on Saturday evening.

Lustful Ways . . .

Dear Journal,

After Drake turned me out orally, it was on. My body had never felt that way before. And we hadn't even had actual sexual intercourse. Imagine that. Yes, I was already whipped. You see, I'm one of those unfortunate women who doesn't have orgasms easily. Sure, I've had small ones before, with a lot of hard work on my partner's part, but never the mind blowing, earth-shattering ones that I hear women talk about all the time.

According to Taylor, she is multiorgasmic and she'll have orgasm on top of orgasm if a man so much as blows in her right ear. It has to be her right ear, not her left one. Well, maybe I'm exaggerating, but she doesn't have a problem. If I can have just one, I am doing great.

When I came in Drake's office chair from just his mouth and fingers, I was like "Damn!" I jumped at the chance to see him over the weekend and find out more about this exciting, mysterious, and sexy man.

Our first date was beyond unbelievable. I felt like Cinderella at the ball with her black prince charming in tow. If I didn't think I was in lust with the man before, by the end of our first date, I knew I definitely was seeing stars and hearing sweet violins playing our song; I was sprung. A night out on the town turned into a two-day date. That was one thing I would learn about Drake, he never did anything halfway. He did everything in a big, dramatic way. Drake was very passionate about everything: his career, his hobbies, his woman.

I thought we were simply going out to the movies and then dinner. Therefore, I dressed in a nice but casual dress and heels. We ended up going to an early dinner out in Buckhead, catching a play at the Fox Theater, and capping the night off by going for a horse and carriage ride through Midtown. It was magical. It was perfect. And then to top off all that excitement and my natural high, Drake had reserved a room for us at the Georgian Terrace Hotel, directly across from the theater. I was totally speechless.

I simply adored this man who was able to so easily take control of any given situation. Drake was a man who took charge, and that excited me in the beginning. I noticed the envious looks women gave me when I went out with him. I didn't care, Drake was my man. And I was his woman . . . or so I thought.

* * *

Our room came complete with a Jacuzzi, king-size bed, colorful flowers, expensive champagne, and a great view of the city. Drake didn't forget anything; he attended to the smallest of details. That was impressive. Of course, I hadn't packed an overnight bag, but he came prepared. The man was amazing. He had secretly packed a small suitcase for both of us that he had hidden in the trunk of his car. He bought a toothbrush, toothpaste, and other essentials for me. He even purchased a sexy purple teddy, his favorite color, for me to sleep in. Not that it stayed on very long.

That night, Drake and I ordered room service after deciding to have a midnight snack of assorted cheese and crackers, and we sipped on chilled champagne. Drake gave what I thought was a heartfelt toast to having me in his life. Afterward, he didn't rush to get me in bed or attempt to get intimate with me. We actually cuddled on the cozy bed and talked. With my head on his stomach, I learned quite a bit about his upbringing.

Drake had been given a lot on a silver platter. Don't get me wrong. He worked hard for everything he received, but his parents owned a sports apparel manufacturing plant in Los Angeles. Money wasn't an issue for them. He grew up with his mother, father, and a brother. He attended private schools, excelled academically and in sports, and dated girls from affluent families. His family even owned a summer home. After graduating from an Ivy League college and working for the family-owned business for a few years, he wanted to branch out on his own for a change. Be his own man. Test his wings. He'd heard so much about the A-T-L that it was his first choice.

Literally, as the sun was rising over the city, he made the most delicious, sweetest love. Slow and easy. I felt Drake down to my soul. He made me understand and appreciate the meaning of feeling like a woman. With every touch, I grew to crave him. He made love to my entire body, mind, and soul. Drake didn't rush; he reveled in loving and caressing every inch of me. He asked what felt good. He watched to gauge my reaction to things he did to me. Drake wanted to possess me. I wanted him to love me. And love and possession don't mix . . .

By Saturday morning we were so tired that we slept, wrapped in each other's arms, until almost noon. I never imagined being so safe and protected. After I woke up to tender kisses, we made love two more times, took our showers, and had a light lunch in one of the restaurants downstairs. The salmon salad with iced tea was excellent. After checkout, we weren't ready to part company, so we rode out to Lenox Mall and shopped for a couple of hours. We giggled, held hands, and French kissed like two teenagers. Drake bought me a gorgeous Coach bag. It didn't matter that the price tag was almost $750; he didn't bat an eye at the price. When he declared that he had to have his woman dressed to the nines, I beamed because I knew he was claiming me as his woman. He had already claimed and tamed my pussy.

Yeah, that was the best date ever! It was perfect. Unfortunately, Drake wasn't. Not by a long shot. However, it took months for me to discover that tidbit of information. That revelation would have saved me so much heartache and pain. Looking back, the signs were there. Hindsight really is twenty-twenty.

Before the Storm . . .

Dear Journal,

"Kennedy, I could stay like this forever," Drake whispered, leaning down and kissing me on the forehead. His body was warm and solid. I felt protected, secure, and wanted.

"Me too," I barely answered with closed eyes. I was still coming off my high. We had made love and I was relishing the moments before the sweetness fled into the darkness and cover of night. Candlelight flickered off the walls in my bedroom, creating strange shadows in their wake. And there was a strong and strange mixture of berries and sex that clung to the air.

Drake was slowly tracing his fingers up and down my arm. Each touch sent shivers throughout my being. And lying, wrapped in his arms, I felt happy.

"How you feeling?" he asked.

"Great, babe, as always. You?"

"Satisfied."

"I love you, babe."

"Ditto."

"Ditto? What does that mean?"

"You're special to me. You know that, Kennedy." Still tracing patterns on my arm.

"Special?" I questioned with a pout.

"I've dated a lot of women in my past, but you—you are, by a long shot, different and very special."

"How many are a lot of women?" I asked jokingly, but curious at the same time. I rose up on one elbow so I could see his face.

"Oh, come on, Kennedy, I've told you of my past. I've never had a problem meeting women. Women are always throwing themselves and their pussy at me. You are with me now. So, it doesn't matter how many," he said, slightly agitated. The candlelight cast dark, contorted shadows across his face.

"You're right, babe," I crooned, relaxing back into his arms.

"Wait a minute. Different? Is that good or bad?" I laughed, pulling myself up to look into his eyes again. Drake had the sexiest eyes. A woman could get lost in them, and before she knew it, she could simply drown. Sometimes I felt like I was drowning in his presence. I couldn't breathe or catch my breath.

"Baby, of course, different in a good way. It couldn't possibly be in a bad way."

"How am I different, babe?"

"You really want to know?" he asked, absently cupping my breast in his hand.

"Yes. I really want to know," I laughed on a natural high. The moment was perfect. A light rain had started to fall outside, and my apartment was warm and cozy on the inside.

"Well, for one, you don't try to be the man."

"What?" I laughed. "You're joking."

"You know what I mean. There are so many women who are kidding themselves and thinking that they can do it all, have it all, all without a man."

"What is wrong with that?"

"Baby, a man wants his woman to need him. He doesn't want to feel like he's not wanted or appreciated or needed. There can only be one leader in a relationship. The man."

"I see." I was hearing this theory for the first time.

"Women in Atlanta are notorious for that type of bullshit, feminist attitude. I don't need a man; a man can't do anything for me that I can't do myself . . . Bullshit! Then why are they at the club with a dress on two sizes too small showing all their ass, leaving absolutely nothing to the imagination? Why are they always in search of some dick? Answer that. Well, you aren't like that."

"Are you saying I'm not independent?"

"No, baby. I'm saying you act like a woman. You are content with letting me be your man. Your girl Taylor could learn from you too."

"What? How did Taylor get brought into this conversation?"

"I don't care for Taylor, and it's obvious that she doesn't care for me either. Taylor thinks her shit don't stink."

"I wish the two of you would try to get along. She's my best friend and you're my man. I don't want to be caught in the middle."

"I don't like her putting crazy ideas into your pretty head. I like the way things have gone with us these last few months, and I just don't want anyone to destroy that."

"Oh really now?" I said as Drake planted a kiss, then another, on my neck. He knew that was one of my weak spots. The meltdown began.

"Definitely. I like how you let me order for you in restaurants, how you accept my advice and opinions, surrender to me in the bedroom."

"Do you?" I asked while he traced a line up my arm.

"Yes, Miss Logan, I do." He tweaked a nipple between his thumb and forefinger. I moaned loudly.

"And a woman shouldn't be vocal and proactive in achieving her goals?"

"I'm not saying that. I'm simply stating that a real woman should make an effort to please her man and take care of his needs. If I tell you to get down on your knees and suck my dick, I expect you to do it. No questions asked. Again, there can only be one leader in a relationship. That's why Taylor can't keep a man; she thinks she's one."

"You are sounding like a male chauvinist, babe."

For a moment this angry look crossed Drake's face, and just as quickly disappeared. Then he broke into a huge, mischievous grin. He reached for me.

"Call it what you want, now come here and surrender to me again," he said as his hand found the warm place between my legs. "Dance for me."

"What? Dance for you? Are you serious?"

"Yeah. Don't I look serious? Stand up and do a strip tease for your man."

"No, I don't think so."

"Come on, just a small one," he said, tugging on my arm to pull me into a standing position.

"I don't know," I said, pulling the sheet tighter around me.

"I thought you loved me."

"I do."

"Well then, do this for me. Kennedy, it's just you and me here. We are behind closed doors, and I thought you were my woman."

"Okay, but just a little one," I said, motioning with my fingers.

"Just a little one, then," Drake stated, assaulting my neck with kisses.

I hesitated.

"Okay, let's see what you got," he said, placing his hands behind his head and leaning back against his pillow, waiting for the show.

I shyly released the sheet and stood up in all my glory. Slowly, I started moving around, doing a belly dancer type routine. Drake was taking it all in.

"That's it. Lower your hands so I can see those gorgeous tatas. You know I'm a breast man."

I continued to dance as I slowly lowered my hands, then raised them above my head, twirling my fingers in midair.

"Yeah. Nice. Show me my titties. Turn around, slowly. Tease me . . . Not too fast. Now, touch yourself for me, baby."

"What?"

"*Touch yourself. Play with your breasts and nipples. Real slow. We got all night.*"

I paused for just a moment. Drake's lust-filled eyes never left mine.

"*Yeah, squeeze your nipple. A little harder. The other one. Harder. Make 'em stand at attention for me. Salute me.*"

"*Drake?*"

"*Shhh, you're doing great. Now, keep one hand on your breast and move your other hand down between your thighs.*"

"*I don't know.*"

"*Come on. Right now, you are sexy as hell. You got my dick hard as bricks . . . That's right. Don't stop; touch yourself. Stick two of your fingers in. Deeper. Pull 'em out. Back in. In. Out.*"

"*Look at you. Yeah, you're getting good and wet for me.*"

"*Moan for me.*"

"*Keep stroking. Stick your fingers all the way in. Do it harder. Faster. Open your legs wider.*"

With my eyes closed, head thrown back, my breathing was getting more erratic.

"*That's my girl. Get yourself off. Get yours.*"

"*Come here, let me taste you,*" he said, sticking my fingers in his mouth and sucking. "*Hmm, finger lickin' good. Delicious. Come here,*" he said again, this time pulling me down onto the bed, on top of him.

Drake entered me quickly and roughly, a sigh of surprise escaping me. Tonight we weren't making love; tonight was fuck night. We had those too, just like costume night. Drake was going to fuck me unmercifully as he frantically gripped and maneuvered my hips up and down to the steady, rhythmic beat of his relentless dick. With every thrust of his rod, my womanhood eagerly anticipated and accepted the next.

Later, still not sated, he smacked my butt as he leaned me over a chair and entered me from behind, pulling me into him as he bit down on my neck and gave me all he had. Over and over.

Smack! *"Work that ass."*

Smack! *"Take this dick."*

Smack! *"Open that pussy up for me. That's right."* Pushing my legs open with his knees.

Ohhh. Ahhh. Ohhh.

"Yeah. You like this dick, don't you?"

Smack! *"Don't you?"*

"Ohhh, yes, babe."

"You ready to come? You almost there?"

"Ohhh. Yeah."

"Come on this dick."

"Ohhh. Ohhh. Oh . . . my . . . God."

"Yeah, this is mine. My pussy."

It's Over . . .

Dear Journal,

Sometimes I close my eyes and dream of the day when Drake will love me. However, it's just that, a dream . . . a carefully crafted illusion. I used to think I needed him next to me. Sometimes, I craved him so much I couldn't sleep at night. Thoughts of him kept me at full alert. Drake was my natural high.

Now, that's never going to happen—Drake loving me. There are situations and events that occur in one's life that never allow you to go back. There aren't any "what ifs," "buts," or "ands." Some things are totally unforgettable, unacceptable, and unforgivable. In some situations saying "I'm sorry" is simply not enough. Not good enough. The only feasible solution is to go your own, separate ways because hate is your constant companion.

We were once happy, though, at least I was. I'll admit that. Drake, I think he was happy with me. At first anyway. There were many smiles, gentle moments in time, sincere mutterings of truths. I hope everything wasn't a lie. However, I know, once you tell one lie, you have to continue to keep up with the first one. Eventually, your reality becomes based on myriad lies on top of lies, and that's no way to live. You're simply existing under an illusion of untruths.

I figured out, much too late, that Drake is all about the chase. The thrill of the game. He gets off making women love him. That gives him an adrenaline rush. Once that's accomplished, he's gone . . . like a thief in the night. Game over. He is very competitive by nature. Love, just like business, is all about dividing, conquering, and winning. Once it's accomplished, it's another notch on his belt. Another line or two on his glorious résumé. Broken hearts his souvenir.

Drake realizes he is a very attractive, gorgeous, charming man, and most women's fantasy. He uses that to his advantage. He has cultivated it to an exact science that turns women to putty in his strong hands, and then he attempts to mold and sculpture that clay to his heart's desire.

So yes, in the beginning we were happy. Very happy. Drake wouldn't have had it any other way. It was all part of the illusion he expertly crafted. In order to love him, you have to be happy first. And believe me, Drake knows how to make a woman feel special and desired. Special, intimate dinners, weekly deliveries of fresh fragrant flowers, luxurious weekend getaways, whispered promises during midnight phone calls, "just because" cards that speak of love and devotion; these were all part of that total facade to make one love him. He succeeded.

I thought Drake was the one who could make my life complete. Now, I think that whole concept is totally ludicrous and I was crazy for thinking it. Neither Drake nor anyone else can make my life complete. I have to do that for myself. I didn't come to this realization overnight; I won't give myself that much credit. It took a near fatal mistake, reflecting, and growing up.

Looking back, I was at Drake's beck and call. I'd drop everything to be with him. My family, friends, even myself, played second fiddle to Drake. I used to upset Taylor so much when I'd break an outing with her to be with Drake. All Drake had to say was jump, and I'd ask how high. I had no shame. Drake became my entire world, and that's when he became dangerous to my soul and well-being. Never make a man your entire world! Don't give him that power.

The Aftermath . . .

"Hey, I'm in the lobby. Come on down, girl. I'm starving," Taylor screamed into the phone, hanging up before I could manage more than a simple greeting.

"I'll be right down," I said to a dead line.

Today was Valentine's Day, and I almost didn't come to work. I seriously contemplated calling in sick. I didn't feel like seeing my coworkers' cubicles overflowing with beautiful red roses or hearing them boast about what their boyfriends or husbands were doing for them or taking them for Valentine's Day. It seemed everyone was in a relationship or had that special someone in their life to love and adore them, but me. I had no one. I was all alone. Drake was history. After what went down.

Even Taylor, who went through men like ruined and discarded stockings, had been dating this one guy on a regular basis. Regular for Taylor meant for more than a month. I have to admit, I was more than a bit jealous. Sometimes, I wished I were more like her. Taylor was outgoing, chipper, and gorgeous. I don't think she ever met anyone who wasn't a friend. She was the type of person who would strike up a conversation in an elevator with a complete stranger, while most of us would stare at the ceiling or the doors and wait for them to open. She'd walk out of the elevator with a phone number and plans to hook up later at happy hour.

After making it down to the lobby, stepping off the elevator and glancing toward the gold and black security desk, I spotted Taylor right away. She wasn't hard to miss. With a dress that was fierce, but not too sexy for work, she was dressed from head to toe in red. She had on red shoes with straps that enclosed her ankles, which I'm sure cost her a small fortune.

Her long brown hair was pulled back off her face and cascaded in waves down her back. Taylor would tell you in a minute that her hair wasn't a weave either. Don't even think it. Resembling a young Janet Jackson, she looked gorgeous. However, Taylor always looked great, like she just stepped off the pages of a fashion maga-zine or perhaps a catwalk in Paris.

The thin and very married security guard closest to her was try-ing to check her out without being too obvious. Taylor was so busy checking her lipstick and hair in her small compact that she didn't even notice him. Yet, all the men passing by noticed her and gave admiring stares and no doubt wished they'd be lucky enough to spend even one night with her.

After putting her compact away, she looked up and spotted me. Instantly, a huge smile spread across her face. A smile that lit up her deep dimples. Her happiness made me grin, and I momen-tarily forgot my situation. Taylor met me halfway and linked her left arm through my right one.

"Hey, sweetie," she said, giving me a quick kiss on the cheek. "Happy Valentine's Day."

"Is it? I wouldn't know."

"Oh, Kennedy, come on. It's not that bad. Today is just another day. A day for big corporations to make money off of the buying public who get caught up in yet another holiday. Next month it will be Easter."

"That's easy for you to say. I bet your new boyfriend, what's his name, hooked you up."

Taylor didn't say anything, just continued confidently walking toward the revolving doors to the outside.

"Well?" I asked, stopping halfway out the door.

"Okay, Kennedy, I did receive some flowers. But so what?"

"Someone in the world cares about you. That's what."

"I care about you, and so do your parents."

"Thanks, but it's just not the same," I declared, walking outside.

"Well, I'm going to put a smile on that pretty face of yours if it kills me. What do you want to eat?"

"I don't care. Food is food. I'll go wherever you want to."

"See what I mean? K, you have to start making decisions. Quit being so indecisive. That's why Drake bossed you around."

"Whatever."

"I'm treating you to lunch. I haven't seen you in weeks, and here you are, acting funky. Snap out of it."

"Well, thanks a lot. We can't all be the charming, sexy lady in red," I stated sarcastically.

"What am I going to do with you?"

I rolled my eyes upward. Before I could answer, Taylor was off on another tirade.

"Since you can't decide, I'll choose for us. Let's do Mick's for lunch. I've been feening for some of their chocolate chip cheesecake; I haven't had any in months."

"It doesn't matter. Sounds good to me."

"Okay, cool. Let's do it. Ooh, I'm so happy to see you," she declared, squeezing me into a gentle hug.

As we walked the couple of blocks up to Mick's, Taylor was a complete chatterbox. I couldn't help but notice the appreciative glances and outright stares that were directed our way. Whenever Taylor and I hung out, men seemed to come out of the woodwork like roaches. I couldn't remember a time we'd ever had to buy ourselves drinks in the clubs. As for Taylor, I couldn't recall when she didn't have a man she was dating or one or two waiting in the wings. I met plenty of men, but I guess my personality spoke volumes for me. Men saw me as standoffish, and I wasn't into dating every Jamal, Brandon, and Malik who asked me out. I was looking for quality, not quantity. Taylor, on the other hand, was following her mother's example. By the time I met her, Taylor's mother had already gone through four husbands.

"Here we are. Crowded as usual, just as we expected," Taylor said, opening the door for us to enter. The noise level, as always, was in maximum overdrive. We had to nearly scream to hear what each other was saying.

"Table for two, nonsmoking," she requested of the friendly waiter dressed in black and white.

Taylor and I were in luck because we were immediately led to a booth, near the kitchen, over in the corner of the busy restaurant. I didn't have to study the menu since I had eaten at Mick's on numerous occasions, but I pretended to check out the selections to shield myself from her scrutiny and pending questions. As I pretended to peruse the menu, I could feel her eyes on me.

"Well, friend, what's up? Looks like you've lost some weight," Taylor said, carefully looking me over.

"Have I? I haven't noticed." Actually, I had, since my clothes were too loose, but Taylor didn't need to know all that. I knew it was only a matter of time before the fifty questions began.

"And don't tell me nothing's up because I know better."

"I'm sorry to disappoint you, but nothing is up."

"Kennedy, I've been your best friend for how many years? I know when something is bothering you," she said, squeezing my hand across the table. "I love you. When you hurt, I hurt."

After hearing the sincerity in her voice, I had to close my eyes shut because I longed to tell her everything that was wrong in my world. I wanted to inform her of my unhappiness with myself and my failed relationship with Drake. I longed for her to know of my attempted suicide and how Mother was smothering me with her unwavering love and devotion. Living down in Florida, after their divorce, Daddy was not aware of what happened.

I ached to ask why I couldn't find love, only sorrow, and to ask why my life wasn't going the way I wanted it to go. I yearned to tell her how I daydreamed about finding my birth mother and asking her why she gave me up. There was so much I desperately needed to share with Taylor as she sat there with her perfect manicure, expertly lined MAC lips, beautifully coiffed hair. But, I didn't; I couldn't.

I lied and told her half-truths because the real truth hurt too deeply. My truths weren't pretty, and I wanted to be pretty in her eyes. I didn't want to disappoint Taylor or take the smile from her lips. Her smile let me know that there was joy in life. It wasn't impossible.

"Taylor, so much is going on. It would take three lunches to discuss everything."

"I have time. I have all the time in the world for you, K."

"I know and I appreciate it."

"Girl, is Drake still bothering you?"

At first I didn't speak. I just looked ahead of me and stared at the wall. I hated that I had shared details the other night on the phone of how he'd harassed me after our breakup. Driving by, calling me. Making my life a living hell . . . after all that happened.

"Well, is he?" Taylor asked impatiently.

I had to let some of my confusion out. "Not lately. But I can't get him off my mind. I have a love-hate relationship playing out in my head and heart. I despise how he treated me, which is what caused our relationship to end; yet I still love him when I think of all the good times we shared. And yes, Taylor, we did share many wonderful times," I declared, staring at her and praying that she'd understand where I was coming from.

"I know, sweetie. I'm sure you did. I know you are hurting now, but there are more fish in the sea if you'd only give them a chance. Drake wasn't the one. He wasn't right for you. He was more like a piranha. I sensed that. I don't know what happened to permanently end your relationship, but I assume you will tell me in time. I'm just glad he's out of your life. For good."

"Yeah, you're right."

"What can I do? What can I do to help?"

"Nothing. I just need time to see where I wanna be."

"Take it. Take that time."

I didn't say anything, just looked up as our waiter approached the table with pen and pad in hand.

"Are you lovely ladies ready to order?"

Taylor answered for us. "Yes. I think we are."

We placed our orders and settled into a comfortable silence, as friends do.

"Kennedy, you know I don't usually get involved in your love life."

"Since when?"

"I want to discuss Drake. You know I don't like how he treated you."

"Here we go again."

"Yes, here we go again. When you love someone, you just don't treat them bad."

"He is no longer in my life. Between you and Mother, y'all are driving me crazy over Drake Collins."

"Well, maybe you should listen to us. Underneath all that bullshit charm and good looks, he is an arrogant, conniving, good for nothing, lowlife. I think he secretly hates women," Taylor exclaimed in her usual animated way, with hands and hair flying all over the place.

"You really don't like him do you?" I asked with a genuine smile on my face.

"No, I don't, and I don't feel that you—" Taylor stopped in mid-sentence when she realized I was making fun of her.

We laughed for a good two minutes.

For the remainder of lunch my mood soared. It was good to be back in Taylor's presence. Her aura was so positive and full of intoxicating energy. She was perfect for her role as an account executive over at Coca-Cola.

"Are we still going away in June?" she asked out of the blue.

"I don't know."

"What do you mean you don't know? We can't break with tradition."

"Well, yeah, I guess you're right. I'm going."

"Oh, oh. And we have to go shopping for swimwear."

"I'll wear my suit from last year."

"No. We have to pick out something new and sexy. Something

that will make the men fall out of their lounge chairs with their tongues dragging the ground."

"Maybe I don't want them falling out of their chairs over me."

"K, you are no fun. That's the thrill—to see how stupid and juvenile they act just to see a little ass and cleavage."

"That's your idea of fun?"

"Yes. I'm seriously thinking about writing a book called '1001 Stupid Men Tricks.' I've seen enough dumb shit at the clubs to fill up two books."

"I wouldn't have enough material for a quarter of a book."

"K, you've got to get out more and be more observant. You've never noticed how you can bat your long eyelashes, toss your hair, and just look at men with those big innocent eyes, and they'll be at your beck and call . . ." With that, Taylor was into chatterbox mode again. I listened for a few more minutes before my attention span floated away.

For as long as I could remember, Taylor and I always went away the second week in June. It was a tradition we started right after college. We'd do the girl thing, pack our swimsuits and sunscreen, and head off for a wonderful week full of fun and sun. We always rebond during those times, and I realize what a true and real friend Taylor is to me. We have some really deep conversations, and of course, we party!

Our waiter brought our meals and drinks to the table and went to greet new customers who were seated at his other stations.

"Sweetie, how's your salad?" Taylor asked, digging into her lunch with gusto.

"It's good."

"Well, you're not eating like it's good. You are barely touching your food. We've got to get those pounds back on you."

"Yes, Mother."

"Men don't like twigs. A sistah got to have some meat to hold onto."

"Yes, Mother. I hear you, Mother."

Taylor gave me this look like she wanted to say something but then stopped.

After taking a long lunch, I was actually feeling better. Taylor is good for me. She had me cracking up with her antics and good nature. At one point she was feeding me pieces of my grilled chicken Caesar salad with her fork.

"Come on, open up. Here comes the choo choo. Oh, I forgot to ask you, how's your Coke?"

"Delicious, ice cold, and packed full of caffeine."

"Good. Well, let's make a toast to Drake."

We held our glasses up and clicked. Taylor had witnessed Drake's tirades on me drinking Cokes. I'd come to realize it wasn't an issue of my health; it was an issue of control with Drake.

"Good riddance."

"Ditto."

We were laughing our heads off. Being silly. It felt good to laugh. In passing, our waiter asked if we'd slipped some liquor into our cherry sodas. We giggled some more. But like they say, all good things must come to an end. I glanced down at my watch and realized I had overstayed my lunch hour, and my desk held tons of paperwork that was calling my name.

Suddenly, I noticed the atmosphere at our table had changed. It became ice cold. I looked up at Taylor and saw her staring toward the entrance. Since my back was to the door, I turned in my seat to see what had stolen her attention and evidently her good mood as well.

I froze and my hands literally started shaking as Drake's eyes met mine. I could see the familiar specks of green dancing in his pupils. Taylor sensed my immediate distress.

"Calm down, Kennedy. Be cool. We can leave," she whispered between clenched teeth.

"Yeah, let's go. Now," I barely muttered.

"Shit. His ass showing up made me miss getting my slice of cheesecake," Taylor nearly screamed in anger.

As she attempted to pay the check and leave a tip, Drake approached our table with a huge smirk on his face. He was looking as handsome as ever in his gray pin-striped suit, and it looked like he had gotten some sun because his skin tone was radiant. He didn't look like a man who was pining over his woman or the loss of a doomed relationship.

"Hello, ladies. You two are a sight for sore eyes. Two beautiful ladies at one table."

Taylor answered. "I wish I could say the same because my eyes have seen enough."

"Taylor, how are you? Good to see you too," he said sarcastically. "I see your attitude hasn't changed."

"No. Still not willing to let you treat me like a second-class citizen."

Drake ignored her and directed his full attention on me.

"Happy Valentine's Day, Kennedy. I started to send you some flowers, but then I remembered how you kicked me to the curb. You and I must talk," he stated, reaching over to touch my left shoulder.

"Don't! Don't touch me! Don't you ever place your hands on me again!" I managed to utter through clenched teeth as I pulled away.

"You heard the lady!" Taylor screamed, pushing Drake out of the way and making her way from our table.

Following her, I sideswiped people in my path and was almost out the front door when I barely heard Drake call out, "Kennedy, we will talk. You can't run from me forever." When I glanced back, our waiter and Drake were staring at us. There was amusement on Drake's face and disbelief on our waiter's.

On our walk back to my building, Taylor managed to calm me down a little.

"K, don't give that man your power. I don't know what went down with you guys, but Drake is obviously getting joy out of your pain. Don't let him. Don't give him the satisfaction."

"All I did was love that man. That's all."

"I know, sweetie, but sometimes love isn't enough. He'll miss you one day. He'll realize what he lost in you, and you'll under-stand what you have to offer a *real* man. In time your heart will heal and you won't feel so sad."

We made it back to the front of my building, and all I wanted to do was walk the two blocks to my car and drive home.

"Listen, K," Taylor said. "Call me if you need me. I have a two o'clock meeting, but I should be at my desk after three o'clock, no later than three-fifteen."

"I will."

"I mean it. Call me."

"Thanks for lunch."

"K, you are gonna be all right. Time heals all wounds. That and a new man with a big dick." She laughed. I didn't.

As I headed into the building, I didn't look back. I tried to walk tall and confident. If I turned around, Taylor would see the begin-nings of tears forming in my eyes. I didn't want her to see how weak I was. I used the ride up in the elevator to mentally compose myself. I somehow made it through work for the rest of the day and managed to make it safe and sound through rush hour traffic.

All I could think about was my bed; it was my single focus. As soon as I entered my apartment, I left a track of clothes down the hallway. I stayed up long enough to write an entry in my journal before I was in bed with the covers pulled tightly over my head. I wrote:

Dear Journal,

Today was not a very good day. In fact, today was one of the worst in a while. When I saw Drake at Mick's, I wanted to die again. With him standing there, gloating down at me, I felt smaller than minuscule. I hate that man. I despise him so much. What does he want to talk about? There's nothing more to say. We are history, kaput, done! After what he did, there's nothing more to discuss. I hate him for that.

Happy Valentine's Day. Yeah, right.

I recalled another holiday season. It's amazing how a day that started out so normal would turn into my worst night mare. It was a few days before New Year's Day, a Friday night, and Drake and I had attended a post-Christmas party with some of his friends. I swear, the man had been in Atlanta only briefly, yet he had more friends than I did, and I had lived here all my life. People were naturally drawn to him.

Drake and I had a great time. It was a small, intimate affair. There were about six couples total and we sat around and sipped wine, ate delicious food, played board games, and talked. A real low-key event; just my speed. Drake was very relaxed and especially attentive to my needs.

I drank a bit too much, which was anything over two glasses, but I'd noticed that whenever I was with Drake, he encouraged me to let loose. I knew if I were with him, he'd take care of me and not let anything horrible happen.

I truly enjoyed myself, and no one could have told me that would be the last time Drake and I were together as a couple. We laughed, we cuddled, and we kissed under the live mistletoe. It was a magical evening, and there were even a few snow flurries in the crisp air that added to the magical spell. We left the party around midnight and I convinced him to drive around to look at Christmas lights and decorations before they were taken down.

Drake and I drove around, listened to Christmas music on the radio, laughed and had a great time in the sanctity of his car. It was like it was just he and I in our own little world. We sipped on some hot cider, taken from the party, that was laced with liquor, and I was feeling no pain. I was buzzed, but I didn't care. I felt free and in love. I knew Drake had his imperfections, but I knew he'd change for me. Love could do that . . . change a person. It was almost a new year, with new beginnings.

We arrived back at my apartment a little after one A.M. The apartment was nice and cozy. Without turning on the lights in the living room, I asked Drake to turn on the Christmas lights on my tree while I took a hot shower. I wanted to slip into something sexy, this Frederick's of Hollywood outfit I'd purchased complete with Santa boots. It was Drake's last present that he had to open. Ho! Ho! Ho!

After I couldn't convince him to join me in the shower, I slipped in alone. I turned the water to as hot as I could stand it and placed my face under the shower head and enjoyed the feel of the water streaming down my face. I relived our night together and smiled because it wasn't over yet.

I vaguely heard Drake rambling around in the bedroom and kitchen. He had said that he was going to get the rest of the champagne out of the fridge. We had a leftover bottle from a few days earlier that he'd spent an enormous amount of money on. I stepped out of the shower, layered myself with body lotion and spritz, and slipped on my sexy lingerie. I pinned my hair up on top of my head, pulled on my black and red Santa boot slippers, and walked back into the bedroom.

Drake was already under the covers, completely nude and waiting for me. He reached out his hand, pulled back the covers, and I slipped under after tossing my boots to the floor.

"You are so beautiful. You know that," he stated, propped up on his elbows, caressing my cheek.

"You are too."

He gave me a funny look.

"What? Men can't be beautiful. Well, you are, babe."

"I think you have definitely had too much to drink," he declared.

"You think so?"

"I know so," he said, pulling down my red spaghetti strap and pouring some chilled champagne, from the nightstand, on my nipples.

He proceeded to lick it off, and I proceeded to melt.

"Oh, you like that, huh, Miss Claus?" he asked, searching between my legs to see if I was ready.

I nodded my head.

"Well, Santa has more where that came from."

"Oh really?"

"Have you been a naughty girl? Or a good girl?"

"Good."

"Come here. We'll have to correct that." Drake flipped me over on my stomach and discarded my gown. So much for the $125 I'd spent. He poured champagne in the arch of my back and proceeded to lick and suck it off, all the way down to my buttocks.

That night it was all about me. Drake pleased me from the tip of my toes to the top of my head, and I got to ride his reindeer. Afterward, we lay wrapped in each other's arms with our legs entwined. I let out a pleased, satisfied sigh.

"I could get used to this, babe."

Drake had his eyes closed and his arms wrapped protectively around me.

Silence.

"Did you hear what I said?"

"Shhh. Just relax. Go to sleep," he murmured in a drowsy voice.

Cradled in his arms, the man I loved, I did just that. I dosed off into a peaceful, dream-filled sleep while visions of family, children, and marriage danced through my head. In my sleep-induced state, I vaguely remember Drake getting up to go to the restroom. He was soon back, claiming his rightful spot. Nestled next to me. I quickly dosed back off.

I don't know how much time passed; I was disoriented and shrouded in the throes of deep slumber. I felt Drake gently nudging me and kissing my neck. His hardness pressed against me.

"Babe, go back to sleep," I whispered, reaching behind me to stroke his cheek.

Drake didn't say anything. He continued to spoon with me and caress my breasts. As usual, he knew my nipples were one of my weak spots. He started playing with them, squeezing them between his thumb and forefinger, and I started moaning. Sleep was quickly slipping away. We were still naked from earlier, and I felt the heat rise from his body. I reached back to stroke his erection.

"Oh, I thought you'd like that. I see Rudolph the red-nosed reindeer is awake and ready to drive his sleigh," I teased.

I still had my eyes closed as I continued to stroke him up and down. Fast and then slow. Just like he liked. At some point Drake reached around and inserted three of his fingers inside me. I was already wet and very excited. I turned on my back and spread my legs wider so he could continue to do what he was doing so well. My hand pressed down on his to encourage him not to stop.

I wanted him then. He could forget foreplay. I needed to feel him inside me, again. Drake had other ideas, because when I tried to mount him, he stopped me and pulled my head down near his lap. Through the darkness of the room, he looked at me and smiled. I knew what he wanted. I went to work with a passion. I licked, sucked, squeezed, and sucked some more. Taking it all in. I'd glance up and see him trying to hold his moans in.

"That's enough for you, you greedy boy," I joked, coming up for air. "It's time for you to eat your supper," I teased.

Through the eerie shadows of my room, Drake looked at me with this strange glow in his eyes.

"Come on babe, go down on me. You know I love that."

Drake went to work; it was his best performance ever. The man had a true talent for going downtown. When I was on the verge of coming, I pushed him off me. I wanted to feel that delicious dick inside me before I came.

Drake was more than ready to oblige. He eased me onto all fours and slowly eased himself inside me. I was taken back for a moment because he felt larger or wider or something that I couldn't quite put my finger on. His thrusts felt like they were coming out my stomach. They had never felt that way before, and he smelled different too. I assumed it was the new cologne he had purchased at Belk's.

"Oh, babe. You feel so good."

Drake didn't say anything. He continued to ram me with no mercy. His fingers were clawing at my breasts.

"Babe, slow down. There's more where this came from. Quit being so greedy."

I looked back, and Drake had his undivided attention focused on the task at hand. By now he was usually saying all kinds of nasty shit to me. He loved to talk dirty to me during sex. Instead of turning me off, I'd get super hot. I was pretty verbal now myself, and initially that surprised me, but Drake preferred it that way. That early morning, he was uncharacteristically quiet. Too silent. All I heard from him was his heavy panting.

"Oh babe, your dick is making my pussy feel sooo good. You've got me so hot."

He was still ramming me with no sign of slowing down.

"That's right. Take what's yours. Oh God! You've got me coming! I'mmmmm coming, babe!"

We both came at the same time in hard, forceful, spastic shudders. I felt him shoot hot squirts up inside me. At the exact moment that was happening, I heard a cell phone go off in my closet.

Without an ounce of energy left, I collapsed down on the

bed. At first I thought I was imagining things. I dismissed the sound. But then I heard movement.

"What? What is that? Did you hear that," I asked, crouching on my bed, ready to flee.

Sprawled out on the bed, Drake looked at me in surprise and stared at the closed closet door. Then the door swung wide open and there stood Drake. I looked from one to the other in amazement. There were two Drakes.

"What the hell?" I said, jumping up and trying to hide my nakedness.

Then Drake spoke. The one from the closet entrance. "Calm down, Kennedy."

"What do you mean calm down?" I asked, glancing from him to the Drake on the bed. The one on the bed whose dick was now erect and pointing wickedly at me. "Drake, what's going on?" By now I was crying as the realization of what had occurred was slowly sinking in.

The Drake from the closet closed the gap between us.

"That's my identical twin brother, Blake," he said, pointing to the man now hurriedly pulling on his pants.

"What? Your twin? You let your twin brother fuck me? You bastard! I can't believe this! My God, you're sick!"

"Calm down, Kennedy!" Drake was saying, walking toward me with outstretched hands . . .

The Confrontation . . .

Monday morning came before I knew it or was ready for it. I absolutely hate Monday mornings. They are a constant reminder that I'm a slave to corporate America for at least the next five days. Ugh.

I awoke sweaty and tangled in my sheets, with my comforter on the floor. I had tossed and turned all night in my lonely apartment. Every sound was elevated tenfold. I witnessed every creak and groan of the walls settling. I heard my upstairs neighbor when he arrived home and attended to various household duties. I swear the man is a night owl or a vampire. Who vacuums at ten o'clock at night? Faintly, I could even pick up traffic sounds two streets over, on a major bypass. Around six o'clock A.M., just as I was finally dosing off into a deep, restless sleep, the alarm clock blazed me awake. I lay there for another ten minutes, unable to move the few feet to my bathroom.

I felt horrible, and I didn't look any better, with the heavy, puffy bags concentrated under my eyes. I didn't feel like going into work, but if I didn't, I knew I'd mope around the apartment all day. For some reason, I was afraid to be alone with my random thoughts. So, off to work I went, grumpy and all. If I had known what was coming, I would have stayed at home, in bed.

Around nine o'clock, after I'd finished off my first can of soda, I felt much better. I could feel the caffeine and sugar surging through my veins giving me an instant high. It gave me renewed energy to tackle the never-ending phone calls and pile of work sitting on my desk. In need of a diversion from my issues, I dove in.

At ten o'clock my manager informed me there was an emergency meeting upstairs that I was to attend in her absence. She had another client meeting that couldn't be missed, and since she couldn't be in two places at once, I was her stand-in. My stomach immediately fell to my knees because I knew Drake would be a part of the mandatory meeting. I'd have to be in the same room with him for at least an hour or more. That realization frightened me and made me sick to my stomach.

At first I debated faking illness and leaving for the day, but I couldn't run from him forever. Besides, my manager believed in me and confirmed that I was an asset to the company by sending me to represent our department at an important meeting. Today was the day I'd make a stand and prove I was strong. Drake wanted me to bow down and surrender. I refused.

I arrived upstairs ten minutes before the meeting was to begin. I figured I'd need the additional minutes to pull myself together and psych myself out. Plus, I needed to review the agenda. The friendly administrative assistant informed me where the meeting was to be held. I was one of the first to arrive in the large conference room at the end of the hallway. I spoke to the two other women who were already there and made sure I secured a seat near the middle of the table. I didn't want to be up front, where I knew Drake would be. Yet, I didn't want to entirely disappear at the very back either.

Slowly, different managers started drifting in with cups of freshly brewed coffee and pens and notepads in hand. Drake was one of the last to arrive. For just a quick second, I saw the surprise flash across his face when he saw me seated at the massive table. I looked down at my yellow legal pad and pretended to read my briefing. As always, his presence intoxicated and overwhelmed me.

"Okay, people, let's go ahead and get this meeting started," Drake said, chairing the meeting and looking from one to the other of us. "We all have a lot on our plates today, and I apologize for taking you away from other matters. However, we have a small crisis that needs to be addressed and handled as promptly as possible."

He stood tall and confident as he went on to inform us that one of our major clients was threatening to pull out once their contract ended in a couple of months. This company's bigwigs had complaints of inferior service and poor customer service, among other things, and said they could obtain lower pricing elsewhere. They had been a client for many, many years and brought in an enormous amount of revenue. Everyone seated at the table knew there was no way in hell we could afford to lose them. We had to handle them with kid gloves and come up with a planned resolution; our jobs depended upon it.

Drake skillfully went over the history of our client, revenue figures, and then addressed each complaint. When he came to the customer service piece, he looked directly at me for guidance.

"It appears we have Miss Logan in our presence today. For those of you who don't know her, she's a CSR and very familiar with this particular client. Maybe she can be so kind as to address some of these issues concerning customer service." Then he looked at me again and smiled, knowing he'd put me on the spot. I wasn't prepared. I was simply sitting in for my manager. He knew that.

All eyes turned in my direction for clarification and understanding. I felt my face flushing. I swallowed the lump in my throat and gulped.

"Mr. Collins, this is the first time that I've been made aware of these complaints concerning our department. As you know, I'm sitting in for my manager, who had a conflicting appointment. I'll be happy to tag this as a take-away item, investigate, and report back to everyone ASAP."

Drake sat there with this smirk on his face. I wanted to slap it off. Honestly, I just wanted to slap him, period. "Miss Logan, as you know, this is of a most urgent nature. Time is of the utmost importance. Can you shed any light at all on the current situation? And when can we expect to receive your report?"

"Today, by five o'clock."

Not trying to shift blame, I proceeded to explain what little I knew of the situation, starting with high turnover ratios in our department contributing to unusually heavy workloads. Until very recently, several different reps had handled the client's account.

"Very good. Thank you, Miss Logan, for your input," Drake stated, as his eyes looked me up and down. "I'll expect to have that report in my office, in more detail, by five o'clock sharp. Please copy everyone in this room as well."

"Thank you, Mr. Collins," I responded. I was pleased with my comeback in his effort to make me look stupid in front of my colleagues.

"Well, unless there are any more questions or concerns, I suggest we all get back to work, and with your take-aways in hand, be prepared to meet again on Wednesday, same time and place. I'll have my administrative assistant send out an agenda. I would like a manager's meeting scheduled with them by next week. Thank you."

Everyone rose to leave.

"Miss Logan, may I speak with you for a minute, please?"

I wanted to scream out *Hell no*, but controlled myself.

"Sure," was all I said. Drake was now seated at the head of the table. He hadn't looked up again and was reading his notes. By now mostly everyone had filtered out of the room.

"Do you mind closing the door, Miss Logan, so that we may speak privately?"

As I got up to close the door, I could feel his eyes taking me in. Caressing my body. At one time I enjoyed knowing that my man was watching me. Now it made my skin crawl. I stopped myself from scratching. I turned slowly around, didn't make eye contact, walked and sat two seats down from him.

"You did great today. I put you on the spot, but you were quick on your feet. I like the way you didn't tolerate everyone placing total blame on your department for the mess we are in. You are very loyal."

"Loyal to those who deserve it."

Drake laughed and stared at me for a few seconds.

"You look very nice today."

"What do you need to speak with me about?"

"Oh, so now you don't have any manners?"

"You look very nice today."

"Thank you."

Drake reached for my hand. "I've missed you, Kennedy."

I pulled my hand from his reach. "Is that all, Mr. Collins?" I acted as if I hadn't heard his previous comment.

"Did you hear me?"

"Yes, I did. Is that all?"

He chose that moment to move and sit directly next to me. I instantly felt a powerful combination of uneasiness and desire rise from the pit of my stomach. Despite my feelings for him, he was still a very handsome and sexy man. No one could take that away from him. And today, dressed in a black suit with a crisp white shirt, his hair freshly cut and him smelling divine, I couldn't help but notice and wonder how he could look so good on the outside and be so messed up on the inside.

"You are so beautiful. You're all I think about lately. When are you going to forgive me and let bygones be bygones?" He reached over and caressed my face and hair. I froze.

I couldn't believe what he was saying. Let bygones be bygones. Like we'd had a simple argument over something trivial. He was either in denial or totally insane; maybe both.

"How about never? Is that clear enough?"

"You can't mean that. I promise, what happened will never happen again. It was a test."

"If that's all, I have to get back to my desk. I have a report to deliver by five. Sharp." I stood to leave.

He roughly grabbed my arm and pushed me back down into the chair. "This meeting isn't over. I am your superior, Kennedy, and don't you forget that. I can make your life a living hell. With the economy the way it is, now isn't a good time to search for a new job. Do you understand me?" Then he reached down, boldly placed his hand inside my blouse and fondled my left breast, first gently, then rougher as I attempted to pull away.

I jerked away like I'd been burnt. "What are you doing? Take your hands off me!" I screamed through gritted teeth.

Drake grabbed me by the wrist. "We'll continue this conversation later. Believe that."

"Don't hold your breath!"

"Good day, Miss Logan. Like I said, we'll talk later. Real soon."

"Stay away from me. I mean it or . . ."

"Or you'll what? Go to your manager, who is seriously sweating me, by the way, and tell her that I've been fucking you silly and that you've loved every damn minute of it? I don't think so. Kennedy, you don't air your dirty laundry like that. You're too much of a lady. Well, that's what everyone thinks anyway. I've seen the real Kennedy. The real freak."

"Stop!" I screamed, placing my hands over my ears to block out his words.

"Kennedy, you should know by now that I get what I want. One way or the other. And I want you. And I will have you," he stated, tracing a circle around my nipple through the sheer silk of my blouse.

I slapped his hand away. "Why are you doing this to me?"

"Because I can. If I wanted to, I could have you down on your knees doing what you do best. You want to suck my big dick, Kennedy? You're one of the best; I taught you well. I bet I can even get you to sleep with my brother again. It was a trip watching my twin brother handle his business."

I started to cry softly. "You are sick."

"Don't cry now. You were not crying when Blake was hitting it from behind."

"What man would want to watch another man screw his woman, let alone his own brother?"

"A man who can control his woman. Why not my twin brother? It was like watching myself get busy."

"You're sick," I said again.

"Join the club. When my brother Blake was hitting it right, I didn't see any complaints. You were all into that shit. All over his dick."

"I thought he was you. I didn't even know you had a twin."

"You don't know how your own man moves and feels inside you?" Drake asked with disgust in his eyes.

I shook my head sadly. "I can't believe I thought I loved you. You don't even know the meaning of the word. How could I have been so blind? So misled?"

"At some point in time, y'all all do . . . think you love me. Women always confuse a good fuck with love. I, on the other hand, know that good pussy is just that . . . good pussy. Fix yourself up and get back to work."

With that, Drake turned and readied himself to walk out of the room. Not another word was spoken, but the tension in the air could slice through steel.

After I had composed myself enough to walk out of the conference room, I found the administrative assistant sitting at her desk looking at me curiously. I turned away and kept walking. As I stifled a sniffle, I could feel her eyes boring into my back.

The Finale . . .

It was a little over a week later, after our first impromptu business meeting, that I found myself riding the elevator back upstairs for yet another meeting. My manager had asked me to finish it up, since I started the process, and to report back to her. She claimed that this would be good experience for me. The previous week, I had turned in my findings in a detailed, comprehensive ten-page report. Today was to be a follow-up meeting for all concerned and to tie up loose ends.

As before, I arrived early. Again, I wasn't sure what to expect from Drake after the fiasco last time. I knew I wouldn't and couldn't allow myself to be alone with him. I had thought long and hard about filing sexual harassment charges, but I wasn't sure. I had no doubt Drake would drag our so-called secret affair into the spotlight, and I definitely wasn't ready for that. I was totally confused. I had no clue what I should do or how I should proceed. I just knew my life was in shambles and I had to do something to move forward and reclaim it.

This time when I arrived on the floor, the conference room wasn't empty. Apparently, another meeting was going on, which was expected to end shortly. I stood just outside the door and chatted with the administrative assistant. She was an older black woman, with salt and pepper hair, who I heard had started out as a temp and eventually moved into a permanent position.

"How are you today, Miss Logan?"

"I'm okay, and yourself?" I asked.

"I can't complain. I'm here, I'm alive, and I'm kicking. That's a blessing in itself, wouldn't you say?"

I laughed. That sounded like something Mother would say. "True."

"Sometimes you young people forget to count your blessings." She winked.

"You might be right."

"I know I am. I have a daughter about your age."

I smiled and looked toward the conference room door. I didn't want a lecture on religion or the state of the younger generation.

"If I may say, you're smart, gorgeous, and seem like a wonderful person who was brought up right."

"Thank you."

"I mean it. Your mother should be very proud of you. I noticed you months ago. You stand out around here because of the way you carry yourself with such grace. You don't gossip and be all up into everyone's business. You have class."

"Thank you," I stated, again glancing back at the conference room.

I noticed the other meeting was ending, as associates walked out the conference room, scattering in different directions. I saw a few familiar faces and I waved.

"I like conversating with young people, and I think they like talking to me because I call it as I see it. I'm real, as you say. For you, I have just one simple piece of advice. Remember, what looks good isn't always pretty," she said, raising her eyebrows.

I opened my mouth to ask her what that meant, but just then Drake and a very lovely woman with legs from here to eternity and a Halle Berry short hairstyle came around the corner. I'd never seen her on the floor before, and I knew all the managers.

"Excuse me," the mystery woman said in a condescending tone as she stuck her nose up at me and walked around me.

I moved out of the way. Drake barely acknowledged me.

"Miss Logan, the meeting is starting in just a few minutes," he stated, looking down at his watch as if I was running late.

I delivered a half smile to the administrative assistant. "I guess that's my clue to go."

"Sure, darling. You take care of yourself," she replied.

"By the way, who was the woman with Mr. Collins?" I asked.

"Oh, that's Miss Reynolds. She started a week ago. Replacing the management slot that was vacated by Mr. Stephenson."

"Umm. I see."

By the time I made it into the conference room, I had to sit closer to the front and to Drake. I vaguely noticed Miss Reynolds glaring at me out of the corner of my eye. I couldn't figure out for the life of me why I was getting strong vibes that she didn't care for me. This from a woman I hadn't even had the opportunity to be formally introduced to or knew existed until a few moments ago.

"Good morning everyone. Today's meeting should be short and

sweet," Drake announced, his eyes lingering on me for a few additional seconds. I noticed Miss Reynolds catching him and openly glaring at me.

"Before we go any further, for those of you who haven't had the opportunity to meet her yet, I'd like to introduce you to Miss Brittany Reynolds. She's one of our new managers."

She waved and stood briefly. "Thank you, Mr. Collins. I look forward to meeting everyone and fostering a productive and meaningful working relationship."

"Okay, let's get down to business. The first item on the agenda is . . ."

The meeting went by quickly, and the good news was that we were able to pacify our client with some modifications on how we handled their account. Bottom line, they were no longer pulling out and our working relationship would continue, hopefully, into infinity.

Throughout the meeting, I noticed a silent communication going on between Drake and Miss Reynolds. It was very subtle, but there nevertheless. I knew it wasn't my imagination because it was how we used to interact with each other in public. I immediately picked up on the vibes.

Finally, the meeting ended and I couldn't wait to get off that floor. I retrieved my notes, purse, and pen, and was trying to slip quietly away. Of course, that wasn't in Drake's plan.

"Miss Logan, have you been formally introduced to Miss Reynolds?" he inquired. He was trying to be funny, and I hated him for it. I knew what was going on. He was messing with me.

I turned around with a plastered smile on my face. Drake and Brittany were standing side by side, looking at me expectantly. "No, I haven't." I reached out my hand. "Good to meet you. I'm Kennedy Logan."

"Brittany Reynolds. Kennedy, what a lovely name."

"Thank you."

"You're one of those customer service reps, aren't you?"

"Yes, I'm one of those." I immediately didn't like her condescending tone.

"I must come down there and check out the team. I haven't been in the trenches in a while." Then she laughed, a shrill, irritating cackle.

"You do that."

"I told Brittany what a wonderful team you and I made behind closed doors, *working* on our project," Drake injected, emphasizing working.

"Did you?" I said, knowing what he was insinuating.

"Well, Drake and I have spent an enormous amount of time behind closed doors as well," Brittany said. "So, your services won't be needed anytime soon. He now has me to handle that role."

"Good for him."

"Drake is showing me the ropes, so to speak," she laughed, daring me to read between the lines.

Heifer! I silently screamed.

"Well, it was nice meeting you. Take care."

"You too, Kendall."

"That's Kennedy."

"Oh, I'm sorry. Of course, Kennedy."

I bet you are. Heifer!

With them not too far behind me, I started to make my exit and escape. I could hear them whispering and laughing behind my back and having too much fun. Yes, they were very comfortable with each other. As much as I despised Drake, I still felt a tinge of jealousy.

Free at Last . . .

Two months later . . .

I prayed. Prayed some more. Then, I called Drake. Called him for the last time. I pushed each digit of his number like I had done hundreds of times before, but slowly. The phone rang and rang and rang with no pickup other than his voice mail. It didn't matter. It was probably for the best. I wanted to get this off my chest and it didn't matter if I told Drake face-to-face, over the phone, or in an impersonal voice mail. Who knew when he would arrive home? He was probably still out partying from the night before or laid up with somebody. I listened to his voice. Closed my eyes to commit it to memory. He always had such a sexy, deep voice. One day he'd miss me and realize how wrong he was. One day he'd be sorry.

My message, which took two phone calls, went like this:

"Drake, I want to inform you that you are not going to intimidate, harass, or threaten me anymore. I'm sick of running. I've prayed about you. Today, I made the decision to fight. If you ever call me, drive by or come by my apartment again, I swear I will call the police and report you. Everything will come out. Everything!

"One day, you'll get yours, because we really do reap what we sow! I deserved so much more from you. I loved you. Thought you were the one. The man of my dreams. Now, I just pity you. I pity you. Don't ever contact me again. I realize you tried to shape me into someone I wasn't, tried to strip away my integrity, but it doesn't matter. You almost succeeded, but not quite, because I'm still standing! Goodbye, Drake."

After hanging up, I felt free. Free like a bird gliding through the sky. I felt like a burden had been released from my shoulders, and when I turned the car radio back on, guess what was playing? "Jesus Walks With Me," by Kanye West. For the remainder of my drive I felt confident that no matter what went down, I knew I could handle it. I was stronger than I thought. I was humiliated, and had almost sacrificed my soul for a man, but I was still standing! A calmness settled over me and I sensed a shroud of protection and love surrounding me. I was at peace.

These are my confessions. . .

ELECTA ROME PARKS, one of the rising stars in contemporary fiction, is the author of the best-selling novels *The Ties That Bind* and *Loose Ends*, which were originally self-published through her own company, Novel Ideal Publishing and Editorial Services Company, a company now dedicated to quality editorial services.

After successfully self-publishing her debut novels, New American Library, a division of Penguin Group, bought the rights. Mrs. Parks signed a three-book deal with New American Library. Her first novel, *The Ties That Bind*, was rereleased in October 2004, and *Loose Ends* was rereleased in November 2004. Both books were immediately chosen as Black Expressions Book Club selections and embraced as Books of the Month by book clubs across the country. A third manuscript, *Almost Doesn't Count*, which was immediately chosen as the main selection for Black Expressions Book Club, was released in August 2005.

Recently, Electa signed her *second* and *third* book deals with Penguin Group/New American Library and HarperCollins/Avon Red. Her upcoming projects are: *Ladies' Night Out* (NAL, January 2007) and *These Are My Confessions* (Avon Red, July 2007).

Electa Rome Parks has been a frequent guest on radio shows. She's been interviewed by newspapers, *Vibe Vixen*, *Upscale Magazine*, *Rolling Out*, and *Booking Matters*, to name just a few. Parks lives outside Atlanta, Georgia, with her husband and two children. With a B.A. degree in marketing and a minor in sociology, she is following her true passion and working on her next novel.

Please contact Electa at *www.electaromeparks.com*.

Strapped

Cheryl Robinson

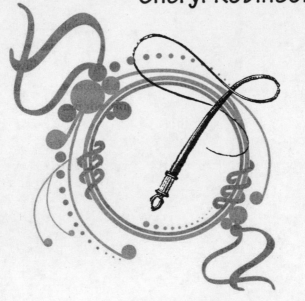

Sex Games

The first man I killed was by accident.

I'd been chatting with him online nearly the entire summer before finally arranging to meet him at Sambuca's, a popular jazz club in the uptown section of Dallas. In his profile, he wrote: I'M INTO PLAYING GAMES, BUT I'M NOT TALKING ABOUT MONOPOLY. During our first of a series of phone conversations, he shared with me that his fantasy was more of a fetish. He wanted to be choked as he was getting ready to come. He said that a woman could use her hands, but he preferred a thin black leather belt to be tightened around his neck for a few seconds just until he went unconscious. To me, it sounded like a dangerous game, but he'd had this done to him before . . . many times . . . and the sensation, he said, was indescribable.

Initially, I had my reservations, which is why I'd decided to meet another man instead, but when things didn't work out with him, I called Lester. I hated his name but I loved his deep and sexy voice. Something as simple as the way he said my name made my pussy wet, and the things he said to me while I was on my way to meet him almost caused me to have an accident.

"You want me to fuck you deep and hard, don't you? I just hope you can handle my big dick, otherwise I might bust your juicy pussy wide open."

I started squirming in the seat of my car from the anticipation. "Are you really strapped?"

"Strapped?" he asked, laughing. "I got a ten inch dick. How big do you need it?"

"The bigger, the wetter; the bigger your dick is the wetter my pussy will be."

Neither of us had a picture attached to our online profiles, so the mystery of how he'd look in person, wondering whether or not he'd truly have what I wanted, and whether he'd find me sexy, quickly turned into my own fantasy. I wanted to know if it was really true that *everything* was bigger in Texas, and was bigger really better.

Quiet as I've always kept it, I do think about having sex just as much if not more than most men. But the men I'd been with didn't have what I wanted. I wasn't asking for a dick that was so big it could be confused with being a third leg; a solid seven inches would do just fine, I'm sure. But if I lucked up on more, like ten inches, I definitely wouldn't turn it down. So after my devastating breakup with my fiancé of three years, I set myself on a mission while on my summer vacation—to find just that, a big dick. Better to get loose in Dallas, a city where I'm completely unknown and detached, than in my hometown of Detroit, where I live and work.

For nearly an hour, I waited at the bar for Lester, sipping on chocolate martinis that were being generously supplied to me by a secret admirer whom I had yet to see. My mind started to drift into a fantasy of being loved, just not with the heart. I'd had that many times before, or so I thought. Words—I couldn't trust. But could I make love to a man without being in love? Could I fuck him? I thought so. I wanted to be someone other than who I'd always been, someone other than a stiff middle school teacher who pulled her hair back into a puffy ponytail and hid behind a pair of granny glasses and ruffled blouses buttoned all the way to the top. But I had to change, not just how I looked, but how I received pleasure. The next time I slept with a man, I wanted him to make my body feel what his words couldn't express. I wanted the truth, and an orgasm never lies; a good fuck, no one can take away. Something like that can stay in your consciousness forever.

After accepting the fact that Lester was a no show, I stood to leave the bar, and that's when a man who was not attractive in the least—or at least not to me—walked toward me. He was stuck in the eighties, still wearing his hair in a curl with a skinny leather tie and a pair of penny loafers with a nickel in the slit. But I was willing to sacrifice good looks and style for some good dick any day, and so I smiled and sat back down.

"Are you Lester?" I asked, assuming he was the man I'd been waiting for.

"Lester?" he questioned.

"Is that your name?"

He shook his head. "No, I'm sorry. My name is Eugene." He sat on the bar stool beside me. "But it can be Lester tonight if you'd like."

"Well, it depends," I said as I placed my hand on his leather tie and then slid it down between his legs to feel his dick. "How big is Lester?"

"Pardon me?" he said, before becoming stunned into silence.

I could have played it off by pretending to be buzzed and then apologize, but why should I? His reaction provided me with my answer—the one I wasn't looking for—that it wasn't big enough.

When I started to remove my hand, he grabbed hold of my wrist and placed his other hand on top of mine, pressing it down firmly. That's when I felt his pants balloon. "Does that answer your question?"

"Part of it."

"And the other part?"

"How's it going to feel when it's inside of me?"

"Would you like to find out?"

I nodded, and this is where it all started to go wrong.

We stood from the bar holding hands. Neither of us said a word, but I knew what was going to happen next. I followed him out of the club into the parking lot, cautiously walking toward his car, and then I stopped suddenly.

"I'd rather follow you in my car."

"Don't get lost," he said with a wink.

I followed behind his convertible Mustang for several miles, ignoring my cell phone, which had been vibrating all night with calls from my friend Melony. Finally I pulled into the parking lot of a luxury hotel, where we parked side by side. After he let his top up, he got out of his car and walked over to the passenger side of my car. I unlocked the door so he could get in.

"You look good enough to eat." He didn't waste any time sliding my dress halfway up my thighs and sticking his head between my legs, but I held him back, wiping the Jheri curl juice from my thighs.

"There's a time and a place for everything," I told him. "I'd rather my car not be the place."

"You have to learn to let go. I prefer to be teased a little and fucked a lot." He took his forefinger and shoved it inside of my pussy. The quickness of his jab made me gasp. He pulled me over the center console with his finger stuck deep inside of me and let the seat go back as far as it could. "Ride this," he said as he inserted two more fingers inside my pussy, "like it's the biggest, juiciest dick you've ever had."

"Fingers annoy me."

"If they annoy you, why are you so wet?"

"I'm naturally lubricated."

He slid his fingers out, sniffed them, and then put them in his mouth to suck my pussy juices. "I love the smell and taste of sex. That's why I like to finger fuck. It gets me in the mood." He started rubbing between his legs. "Are you ready for me to let the beast out?" I looked down at his bulge and didn't hesitate to grab it. "Let's do a quickie right here in the car. I'll still have more for you when we get to the room."

"I'm ready to go up right now and then take it from there," I said, and opened the passenger door. We both tumbled out of the car. I stood, repositioning my dress, pulling my thong from the crack of my ass.

He grabbed me by the wrist and we started walking in the direction of the hotel.

"You ain't never had it like I'm going to give it to you," he whispered in my ear.

"I hope you're not all talk. I've had that type before . . . several times."

He ignored my comment, which caused me major concern. It was bad enough I was getting ready to fuck a man that I didn't know, but it would be even worse if the sex turned out to be a disappointment.

"When you go inside, head straight for the elevator, get on and take it to the tenth floor. I don't want it to seem like we're together. I don't think my wife would follow me, but you never know."

I was slightly offended, but I had to remind myself that I wasn't looking for a relationship. So I did what he said and waited close to fifteen minutes for him to join me on the tenth floor. I'd pressed the down button to the elevator, ready to leave, assuming I'd been stood up a second time, when the elevator door opened and he slid out.

"Sorry it took so long. I had to make a call. The room number is 1027."

I followed behind him without any reservation as to what I was doing, but rather with anticipation of what the two of us would be doing very shortly. When we entered the small but quaint room, he immediately started taking off his tie and shirt.

"Are you in a rush?" I asked.

"Just anxious." He sat on the edge of the bed. "How much?"

"How much what?"

"If I want oral and possibly some anal. How much for all that?"

"What do you mean by how much?"

"You're a call girl, right? Come on. I know that's what you are. I can always tell you high class hoes. You come to a nice club alone and you dress real seductively. You pretend to be into the music, but every so often you look around to see who might be looking at you. I guess it's better than walking the streets, huh?"

"And I can always tell a John. You come to a club alone with that deranged look in your eyes like you need a fix bad and pussy is your drug. What's wrong, you can't get what you need at home?"

"Every now and then I get tired of home cooking and I need to eat out." He pulled two hundred-dollar bills from his wallet. "For this," he said, as he tossed the money at my feet, "I should be able to get all I can eat."

I picked the bills up one at a time and looked over at him. "For this? I guess you're eating fast food, or better yet you might as well go on a fast. For this, I might as well walk the street." I threw the money back to him.

"What, that's not enough?"

"Not for this." I sat on the window ledge, hiking up my dress, and with my legs spread open began rubbing my pussy. His eyes zoomed toward my chest. "Is that all you?" he asked.

"Who else's would it be?"

He shrugged. "I don't know, but why don't you come out of your dress so I can see what you're working with, and I only hope it's not a miracle bra."

"Do you have on miracle briefs?" I walked over to him and turned so that my back was facing him. "Unzip me."

"Look at that fat ass," he said as he squeezed my butt cheeks. I closed my eyes when I realized my fantasy was about to finally come true. He unzipped his pants, and a few seconds later I felt two rock hard taps against my hip.

"Try to imagine how good my dick is going to feel once it's inside of you," he said as he bent down and used his teeth to pull my thong down. "I'm about to give you something you can feel."

I felt a few more taps, but this time they were even harder.

I opened my eyes, looked between his legs, and lay down on the bed with my legs spread wide, "Jump in."

"Am I strapped?" he asked as he stood naked at the foot of the bed, holding his dick in one hand. It was so thick that his hand barely fit around the shaft. He wasn't much to look at in the face, but in the flesh his body looked just as chiseled as Terrell Owens's, and that's who I pretended he was—the NFL player I've always wanted to fuck.

"You still haven't answered my question. Is this what you mean when you say you want a man that's strapped?" I hadn't mentioned anything to Eugene about wanting a man who was strapped, but I had talked about what I was looking for with Lester. "Surprised? No, I didn't forget."

"You said you weren't Lester."

"I say a lot of things. I said I was ten inches when in reality I'm a foot long. I'm into playing games, remember?" he asked as he picked his leather belt from the floor and snapped it in the air.

The crackling sound of the leather both frightened and intrigued me. I felt naughty and nasty, like the tramp that I'd always wanted to become. I'd never seen a dick that big. Correction, I'd never seen a big dick period. "I want to suck on your fat dick head," I said, "until you come in my mouth."

I started crawling toward him with my tongue wiggling. His dick was so perfectly shaped, not just long, but thick also. Even his Jheri curl started to look good. I'd reached the tip of his head and swirled my tongue up and down his slit. I opened my mouth and started sucking his dick, moving up the shaft inch by inch. He wanted his balls tickled with my tongue, and I was more than willing to accommodate. His toes curled, his head fell back, but then when it seemed like he was going to make a deposit, he pulled out of my mouth suddenly.

"I don't want to come that way. I want you to ride me, and then when I'm getting ready to come, I want you to take the belt and strangle me."

"But it tastes so good that I was ready for more. I wanted to swallow." I stood from the bed and pushed him against the wall. He held his hands out and snatched me toward him by my nipples. He was into pain—giving and receiving. That much was obvious.

When he let go of my nipples, I had to feel them to make sure they were still there. My breasts were tender and my pussy was wet and tight. "Can't you be gentle?" I asked as I took one of his hands and rubbed it along my hairy slit.

He pushed me back down on the bed and yanked me toward him by my ankles. "I like it rough." He knelt between my legs and ate my pussy like he was drilling for gold, and before long he struck it. I closed my eyes and thought of Terrell Owens. That's who was eating me . . . not Lester. Every inch that he went deeper caused me to wonder about him. Every swirl he made inside of me had me question his true intentions, but then there was the presence of the black leather belt and knowing what he wanted me to do with it. I should have refused, but instead, when he turned on his back and gestured for me to straddle him, I did. It could have stopped there. I was in control, riding his dick like a bull and taking in as much of it that I could stand. And then he handed me the belt.

"When do you want me to use it?" I asked, still on top of him, enjoying the ride.

"I'll let you know. Just keep going. Keep doing what you're doing, baby. I don't come quickly." It was hard to imagine how I survived for so many years with so much less. "Your fat pussy was made to take a big juicy dick. Look how good you're handling me."

The more he talked, the harder I rode him and the more of his dick I took in, until I'd swallowed him whole.

"Now," he said, "right now. I'm getting ready to come. Do it now!"

Reluctantly, I placed the belt around his throat and then tightened it. It felt powerful, mixing pain with pleasure. At first I didn't think I could do it, but I kept thinking about the men who'd done me wrong, and somehow strangling him with that belt wasn't so difficult. He smiled for a second and I continued choking him until I saw foam oozing from the side of his mouth. His eyes rolled in the back of his head and I knew that I'd killed him . . . accidentally, of course.

Last Day of School

Here is how it all began.

On the last day of school I told my students to enjoy their summer vacation and to be sure to come back next year with plenty of stories to share. Little did I know that I'd be the one with the stories, but none that I'd be able to share. Even though it was the last day of school for the students, teachers had to stick around for an extra week, but on this day I had a half day, and instead of going straight home after work, I decided to check on my best friend. She was on vacation, and since I had to pass her house to get to mine, I figured I might as well swing by there and see how she was doing. Catch up on old times, since it had been a few months since we really talked, and nearly a year since we hung out. But that wasn't the real reason I went to see her. I needed to put my suspicions to rest.

With less than thirty minutes before the bell would ring, I sat at my desk and allowed my students to goof off while I thought about my fiancé Edward. First, I was pretty sure that he was cheating on me. And I was almost positive that I knew with whom— my best friend Nancy, which was the reason I had to confront her. Edward never bit his tongue when it came to assessing a woman's attributes. He always thought Nancy had a nice body, and didn't mind telling me. And Nancy had broken up with her man and suddenly stopped coming around me. It didn't take a rocket scientist to figure out what was going on.

Edward and I had been together for nearly three years. In the beginning, our relationship progressed very quickly, but soon I discovered through calling certain numbers from his Sprint bill that he was still seeing his ex. I should have left him then. To know that he told some other woman that he missed her touch tore my insides apart. I thought Edward and I were close. I honestly thought he loved me, but now I knew that he didn't know how or who to love. And it wasn't just his ex. It was a flight attendant and a female police officer, both of whom he'd met online. I'd talked to all three ladies and couldn't get mad at them, especially not his ex, who was in his life before I was. But my best friend Nancy was a different story. I was furious with her, and she was going to find out just how much.

"Class," I said as I stood. I had to raise my voice. "Please settle down. We only have ten more minutes." What did I expect on the last day of school? There was no work to do . . . just a countdown until the bell rang. I walked down the middle aisle of desks and noticed one girl cover her mouth with laughter as she looked down at my low-heeled Ecco shoes. Maybe in wearing them I wasn't as stylish as I could have been. I hated to admit that in some ways I'd started letting myself go. Several months ago I'd lost a contact, and instead of getting a new pair, I went back to wearing my glasses. The year before, I started letting my hair grow out of the stylish layered cut, and when it became too unruly, I pulled it back in a ponytail and have worn it that way ever since. And now I could barely get my fiancé to take a second look at me, but he stared down every attractive woman he saw on the street.

"Monica, get out of his lap and sit in your own chair. One day maybe you'll learn it's better to keep it to yourself," I said, shaking my head.

"So when *you* gonna learn when to let some go?" Monica asked.

I ignored her comment. I taught seventh grade, yet so many of my students acted as if they were grown, especially Monica, who already had a reputation for being easy.

"What you doing for the summer, Miss Cartwright?" Toy, whose reputation didn't far precede Monica's, asked.

I shrugged. "Not sure yet, but I'm going to try and do something a little different this summer."

"You and your man," Toy said.

"Miss Cartwright don't have no man," Monica said.

"Miss Cartwright, you should come back next year with a whole new look," Scottie, the class clown, said.

"What's wrong with my look?" I asked as I surveyed my students' expressions and the many smirks across their faces. But before anyone responded, the bell rang and they jumped from their desks and flooded through the door.

"You cute, Miss Cartwright," Scottie said, "you just need to loosen up a little. Let your hair down. Listen to some Shawna and learn a little somethin' 'bout satisfying your man."

"Listen to some who, so I can learn how to do what?"

"Listen to Luda's girl, Shawna from Disturbing Tha Peace. You know," Scottie rapped, "I was getting some head."

"Okay, Scottie, I get the point. Enjoy your summer."

"You too, Miss Cartwright. I hope you really enjoy yours too. I really mean that."

I watched as Scottie ran from my class, sneaking behind a female student to grab her ass. She screamed, pushed him, and then he put his arm around her shoulder and they strolled out of the building.

I rushed out of the school and headed for Nancy's house. When I arrived, I pulled into her driveway behind a black 5-series BMW—Edward's. He worked at a BMW dealership and had also sold Nancy's ex-fiancé a preowned 5-series that had the older body style. I walked around to the back of the car to look at the license plate: 1OF2. I guess his car wasn't the only thing that was one of two. I was also one of two, and Nancy, who I thought was my best girlfriend at one time and would never do something like this to me, was a back-stabbing bitch. I ran onto the porch and started ringing the doorbell. Of course, no one answered. So I called Edward on his cell phone as I sat on the hood of his car jingling my keys, fully prepared to use one all over his ride if need be.

"Be a man and come outside and bring that bitch with you," I said.

"What are you talking about? And why are you talking like that? I'm at work."

"You're at work, but your car is at Nancy's house."

"My car is at Nancy's house because I let Floyd borrow it since his is in the shop and we were out of loaners. He's probably over Nancy's house, so please don't start tripping."

"So if I call Floyd right now, he'll confirm that."

"Yes he will."

"Okay, 'bye," I said, and hung up. Edward was the type who would lie until the bitter end. He probably figured that I wasn't going to call Floyd. For one, I didn't like him. We never saw eye-to-eye on anything, and we'd gotten into it a few times in the past over Nancy and the way he did her. But all that aside, I needed to know the truth, and that was just a phone call away.

"Floyd, this is Alexis. I just talked to Edward and he claimed that he let you use his car, but I know that's probably not true. Call me back when you get this message. Don't worry about it. The more I say it out loud the dumber it sounds."

I pressed the End button. Looked at my key and got to writing. I wrote: I'M NOT GOING TO BE 1 OF 2 across the driver's side of his car.

Nancy's front door swung open and Nancy shouted, "What are you doing?"

I turned with evil in my eyes and said, "Me, what about you? What are you doing with . . . Floyd?" I asked as Floyd walked out of the house. "Edward really did let you use his car?"

"Yeah, so why did you do that? Maybe she already knows," Floyd said as he turned to walk back into the house.

Nancy grabbed the tail of his shirt. "She doesn't know. She thought he was over here with me," Nancy said, then looked at me. "And for the record, I would never do some low down shit like that to one of my girls. But don't worry about what you just did to his car because he deserves it. Tell her why he deserves it, Floyd."

"Look, I'm not in all this."

"You in it if you want me to take you back. Tell her."

"What do you want me to say?"

"Tell her what you told me."

Club Flirt

Well, Floyd told me. And the only thing that I could think about was that all school year while I was busy planning what Edward and I were going to do over the summer, what trip we were going to take—a three-day cruise to Jamaica, which was one of his favorite places to visit, or a leisurely drive to Toronto, which was something he'd always talked about doing—he'd had other things on his mind.

I wanted to do something different. Something that could possibly help reignite our dying relationship, and Edward, well, I found out he was already doing something different, or should I say doing someone different. Her name was Black Exotica, and it wasn't too hard for me to figure out what she did for a living. My fiancé had, like the song said, fallen in love with a stripper. It would have been so much better for all involved if Edward had just told me himself. I would have been upset, but I would have had to deal with it. At least, I would've been able to tell myself that he finally decided to be honest. But no, he wanted to continue to play me like a fool, and of all the people I had to find the truth out from, it had to be from one of my least favorite ones, my best friend's man, who was trying to get Nancy off his ass when he admitted that he'd gone to the strip club but only stayed an hour . . . but guess who was there and who seemed more than a little comfortable with the star stripper—Edward.

I really didn't feel like going all up in Club Flirt to front him and Black Exotica. What would I, a woman with a master's degree in education from the University of Michigan, an educator, a member of one of the largest black sororities, and a volunteer with Big Brothers/Big Sisters, look like going into a strip club? But that didn't stop me from storming in there to confront my man and his new woman. I felt like I didn't have a choice. Edward forced me to pull out my ghetto card. And I didn't go alone. I took Nancy and her half sister Veronda along for moral support. So there the three of us were at Club Flirt, looking just as lost as ever.

As we approached the door, there was a bouncer seated on a stool in front of the roped-off entrance. His massive muscular arms were folded and his eyes were concealed by dark shades. And even though I had come there on a mission to catch my man in the act, I couldn't help but notice the bulge in the center of the bouncer's pants. Oh, how I wanted so badly to take his dick out and get some pleasure for a change, because Edward sure hadn't given me any, and not just in a long time . . . never.

"Ladies, the club's closed," he said.

"Closed," Veronda said. "It's just eleven o'clock. The club ain't closed."

"Who you going in there to see?" the bouncer asked.

"What you mean who we going to see?" Veronda responded. "Is

that a question you asked all those horny men who came through here?"

"Are you coming in here to see women or you coming in here to find your horny man, because we don't want nothing jumping off tonight."

"The sign outside was blinking girls . . . girls . . . girls. So let us in so we can see some."

"All right, shorty," he said as he removed the rope from the entrance. "I was just making sure."

Veronda winked as she led us into the club. We wanted to sit at a table in the back because Floyd had already confirmed that Edward was going to be there and I definitely didn't want him to see me before I saw him, but even more importantly, before I saw her. It was standing room only, so we stood along the side in front of two large red neon hearts. We knew that Black Exotica was the last stripper to dance, and we didn't have long to wait because she was up next. We'd walked in on the tail end of Skin Tight's routine.

"I wonder how many of these men are married?" Nancy asked.

"Mmm," I said as I looked around at the faces concealed in darkness. For those who were, I wondered where their wives thought they were that night. I started thinking once again that I was with a man that I really didn't know, a man I would have sworn wouldn't be caught dead in a strip club. But I guess that was a naive way of thinking. I know men like to see naked women. I guess most men would love to see nude females sliding down poles and to get a lap dance from them, but why did my man have to be one of them?

"Half these women are lesbians," Veronda said.

"How do you know?" I asked.

"I don't know. I'm just talking. Got to find something to say about these bitches since they're packing 'em in like this."

When Skin Tight left the stage, the table in front of us became available, so we quickly filled the empty seats. During the half hour delay between sets while the stage was being changed before Black Exotica came out, we started drinking. I could feel myself getting buzzed right when Black Exotica's theme music began playing. I was so anxious to see her that I was practically bouncing in my seat.

"By the looks of all the money they make on an average night, I might need to consider stripping. At least I wouldn't have to worry about layoffs," Veronda said.

The men went wild as soon as Black Exotica hit the stage in her fishnet outfit. She had a small chest with very large nipples that were poking through the holes. She was wearing a black half mask over her eyes and a platinum blond ponytail that hung to the middle of her back. Even I, as a woman, had to shake my head. She had a tiny waist and the biggest ass I'd ever seen. I wondered why she'd picked my man. I could see why he picked her. I mean, if I were a man, I'd be interested in that. She was an exotic looking black woman with a body that I'd love to have as my own. But why did she want him? Out of all these men, there had to be one with more to offer, and I wasn't talking about money. My man's thing was barely five inches. So it must have all boiled down to money. My man was generous when he wanted to be, and more importantly, when he wanted something. At one time it was me he chased because I was a hard one to get, but once he had me, my good times were over.

"Maybe this was a bad idea," I said to Nancy. "I've seen all I need to."

"I thought you wanted to talk to her? We didn't drive all the way over here just to leave."

The whole idea of going to the strip club to confront her seemed so ridiculous to me now. Black Exotica was in that place handling her business, and to be honest, the more that I watched her on stage, the more I started to desire her lifestyle. How nice it would be to have the full attention of a room full of men with hard dicks.

As I was heading for the door, I bumped into Edward as he walked in. Our eyes met, but he tried ignoring me until I said. "I guess you're surprised to see me here, huh?"

"Not really," he said as he attempted to brush pass me. "You're doing what you do best—stalk. And if I wasn't on probation, I'd kick your ass right here for fucking up my car."

I grabbed his arm and dug my acrylic French tip nails into his shirt. "I wish you would."

He turned to face me. "I wish I could," he said as he snatched my hand away from his arm.

"Enjoy your life because I'm moving on to bigger and better things." I looked down at his crotch. "Much bigger and honey so much better." My girls walked passed him and giggled.

"That's fine, because I've already done the same."

"Go to hell, Edward."

"I left there when I left you."

My girls pushed me out of the club when they saw the rage in my eyes and the bouncer in our path.

"Did you hear what he said?" I asked Nancy and Veronda as I stepped out of the door. "He left me? No, I left him. He had nothing when I met him. Not even a decent job. Now, just because he sells cars and has a BMW, he thinks his shit doesn't stink."

"Let's go," Nancy said as we stood in the parking lot.

"I'm not going anywhere until I can confront the two of them."

The three of us waited in the car for nearly an hour, exchanging relationship horror stories, until finally Edward stormed out of the club alone and sped off. After another thirty minutes or so with still no sign of Black Exotica, I decided to walk to the side door and knock until someone answered. One of the dancers let me in.

"I'm outside waiting for Black Exotica. I'm her ride."

"You seen Exotica?" she asked a dancer who walked down the hallway topless.

"She's in the champagne room with a customer."

"Oh, she might be a while," the dancer who let me into the building said. "You can wait in her dressing room," she added, standing in front of a door that had a large red star plastered to it with the name BLACK EXOTICA written on it, "or in your car, and I'll tell her you're out there. I thought for sure she drove," she said as a baffled look came over her face.

"I'll wait in her room," I said, then walked inside and sat on the vanity stool. When the dancer walked into another room, I started looking around. There were pictures of Black Exotica with men—some prominent figures—local politicians, athletes, and famous entertainers.

"You a new girl?" Black Exotica asked as she glided into her dressing room with the smell of sex hovering over her naked body. She had a tattoo of a rainbow above her hipbone.

"No, I'm just here to talk."

"Talk? Do I need to call Security?" she said as she stood by the open door, holding the handle.

"No, please don't call Security. I'm just here to talk. I'm Edward's fiancé. Did you know that he had one?"

"Who's Edward?" she said as she remained standing. "Security!" she yelled.

"You don't need to call Security. I just want to talk." I closed the door. "Please."

"I don't know any Edwards. And if he's one of these perverts who come to gawk at me, I can't help that."

"He's in love with you and you don't even know who he is?"

"Do you know how many of these fools are in love with me? Narrow it down."

"He has a small dick."

"Keep narrowing."

"A real small one. He sells BMWs at Euro World."

"Itty," she said, twisting her nose. "How did you manage to work with that little string bean dick? It just slips right out of me." She locked the door.

"A lot of faking."

"I make a living from performing, but with Itty it's only so much acting I can do," Black Exotica said as she walked over to the sofa, where she plopped down and crossed her shapely legs while eyeing me seductively. "Besides, I'm more into women." She patted the empty spot beside her. "And it's nothing better than getting some pussy after I've just had some dick. Come over her and let me show you."

"Oh, I'm not like that."

"No one said you had to be. All I want you to do is sit beside me."

I hesitated before reluctantly walking over to her.

"The only way a man is going to see my body is if he pays me. If he wants to touch me, he's going to pay even more. And if he wants to put his slimy worm inside my precious hole," she said as she used two fingers to spread open her pussy, "then I'm getting his whole damn paycheck because I don't even want a man." She picked up my index finger and inserted it deep inside of her, guiding it in and out. My finger was soaked with her juices. "Your hands are so soft and your fingers are so delicate. Men just want to stab me with theirs." When she let her hand go, I continued to wiggle my finger inside of her. She dropped her head back and then turned to face me. She caressed the side of my face with the back of her hand. "I don't want your man; I'd rather have you." I pulled out my finger. "Don't be frightened. Be open to new experiences." She put my finger back, and I continued wiggling it inside of her. She leaned toward my face in an attempt to kiss me but I drew back.

"I'm not like that."

"You're not?" she asked with laughter as she looked between her legs. "Are you sure? You seem to be enjoying it just as much as I am. Have you ever been with a woman?" I shook my head. "Because once you do that . . . you really won't go back."

"I just came here to talk about Edward." I took my finger out again.

"I don't want your little man. Girl, I only messed with him for the money. For me, it's all about money. And we could make a lot of it if we did a porno together. We could call it—the school-teacher learns a new lesson."

"He told you that I was a teacher?"

"He didn't have to," she said, pulling my hair from its bun, then taking off my glasses. "You have long, pretty hair that's perfect for tugging." She ran her fingers through my strands as she slid over closer to me. Her hands crept underneath my top, unsnapped the front fasten to my 38D cups, and started juggling them. "Wouldn't you love to go back and tell your man that you got with me? That you'd done something that he couldn't, which was made me come?" She got onto her knees on the sofa then, in front of me, grinding her "precious hole" over my nipples while she squeezed both of my breasts together. "Are you going to let me eat your pussy?"

"I have to go," I said as I stopped her from using my breasts to jack off with.

She slid her knees off the sofa onto the floor and began kissing the fabric between my legs. Her long stiff tongue rode up my zipper and struck a nerve that caused me momentary pleasure. She untied the drawstring to my linen pants, pulled down my zipper with her teeth and began fingering me through the material of my panties until they became soaking wet. She snatched off my pants and panties.

How did this evening turn out this way? I wondered. I'd come to Club Flirt to confront my man, but now I was in Black Exotica's dressing room sitting on her sofa with my bra unfastened and my top pulled up, exposing my bare breasts. I was completely naked from the waist down, and the star stripper had just started drilling her long pierced tongue inside of me, her head bobbing up and down. This was wrong and I knew it. It went against everything I morally believed in, yet I couldn't stop her because she was making me feel too good to end it.

She stopped for a second and looked up at me. Her lips were dripping wet with my pussy juices. "I'm not going to stop until I turn you all the way out," she said.

I pushed her head back down between my legs so she could continue doing what Edward never would . . . at least not to me. My eyes closed for a minute. I felt in control and realized that was how men must have felt when they were getting head. My cell phone started ringing from inside my purse. It stopped after several rings and then started back up again. That's when I struggled to come to my senses. "I have to go. I have people waiting for me outside in the car." I stood, pulled up my soaking wet panties and my pants, fastened my bra, pulled down my top, and started pinning my hair up.

"But we were just getting started. I have so much more in store for my virgin."

"I'm sorry. I don't know what I was thinking. It was a big mistake," I said as I made my way to the door.

"Mistakes don't taste that good. You'll be back."

I unlocked the door, rushed out of her dressing room and the club to get back to my car.

"Well, what happened?" Nancy asked.

"Did you tell her ass off?" Veronda asked.

My heart was pounding a million miles a second. I shook my head. I was too afraid to talk because I wasn't good at lying. I pulled out of the parking lot.

"What's that smell?" Veronda asked. "Smells like fish." Both Veronda and Nancy let their windows down.

"I don't smell anything." I tried to focus on the road but my mind was back in Black Exotica's dressing room wondering what it would have felt like if I had let her go all the way.

"He left hell when he left me," I said aloud as I entered the house and slammed the door leading from the garage. I tossed my purse on the sofa and walked through our bedroom to the bathroom. I had to take a shower and wash that fish smell away. I stepped out of my clothes and put on a shower cap. I turned on the shower, adjusting the setting so the water would run out warm, then stepped in. I watched as the water beaded on my dark skin.

Black women hate to get their hair wet, so I decided to prove to myself that water was not our kryptonite. I pulled off the shower cap, removed the bobby pins from my hair, and stepped underneath the shower head with my eyes closed. I smiled. This wasn't so bad, especially since I was getting my hair done the next day. I was feeling sexy and free. My man wasn't all that, and now our breakup was going to allow me to look for one that was. I cupped my breasts and squeezed them tightly as I slid my hand between my precious hole. The hair down there had gotten long enough to braid; it was time to shave again—time to become a bare naked lady. My index finger wiggled inside my opening. In and out . . . in and out . . . the way I'd done Black Exotica. But that only frustrated me because it wasn't nothing like the real thing.

I felt soap suds on my back, but I didn't know where they were coming from. Then two hands were placed firmly on my shoulder, turning me around to face a tall muscular man who had to be a figment. He had a tattoo on his chest of a long red arrow pointing down to his dick. He didn't have a "slimy worm." He had a dangerous python that was hissing for me.

"Are you real?" I asked.

"Do I look real?"

I nodded.

"Jump on me and see if I feel real."

We started kissing passionately, and then he sat on the shower bench and pulled me toward him. I started to climb on him but he turned me around so I sat on his snake while he spread my ass apart. I began bouncing on him. It was what I had needed. There was no way I was gay. I'd had too much to drink and so I let Black Exotica take advantage of me. But who was this man who suddenly appeared in my shower, strapped. Had he followed me from the strip club?

"Where did you come from?" I asked right before my home phone rang. I bounced off his dick, and on the way back down my ass fell flat against the marble shower seat. He'd vanished. I shook my head. This was why I didn't go out drinking.

My phone was still ringing. I didn't bother with an answering machine, figuring if a call was important enough, they'd call back, but this person wouldn't hang up. I rushed into the bedroom and picked up the phone, hoping it was Edward calling to tell me that he'd come to his senses and that he was on his way home, because even though he had a little one, little ones were better than none at all.

"I got your message about wanting to come visit me for the summer," my sister said. "But what about Edward?"

"What about him? He's history."

"Are you serious? You finally took your garbage out. I hope you dumped him on the side of the road."

I sighed. "Can I come for a visit and stay with you?"

"Girl, I been begging you to come visit me for years. Of course you can."

"I'll be there next week. I just need to go the salon for a touch-up and to Vision Matters for my contacts."

New Girl in Town

I arrived at Dallas–Fort Worth airport on a Saturday with nothing but the clothes on my back, because the ones I left behind in my closet weren't fit for the adventure I was going on. My sister and her boyfriend were a little late picking me up, which didn't surprise me because my sister was late for most things except her job with the Dallas Police Department. She'd made detective a few years back and had the exciting task of investigating murders. I sat outside the terminal reading the *Dallas Morning News*. On the front page was a story about the Black Widow serial killer. She'd killed five men in Texas over the last two summers, mostly in Dallas.

After about a twenty minute wait, my sister and her boyfriend pulled up. He was driving a black Escalade with fancy rims. I didn't know much about my sister's man . . . just that his name was Tony. I was shocked when I saw his physique because usually my sister's men were fit like her. But Tony had a little more than a few extra pounds. But even though he was wide, he didn't have a big stomach. He was wearing shorts and showing off his chicken legs, which I found to be hilarious, but I could tell he was nice, and doubted that it was his personality that hooked my sister. Had to be something I couldn't see.

On the ride to her home, I couldn't stop thinking about Black Exotica. It bothered me that I could still feel her tongue swirling around my pussy.

"I'm taking you to my book club meeting tonight," my sister said to me. "You'll have fun. The girls are so crazy, and the book we're discussing is off the chain."

"What's the name of it?" I asked.

"*In Too Deep*. It's erotic."

"*In Too Deep*," Tony said, looking over at my sister. "What's that about?"

"Men like you . . . men who are well-endowed."

"And women say men have a one-track mind," Tony said. "You women are no different."

"Some of us aren't. You're right, baby," my sister said.

My sister and I made a detour and went shopping for some sexy clothes to wear to Club Knubian Fantaciez, a male strip club, where the book club members were all going later that evening, and because I hadn't brought any clothes, I picked up several out-fits. By the time we left the mall in our new outfits and headed to the book club meeting in someone's home, we were late. On the ride there, my sister filled me in on some of the members. Most, but not all, were DPD officers, and a few, like my sister, were de-tectives. The meeting was only supposed to last for a couple of hours, and then we were hitting the strip club to follow along with the theme of the book.

"I'm too ready to discuss this book," my sister said, clutching her copy as we entered. In so many ways my sister and I were night and day. She'd always been the life of the party, while I'd been the shy one.

"You're an hour late," one of the ladies said as she walked from the kitchen into the living room carrying a bowl of chips. "We already started talking about the book, finished talking about the book, and now we're on to something else and almost ready to go to the strip club."

"Well, start over," my sister said. "I was the one who was supposed to introduce the damn book, and you already started talking about something else . . . let me guess . . . why are men such dogs?"

"No matter what book we discuss, don't they always find a way to ease that topic back into our discussion?" one of the other ladies said. "I see you brought along a friend." She smiled in my direction.

"I brought my sister."

"Hi, sis," the same young lady said.

"Hello," I said with a smile.

"I'm Melony. Your sister and I go way back. We were in the academy together."

"What did I miss?" my sister asked as she hurried to take her seat on the sofa next to Melony. I stood, since there were no available seats, but another young lady rushed from the kitchen and handed me a bar stool.

"Karen was telling us about that man she met online—the ex-cop who she asked us about a while back."

"Oh, yeah, I didn't know him when he was with the department," my sister said. "Whatever happened with him?"

Funny, when you're going through the heartbreak and pain of

losing someone you truly loved, it's always a little easier to handle when you know you're not alone.

"Let me get your sister caught up. I met this man on the Internet about a year and a half ago. That was my first mistake. Never go online to meet a man for anything other than sex because that's what those cyberspace men are looking for. While they're dating you, they keep their profiles up, and still meet women. I would wake up at three o'clock in the morning just to find him surfing the Net."

"What did he say he was doing?" I asked.

"He said he was doing research . . . as much research as he did at that time every morning he needed to have a damn doctorate degree."

"So you think he was still meeting women online?" I asked.

"Do I think? He _was_ meeting women online and visiting porno sites. He was doing a little bit of everything. I knew something wasn't right about him. First of all, the photo he had was of him standing in a real nice kitchen with stainless steel appliances and a large island in the center. The profile said he lived in Plano, and usually that means you have a little money, am I right?" The ladies nodded. "Well, I never got to see his house in Plano because as soon as we started talking on the phone, he told me that he had to move out of that house because he was renting and the owner decided to sell."

"In other words, he got evicted," Melony said.

"Pretty much. First red flag, but I looked past all that because by that time we'd met in person and I was really attracted to him, things were all good, or so I thought. He rented a U-Haul truck and wanted me to help him move. Now, if you're just now moving out of your house, why was all your shit already in storage? Second red flag."

"Stop," said one of the other ladies, who was milling in and out of the kitchen. "Did he fuck you so good that you lost all sense of reason? Did you let him get in too deep?" We all laughed at her play on the book title.

"Girl, we hadn't even had sex yet, which was why I thought this man was not like all the others. And he wasn't. He was worse."

"Karen, can you make a long story short?" Melony asked.

"Not this one . . . no. I want all the women in here to beware of him and men like him. This man did things differently. He took me to Shreveport to meet his parents. We spent the holidays together. He cooked for me, fixed the viruses on my computer, but he was also online on several dating Web sites with about twenty aliases, trying to meet other women."

"And if the woman is fool enough to fall for it, is that his fault?" Melony asked. "I'm tired of women crying that men have done them wrong. You all are the fools that mess with the men who you already know aren't shit."

"Well, Melony, maybe you're being a little impatient because you're not a woman who has to worry about something like that ever happening to you," Karen said.

"You damn straight I don't."

I figured she told Melony that she never had to worry about that happening to her because Melony was very attractive. Not that pretty women don't get hurt—look at Halle Berry—but I guess when they do, it might not take them as long to bounce back into another relationship.

"You've already told half of us this at least a dozen times. It's time to move on. What is our motto, ladies?"

"Move on to bigger and better things," we all said; I'd heard that motto from my sister.

"Let me help you get to the punch line," Melony continued,

"He convinced you to put a car in your name for him and he never paid one note. The two of you built a house. Once again, it was in your name, he lived there, and never paid a dime, but was telling people it was his house. The utilities were getting shut off every other month."

"I worked my ass off, had to borrow from my 401(k), take out a home equity loan just to keep us afloat. He kept saying he was about to close on this house or that house, and never closed on one, or if he did, I never saw any money come through."

"And was he cheating too?" I asked.

"What do you think? That part goes without saying. Yes, he was cheating on me with a twenty-five-year-old who told me that he drove to her job and picked her up in the car I financed when it still had the temporary tag on the window."

"Mmm," I said, shaking my head, because oh how I could relate.

"He didn't have any male friends," Karen continued. "Every last one of his friends was female. And he used to say, 'I need to tell you in advance that in my line of work I mainly deal with women because most of the real estate agents are females, so don't get jealous if I'm talking to a woman from time to time because it's business.'"

"If you didn't know that was game, shame on you," Melony said, shaking her head. "I'm so glad I don't have to worry about that shit. I've never been treated like that, and I would never treat a woman like that."

"Man," I said, correcting her.

"What, sweetie?"

"You said woman, and I was just correcting you with what you meant to say . . . you'd never treat a man like that."

Several of the other women in the room began laughing. "No, she said what she meant to say," my sister said.

"That's right, I meant to say woman. I don't date men," Melony said.

"Oh, I see."

"Well, was the sex at least good?" my sister asked. "Shit, was he at least strapped?"

"Yeah, he was strapped . . . financially. Owed child support from a previous marriage and everybody else."

"So the sex wasn't even good," Melony said, still shaking her head.

"I didn't say that the sex wasn't good, because I'd be lying if I said all that. It was damn good and he was big enough for me. I mean he wasn't strapped, but he wasn't itty bitty either. But I know one thing, though—he was a little too much into anal sex for my taste."

Melony started laughing. "That's because he was probably bi."

"No . . . no . . . no," my sister said, "there are a lot of men that like that."

"Listen," Melony said, "it's nothing like some pussy. I don't get with a woman and ask her to strap on a dick. When I strap on a dick, that's because I'm with a woman who is bi and she needs that to achieve her climax. If you're with a so-called straight man and he's always trying to poke you in the other hole, he's a bisexual, and I'm not debating that shit with anyone because I know too much about that. He may not have ever been with a man . . . may not even know that's why he wants it so much, but I guarantee you, you get that punk behind closed doors with one of my gay male friends, and when they stick their ass in his face, guess what he's going to stick in their ass?"

"Oh, my," I said.

"That's right, oh, my," Melony said. "I mean, Karen, you can't be mad at that man, because deep down you knew what he was about from day one. As far as a man cheating on you, a man who isn't married isn't cheating. I don't even care if he's living with someone. You have to know what's out there. Sex is plentiful. Cheating is abundant. Pick yourself up, brush your shoulders off, and keep it movin'."

"Yeah," my sister said, "instead of looking for a man you can get into a relationship with, look for a man you can have great sex with. A man who can fill you up. How long it is really doesn't matter. Just as long as it's fat. The thicker his shaft, the better the sex will be. Trust me. And don't have him top it off with a big head too, girl, please. Why do you think I'm with Tony?"

"Personally, I believe that it all boils down to not just the man's size, but how it's shaped," Karen said. "I have a preference for a penis shaped like a lollipop. You know what I'm talking about. You have a big knob for the head and a thinner shaft. That's the perfect shape for sucking."

I looked over at Melony, who had just turned up her nose and shook her head.

"See, I'm the opposite of you," another woman said, "because I like the ones where that head is a little smaller than the shaft because, I'll admit it, I'm one of those naughty girls that like to be poked in that other hole, my little brown eye, and that's when a small head comes in handy."

I was trying my best to stop staring over at Melony, whose nose couldn't stop twitching from disgust of what the other ladies were saying, but it was difficult because I assumed that a woman who was a lesbian would look, act, and dress like a man. But Black Exotica and Melony were two very attractive and feminine females, so my perception was all wrong, and it freaked me out. The other reason I found myself looking over at Melony was because I could feel her eyes climbing my bare legs before stopping at my plunging neckline.

"Okay, I have a question," Melony said, standing with a glass of wine in her hand. "How many of you have been with a woman? Raise your hand."

No hands went up, but I was tempted to raise mine and then explain that even though I'd been with a woman, it had only been once and I didn't take it as far as it could go. But I couldn't say much since my sister was there.

"It's obvious you didn't read the book," my sister said to Melony, "but did you at least read the back cover? The author's not talking about women. This book is about men. Men with big dicks. It got me so hot while I was reading last night that now I'm ready to go to the strip club and feel on some. I brought my dollars with me." My sister pulled out a bank envelope stuffed with one dollar bills.

"We're getting ready to go to the club now," a woman named Belinda said.

"I'm not going," Melony said, then sat back down. "I wouldn't waste my dollars on some dicks."

"Just come on," my sister said as she stood and snatched up Melony. "You're going. We're all going. I can't wait to see Miami Splash, Black Thunder, Hardcore, Sexy L, Orgazm, Hurricane, Flight 69, Playboy, Just Enuff, Mr. Biggs—"

"Damn, just say that you know them all," Karen said. "You must be a regular. Does Tony know about that?"

"Let's just say I've been to my fair share of bachelorette parties. And if you want to talk about men who are strapped . . . you'll get an eyeful in there, especially if it still becomes all nude after midnight. Oh, and grab a few bottles of wine because it might still be BYOB."

* * *

I'd never been to a male strip club before . . . well, once before, but it was so long ago that I couldn't remember much. There was definitely a difference with how men behaved at a strip club versus women. The women were actually louder when the acts came on stage, and they were more aggressive with touching the dancers. I never thought I could get personally wrapped up into watching men strip, but after a couple of drinks and a few overly inflated G-strings flopping in my face, I lost it, especially when they started taking it all off.

One of the dancers came to our table and started giving me a lap dance. He stood in front of me flapping his red elephant G-string in my face, and before I knew what had come over me, I'd grabbed hold of his long trunk and didn't want to let go. I placed a ten dollar bill between the string that was flossing the crack of his ass, and if not for the fact that Melony had started to squeeze my thigh under the table, I probably would have rubbed on his big round ass, but she'd shocked me still. I tried to move her hand away, but her grip was too tight.

"What are you doing?" I asked her.

She leaned over and whispered in my ear, "I'm not interested in what's going on in here." I looked at the other ladies, who were too focused on the dancers to pay Melony and me any mind. "I'm more interested about what's going on in here," she said as she slid her hand under my dress and inside my thong. I gasped loudly. That's when all of the ladies at our large table turned to look over at me.

"What's wrong?" a few asked in unison.

Melony discreetly snatched her hand away.

"Look at the size of Mr. Biggs," I said, trying to play it off. They all turned back toward the dancers. I rolled my eyes at Melony.

I won't tell, she mouthed.

I turned my chair away from her and started waving my dollars in the air so the men would come my way, and a couple of them did. Several minutes later, when I looked back in Melony's direction, she was gone.

Swingers

After being in Dallas for a couple weeks, my patience level was at an all-time low. I'd see them on the street—attractive men that I wanted to get with. But I had no idea how to go about meeting them. Maybe if I was into flirting, but I wasn't; in fact, I could barely make eye contact. I'd gone online and met a few male friends that I chatted with. One man, named Lester, I'd given my number and we talked every day, but I wasn't interested in meeting him. Something about him and his name seemed creepy.

My sister said that a lot of her friends had met men in grocery stores, so I decided why not see if the same could happen to me. I drove downtown to Urban Market and walked around for a little less than an hour before I met a man in the frozen foods section. I was wearing a white T-shirt, but even with my black bra, you could still see my nipples protruding, especially after I opened the freezer door and they became frozen stiff.

"You look cold," the man said as I closed the door. He was slender, so light he was almost white, with red low-cut hair and deep dimples. Above average looking, but far from the drop dead gorgeous men I'd seen in Dallas. Besides, I wasn't much for yellow men.

I placed the pot pie in my basket. "I'm actually hot," my ultra-sexy alter ego said.

"Are you?" He extended his hand. "I'm Bates."

"Is your first name Master?" I said with a giggle. "It was a joke."

"Oh," he said as he put his hand down before I could shake it.

"I'm Alexis. Nice to meet you."

After a few minutes of small talk, we exchanged numbers, and by that evening he was already calling me. He seemed like a normal guy, so I agreed to meet him at a get-together in Deep Ellum. The street leading to the warehouse where the get-together was being held was packed with cars all moving at a snail's pace. Bates had given me the code for the underground garage structure that was attached to the building where the party was. I could see the building less than a block ahead of me, but I wondered how long it would take me to make my way over there. Twenty minutes later I was punching in the five-digit code, with Bates in the car directly behind me.

I parked and waited for him by the elevator. I noticed several people with half masks and long trench coats walk onto the elevator. The women were all wearing high heels, and most of the men had on hiking boots.

"Is this a masquerade party?" I asked Bates as he walked up to me.

"Not really, but most people prefer to partially cover their faces," he said as he handed me a black half-face mask.

"Why do I need to wear this? What's really going on?"

"Nothing, as long as you have an open mind."

"Why do I need one of those?"

"This is Dallas, and in this city you can find almost anything you want."

"All I'm trying to find is a man with a big dick."

"And that's all I'm trying to find."

"What?" I said, convincing myself that I couldn't have heard what I thought I had.

"There'll be plenty of those upstairs."

The elevator door opened and we walked inside. He pressed the button to the top floor. "I know I told you a lot about myself over the phone, but what I didn't tell you is that I'm a swinger."

"A what?"

"A swinger. I'm into group sex. I don't sexually hold myself back from too much of anything."

"But you're black."

"There a lot of black swingers, baby."

"So this get-together is for swingers?"

"Yes," he said, and seemed to grow impatient.

"Wait, you can't just spring something like this on me and expect me to be all down for it. How did you get into this? How do you all find each other?"

"The Internet. That's how I got connected. Relax, everything's going to be fine. I'm sure you're going to enjoy yourself."

I shook my head. "This is too freaky for me. I'm not into all that. Don't you worry about diseases? I mean, I am looking for a man with a big dick, but not one he's been swinging all over town."

"Just go inside and judge for yourself. The beauty for you is that nobody in there knows you and you're not from here."

He was right, and that was the whole point of this summer to sexually explore, but swinging?

The elevator stopped and the door opened. "Put on your mask. And don't be frightened. Just be open," When we walked through the door, there were two big burly men standing behind it. "You'll need to take off your clothes so they can check you."

"Check me for what?"

"You have to be naked in here. They want to make sure that no one is hiding cameras. None of us want to end up on a *Dateline* or *20/20* special," Bates said as he started to undress. "And besides, you don't need to be dressed for what goes on in here."

One of the men started searching Bates, but he was stroking his dick a little too long, and judging by how hard he'd gotten, it was turning him on. Next thing I knew, the body checker got on his knees and put Bates's dick in his mouth and started sucking it like his life was depending on it. Bates extended his arms out and started grabbing hold of the wall.

"You need to get undressed, sweetie," my body checker said to me as I stood in shock, watching the other body checker continue to perform oral sex on Bates. "Take it all off."

I unbuttoned my blouse while I watched Bates begin pounding his dick inside that big burly man's ass. Made me think about what Melony said at the book club meeting about gay men. I was nervous when I stripped down to my birthday suit. Nervous, as I stood in front of my body checker trying not to eye him as he rubbed his hands over my silhouette.

"You're not hiding anything in here, are you?" he said as he rubbed the light fuzz on my pussy.

"No, I'm not," I said as I jerked his hand away from me. Then I walked to a dark corner in the house so I could observe and hopefully not be forced to participate.

A man came up to me—a man who had just finished slipping off a rubber after having sex with some other woman—and for his introduction, he rubbed his stiff dick on my thigh. This wasn't right. Not the kind of scene I was into. I wanted to explore, but not with a house full of freaks. "Let's fuck," he said to me.

"No, I don't want to," I said firmly.

"Isn't that what you're here for?"

"You just finished doing that other woman. Why would you think I'd now want you?"

"Well, in case you haven't noticed, that's what we're all in here doing." He tried moving his dick from my thigh to my pussy.

"Get off of me," I said as I pushed him away.

I moved to another corner. Now, I was standing beside a man who was sitting on an ottoman jacking off with a red spotlight shining on him, while a very thin, blond white woman danced in front of him. He took my hand and squeezed it while he climaxed. I couldn't do this. I didn't bother to find Bates to tell him I was leaving, I just left.

The next night, while my sister was at work, I did a Google search, typed in *swingers* and *Dallas*, and came up with a site that was full of thousands of posts. From the search results I found a sex site that announced: ENTER THE WORLD OF ANONYMOUS SEX. But it wasn't too anonymous because many of them included their picture. I started to put up my own profile, but decided instead to reply to a few. I wasn't looking for much. I just wanted to be fulfilled by one man, if possible. Hopefully someone would respond. Someone I could have my summer fling with.

Nice-N-Wet Looking for a Girlfriend to Play With

A few men responded to me from the Web site, but when I logged back on, I kept clicking on the women seeking women category. I had to get whatever had entered my system out so I could focus on my mission at hand, which was to have fun with some men who were strapped. There were plenty of them on the site, but first I needed to fulfill a fantasy that I'd never known existed before my encounter with Black Exotica, and that was to be with a woman. There were two pages of ads and over two dozen women with pictures showing off their best assets.

I was torn between Nice-N-Wet, who was the same age as me, thirty-one, and lived in Cedar Hill, which wasn't too far from my sister. Her ad read:

> *I'm looking to meet an attractive female for a*
> *serious relationship. I'm very ladylike and I wish*

to find a woman who is the same. I have my own place and all the essentials. I'm professionally employed with no kids or responsibilities other than pleasing me and the woman who I decide to let enter my life. I'm tired of men so you need not continue to respond hoping you'll change my mind. I have a preference for a woman with a big fat ass like mine and long hair, no weaves please and no strippers.

The other ad had the heading, LOOKING FOR A GIRLFRIEND TO PLAY WITH:

I am a black female, 30, seeking a companion to hang out with that can meet my sensual needs. I would like to go out for drinks, shop, and eat more than good food, and of course play. I am in a relationship with a man, but I need the touch of a woman every now and then. I am sexy, 5'6, 130 pounds, and uninhibited. My man knows of my preference and will not interfere. If you are a slim female, race unimportant, d/d free slim with big breasts. E-mail a picture of your best assets and I will do the same.

It was a toss-up, so I decided to write both names on a tiny slip of paper, mix them up and pull one. And the winner was . . . LOOKING FOR A GIRLFRIEND TO PLAY WITH.

I used my sister's digital camera and snapped a few pictures of my breasts, legs, and feet, which I felt were my best assets, and I waited for her response. Every day for over a week, I checked my e-mail. Finally I received an e-mail from *sxyblkldy* with an attachment. She wrote:

> hey got your picture and i definitely like what i see. love those pretty toes and sexy legs. everything you sent was all good. sorry it took me so long to respond but my schedule with work and school is real hectic. i'd love to meet you face to face asap. take down my number and give me a call if you like what i have to offer. here's a picture i recently took to let you see what you could be holding on to real soon.
>
> —tricia

I scribbled her number on a Post-it and proceeded to cautiously open the attachment, since my sister had complained that her computer had recently gotten a virus and her e-mail was filled with porn, but I was curious and so I took the risk. The file opened a picture of Tricia bending over a chair, with her large butt and thighs nearly filling the nineteen-inch screen. When I heard the doorbell ring, I quickly closed all my open screens, logged out of the Internet, and then rushed to the front to see who was there.

"Hello again," Melony said when I opened the door.

"My sister isn't home."

"Do you really think I'm here to see your sister? I came by to see you. I thought that you might want to go out to eat."

"I have some company on *his* way."

"Listen, Alexis, I'm not one to bite my tongue. I prefer to do other things with it, and I'm sure it's probably pretty obvious what those other things are and who I'd like to do them with. I can tell when a woman's interested in me . . . and I can tell that you are. Don't worry, this isn't something that your sister has to find out about."

I was attracted to her, and thought that maybe it was better to meet a woman for my first experience this way then over the creepy Internet, where anyone can be lingering.

"Let me just take you out for some drinks so we can talk," she said.

"Where are you going to take me to, some gay club?"

She laughed. "No, guess what? We go to Ruby Tuesday also."

"I hate Ruby Tuesday."

"I wouldn't take you to a chain restaurant while you're visiting Dallas. Have you been to Pappadeaux yet?" I shook my head. "You'll love it. I don't think I've tasted anything better, but I haven't tasted your pussy yet either."

My eyes widened and my mouth partially opened from the shock of her statement. Looking back on it, if there was ever a turning point, something that caused me to go over to the dark side, it had to be the day I met Melony. Aside from the fact that she was a police detective who carried a gun and a stern look, she was a very feminine woman whom I was drawn to in some way. She had plenty of curves to her body, pretty light brown eyes, and extremely long golden brown hair. Seeing the two of us together, no one would have thought that we were anything other than girlfriends.

Men flirted when we walked into the restaurant during happy hour, and they bought us drinks all night. Before long the two of us had an obvious buzz.

"What are you thinking about right now?" I asked, hoping to break her stare.

"Eating you. I bet you taste so sweet. Don't you?"

"I don't know, I never tasted myself."

"Oh, yes you have. I'm sure you've had a man eat you out and then kiss you."

"I've had them try. But I'm not down for that. I don't want to taste my own or anyone else's."

"Well, I'm a firm believer that it's better to give than receive, anyway. So, when are you going to let me give some to you?"

I shrugged. "I enjoyed our talk, and I know that you're attracted to me, right?"

"I want to take you home and show you just how attracted to you I am. Is that okay with you?"

"Melony, listen to me," I whispered. "You're pretty. If I was leaning that way, I'd jump all over you."

"I'd let you."

"And I'm sure to a certain extent you might be able to satisfy me, but then, there would come a point when I'd need something to finish it off, and you don't have that something else."

"Oh, I do have something that can finish it off. Don't you worry about that."

"Oh, really, what, you're going through a sex change?"

She smirked. "Not quite."

"Then you don't have what I'm looking for. I came down here to find a man who's strapped."

"And you found yourself a woman who can strap one on and work it better than any man can."

"So you're the dominant one?"

"I carry a gun, don't I? Look . . ." She stood from the table, walked over to my side and bent down to whisper in my ear, "I'm ready to take you back to my place and fuck the shit out of you. How is that for honesty?"

One of the men who'd been buying us piña coladas all evening walked up and introduced himself to Melony and me as we were getting ready to leave.

"Thank you for the drinks," Melony said, "but we're not interested in getting to know you. We're trying to get to know each other. This is our first date. We're gay."

"Oh, shit, okay. They said there were a lot of lesbians in Dallas, so I guess they were right."

"Who ever they are . . . they were," she said as she took my hand, then walked out of the restaurant holding it.

"Why did you tell that man we were gay?" I asked, intentionally slurring my words. "You're gay. I'm not."

"You will be after I get finished with you. Get in the car."

"I'm not getting in your car," I said, still slurring.

She pushed me inside her convertible Saturn Sky. "And stop acting like you're drunk. You had one and a half drinks . . . piña coladas at that. You're fully aware of what's going down, so don't try to detract from my fun."

"How did you turn so gay, as pretty as you are?" I asked. "You couldn't have had any problems getting a man."

"Getting men wasn't my problem. Having them satisfy me has always been." She started rubbing my thighs while she drove down I–20 with the top up. "I like women—sexy, brown women. And I have a breast fetish, and you have some nice big round ones that I can do plenty with."

"They're not that big," I said.

"Let me see."

"See," I said, pulling down the top half of my tube dress.

"They're bigger than mine, which means they're big enough."

"Don't you want to be with a man, Melony? A man with a nine inch dick? There are plenty of them online."

"I'm a woman with a ten inch dick at home, and as soon as we get there, I'm going to use it on you."

"I'm sleepy," I said, struggling to keep my eyes open.

"You're not sleepy, you're faking it."

"I am sleepy."

"Close your eyes. I'll wake you when we get to my place."

When I opened my eyes, I was lying in her bed fully clothed and Melony was sitting beside me with the sheet concealing her bottom half. "How did I get in here?"

"I carried you."

"You must be strong."

"It's not like you're that big. You probably only weigh about a hundred and twenty with your pretty petite self," she said.

"I weigh a hundred and twenty-seven pounds, and you can't weigh much more than that yourself."

"One thirty-five." She smiled.

I sat up and glanced at the clock sitting on her nightstand. "I've been sleeping for almost two hours. And what have you been doing?"

Again she smiled. "Watching you."

I tugged at the peak in the center of her sheet. "What's that?"

She pulled the sheet off and revealed her strapless strap on. At first glance it appeared real. It was the same color as her flesh, and it even had veins and testicles. She inched her way over to me, brushing her thin lips against my full ones, and then gently bit my top lip before placing her tongue inside my mouth. She pulled my tube top down and caressed my breasts, swirling her tongue around my nipples and nibbling on them. I stood to wiggle out of my dress.

"Keep your heels on," she said, lying on her back with her head resting against two pillows.

I straddled her, leaned backward and supported myself with the palms of my hands as she used upward thrusts to penetrate me. Her strap-on was vibrating inside of me while her hands continued to cup my breasts. She rolled me onto my back and pulled off the strap-on. She began sucking my left nipple while squeezing my right breast and fingering me, all at the same time. She was gentle with every movement, and I kept coming over and over again. Her lips gradually traveled down my stomach until her tongue was wiggling inside my pussy. I spread my legs so her long wet tongue could get even deeper. Her long silky hair was resting on my thighs. I was a long way from my mission of finding a man who was strapped, but at least, so far, I had managed to find a woman who was.

My juices were covering her face. Melony spread her legs open and started playing with her clit. I was lying on my side next to her, resting my head in my hand. Her breasts were right in my face. "Yours are bigger than mine," I said as I took one in my mouth and started sucking.

"My breasts aren't bigger than yours," she said, "my nipples are."

While she was playing with her clit, I scooped my hand underneath her bottom half and stuck a finger inside her ass.

"You're getting kind of dominant, don't you think?" she said. "That's supposed to be my job."

She used a little unnecessary force to get me to lie on my back before sitting on my face and telling me to "Lick it like you love it." She was on my face, and I had no other choice but to insert my tongue inside of her, and the minute I did, she came. She came so many times, I lost count. When I was riding her and she had the strap-on, she came, saying that the sight of my breasts flapping in the air was what did it for her.

"Now, are you ready for me to make love to you?" she asked.

"I thought that's what we were doing."

"No, baby, that was foreplay. This is the real deal. This is the way I'm going to take your virginity and you're going to feel your cherry burst."

While I was lying on my back, she straddled me. "Aren't you going to put on that strap-on?" I asked.

Melony shook her head. "For what? I don't need one. I only did that to warm you up since you still think a dick is what you need. I know you've heard the saying that size doesn't matter. Well, it doesn't."

Our pussies began tongue kissing. She yelled out at the height of her climax and then became angry at me when she thought I was holding back. My clitoris couldn't stop vibrating from pleasure, but when I wouldn't scream out and express it, she flattened her body over mine and grinded while she filled my ear with her dirty talk. "You're not looking for a big dick. You're not looking for a dick at all. You want my pink pussy. Tell me what you want and how you want me to give it to you." She used her hand to gather the strands of my hair into a ponytail and then yanked my head back and proceeded to kiss and bite on the side of my neck while she continued rubbing our bodies together, causing so much friction I thought we were ready to ignite. She screamed out again, another climax, and this time her fluids were running down both her legs and mine. "Why are you fighting this when you know you want me?"

"I want a man with a big dick and plenty of veins protruding from it," I said, to piss her off, because I was ready to stop.

My statement made her do just that.

"Fine, go out and get you one," Melony said, rolled off me and sat on the edge of the bed.

"I told you at dinner what I came to Dallas to find."

"How could I forget what you came down here for, as much as you keep reminding me? But if you play with fire, you're bound to get burned."

"*You* seem more like fire than anything," I said.

"I'm not the fire, but those men you're out looking for . . . one of them might be. Don't you know that I'm looking for a serious relationship, and with this HIV epidemic, now is not the time to be searching for big dicks."

"I'm not gay and I know how to use protection."

"You can pretend with yourself but not with me. Tell me the last time a man has ever made you feel as good as I just did."

"Never. But all the men I've been with had little ones, so I'd rather answer that question after I've been with a man with a big one."

She shook her head. "I hate men. And I'd kill one before I'd let one put his hands on you and his nasty thing inside of you. You're mine now, and you're going to do what I say."

"I'm going to what?"

"Do what I say," she repeated with a smile, and then pushed me down on the bed and buried her head in my pussy for a few seconds before raising it. "Starting with growing some hair down here."

"Use your strap-on," I pleaded. "I need to feel something hard in my pussy."

"I'm not using anything," she said as she got up. "You need to come to grips with who you are and what you want. I'm not getting hurt again."

"Who hurt you?"

Melony left the room without answering, and I sat on the bed more confused than ever about my sexuality.

Two for the Price of One

When I returned to my sister's house the next afternoon, she had left for work and Melony had already called a few times to let me know how much she enjoyed having me over. While I was talking to Melony on the phone, I logged on to the sex site that I'd joined, to check my messages.

"And I know you liked it too," she said, "especially when I twirled my tongue all around the inside of your pussy and tickled your clit. I felt it throbbing. Are you going to let me lick you every day? A lick a day can keep those fucking men away."

"I don't see how that's possible."

"Anything's possible. Either I can make a detour while I'm at work to get a quick taste or you can meet me at my house when I get off."

"Melony," I said firmly, because it was time to set the record straight. "I hope you're not the possessive type."

"I can be if I have reason to. So just don't give me any reason to."

"Well, that's really too bad because I was just experimenting. In a few weeks my vacation will be over and I'll be in Detroit teaching."

"With my credentials, I could easily get a job on the Detroit Police Department."

"Whoa, slow down. No need to do all that."

"You weren't telling me to slow down last night when I was eating your pussy, so why are you telling me to slow down with the way I'm trying to love you?"

There was one new message waiting in my fantasy mail box. The e-mail was sent by asexymarriedcouple and read:

> hi, my wife and i like what we read and she'd like for you to be her first. this isn't the sort of thing we'd planned on doing, but we need someone to help us add a little spice in the bedroom. i know you didn't mention a preference for women but if you're open to the experience i'm sure my wife won't disappoint and all i want to do is watch. can you send us your photo? you can check out ours on the home page . . . we just joined and we're featured this week.

I clicked on the couple's photo that opened up to their profile and a gallery of over twenty photographs. I looked at every one, mostly full body shots that were taken while they were having sex. They were very careful not to expose their faces. The profile said that they were both thirty-five and had been married for five years. No children. His wife was "bi-curious," and he said that he just liked to watch. NO BUTCHES PLEASE. MUST BE FEMININE.

"I'll do anything just to be with you," Melony said to me while I read. "I'll even let you have a man from time to time as long as you don't get pregnant."

"What about a threesome? Would you ever be with a man if I wanted you to?"

"Never. And don't ever bring that shit up again."

"So your anything has limits?" I continued focusing on the on-line photo of the nude couple in the midst of a sex act. The caption underneath one of the pictures read, SOMEONE PLEASE HELP ME. I'M CHOKING ON THIS FOOT LONG COCK.

"As long as I don't have to be with a man, I will do anything."

When I ended my conversation with Melony, I typed a quick response to the married couple's e-mail.

> i'd luv to meet w/you especially . . . and as for your wife
> i have a special request. i'd like for my girlfriend to be
> with your wife and i desperately need to be with you.
> trust me, neither you nor your wife will be disappointed.
> think of it as getting two for the price of one.

The Web site indicated that asexymarriedcouple were online, so it didn't take long for a response.

> do you have a webcam?

> don't have a webcam but i can buy one today.

> ever had cybersex?

> no, but i'm up to trying new things.

not sure if you could tell from the photos but we are an interracial couple. i'm black and my wife is white. although race is not important, my wife would like to be with a black woman. she thinks their dildos are bigger.

well i'm black and my girlfriend is mixed. and she does have a pretty big dildo.

while i'm sitting at my desk responding to you she's under the desk orally satisfying me. it doesn't get much better than that, and not sure if you can bring it the way my wife does. can you?

most of the pictures i see you in she seems to be doing just that . . . sucking . . . how is she when it comes to fuckin'? she can continue to take you in her mouth . . . i want to put all twelve inches of you inside a different hole.

yeah, it's hard for her to handle me beyond oral . . . she can take some of me but not all . . . i haven't met a woman yet who could.

allow me to introduce myself . . . i'm the one woman who can and gladly will.

i'm getting excited. only one catch . . . my wife said i could only watch . . . and not participate. so we might have to figure a way to work around that . . . if i like what i see.

you will.

what's your best asset?

my juicy titties that get bigger every day.

yum . . . i'm a breast man. are they juicier than my wife's? she's a d.

so am i . . . but a full d, meaning i pop out of my bra . . . whenever i decide to wear one.

let's not chat the day away. go out and get the cam so we can get the ball rolling.

speaking of balls rolling . . . [I typed]

lol. get the webcam and maybe the rest can be arranged. my wife and i are really into role playing. can you and your girlfriend act something out for us?

don't see why not.

Melony called me while I was standing in line buying the webcam. "You are just the person that I wanted to talk to," I said. "My sister's staying over Tony's tonight. Can you come over and keep me company?"

"I can be there in a couple hours."

"Do you mind if we role-play tonight?"

"Why would I mind that? Anything for my baby," she said.

"I'll be waiting for you. Oh, don't ring the doorbell. Take down the code to the garage door. I want to start our role-play as soon as you enter the house."

"Okay, but who am I playing?"

"The sexy nurse coming for a house call."

"Mmm, there's a few things I can bring over."

I had set up the webcam to record the guest bedroom. I tested the picture quality with asexymarriedcouple to make sure they could see the room. The show was going to start in less than thirty minutes, I assured them, and our show ran without advance previews so their early request for me to reveal myself was denied.

When I heard the garage door open and the alarm chime to indicate someone had opened the door leading from the garage to the kitchen, I immediately went into action and started crying real tears, a gift I'd acquired from childhood.

Melony rushed through the bedroom door and found me sitting on the side of the bed with a thin sheet draping my naked body. "What's wrong, Alexis?"

My eyes popped open when she walked through the door in white lace-up and Oxford platform high-heeled pumps with a red cross on the toe, and holding a doctor's bag. She was wearing a naughty red and white nurse's outfit with red rubber gloves and a stethoscope hanging around her neck that had a purple penis dangling at the end.

"Why couldn't the doctor come?" I asked.

"Well, the hospital has rules about treating patients who don't have insurance, but I could tell from our phone conversation that you were in real need of some emergency medical treatment."

"Nurse Melony, thank you so much for coming over. I'm really worried that I may be sick. I fucked a man with a twelve inch dick and I haven't felt right ever since." Both Melony and I sounded like a couple of B actresses.

"I'll need to give you an exam to make sure everything is still intact down there."

"But I'm so sore I can barely move. My pussy feels like it's on fire."

"A burning sensation could mean a venereal disease. I'll need to take a culture swab. Lie on the table flat on your back so I can take a look."

I did what she'd asked. "Now put your legs in these stirrups," she said, pulled out a pair of wrist and ankle cuffs and tied me to the bed with the straps that were attached. "Slide your lower body toward me so I can take a look."

Melony sat on the bar stool that I'd taken from the kitchen. She pulled the sheet away from my body so she could see my lower half in full view. "I'll need to do a pelvic."

She stood from the chair, walked closer to me and bent down. She opened her doctor's case and removed a metal speculum that she inserted inside of me so she could spread my pussy open. She put her latex-gloved finger inside of me, and it began vibrating while she pressed her other hand down on my stomach. "Everything feels normal. Is that painful?"

"Not at all," I moaned.

She removed her finger, took off the fingertip vibrator and the glove, and then reinserted her bare finger inside of me. "Does that feel any better?"

"Yes," I moaned.

"This is better for me to gauge how wet your pussy is getting. Now let me take some cultures to make sure that big dick didn't give you an STD." She stuck her head between my legs and covered her head with the sheet, and within seconds her tongue was licking my clit.

"That sure doesn't feel like a Q-tip," I said.

She stopped licking and said, "Our clinic is in short supply so I had to improvise."

I held her head between my legs and tossed the sheet off of my body so the webcam could catch Melony in action.

"There are just a few more procedures I need to perform and then I should be on my way."

"Okay, and those are?"

"I need to do a full breast exam, and then a pap smear."

"The pap smear hurts so much."

"I'll try to be gentle. Which do you want me to do first?"

"The pap smear, since I'm already in the stirrups."

She walked over to the light switch and flicked it off. Her purple stethoscope was glowing in the dark. "I need to check your vaginal beat."

"What kind of nurse are you?"

"A nurse that wants your pussy. You said you had twelve inches inside of you. Well, this is eighteen inches long and two inches wide."

"I can't handle all of that."

"I know. That's why we're going to share."

I realized that with the light off, the webcam couldn't record the action. "Can you turn the light back on? I want to see you gettin' some too."

She flipped the light switch on, slid one end of the dildo inside of her, and then stood between my legs. "Do you want me to take it fast or slow?"

"Do whatever you feel."

"I feel like fucking," she said as she rammed the other end inside me.

My moans became so loud, I was afraid my sister's next door neighbors, who were sitting on their back porch, might hear me. She climbed on top of me and I wrapped my legs around her back and enjoyed every second of the vibration her lower half was causing mine to have.

Melony left before morning, afraid that my sister might come home early. A few hours later I logged on to check my e-mail.

Asexymarriedcouple wrote:

> we'd like to meet you and the nurse asap. my wife is also in need of some emt.

"Explain all of this to me again," Melony said on the phone the next day, after I tried telling her about the married couple and how his wife wanted to meet her for sex. She didn't seem to fully understand how I was willing to share her with another woman. She appeared hurt and offended. "I thought your feelings for me were genuine."

"They are, Melony, but I still need to get this urge of mine out of my system."

"And you want to do that by having me screw some man's wife so you can screw her husband? How did you even meet these people?"

"Online."

"Online, Alexis? You met them online, and now you're going to their house to have sex with them? Do you know how dangerous that is? Why would you even want to do that?"

"I'm not sure why, but one thing I don't feel like is being judged.

All my life I've played it safe, and all that got me was a bunch of men who didn't want to do anything for me, just wanted to use me for whatever I was worth. Now, I want to be the one in control for a change. I want to be the person using someone for what they're worth. I'm tired of faking my orgasms . . . I want to have one."

"I don't make you come?" Melony asked.

"Yes, you do, but I want to have an orgasm with a man, Melony." I walked into the garage and got in my sister's car. "I'm on my way to their house."

"Don't go over to someone's house that you don't know. Are you out of your mind?"

I started the engine. "Don't let me go by myself. Meet me there so nothing will happen. You don't want to be the lead detective investigating my murder, do you?" I said as I pulled out of the garage.

"Like I keep telling you, you're playing with fire, and one day, Alexis—"

"I'm going to get burned. I know, but I thought my woman would protect me."

She laughed. "Amazing how I conveniently became your woman when you want me to do something." There was a few seconds of silence. "There is no way I would go to a stranger's house for sex."

"Forget it. I won't go either, but I'm getting some big dick to-night somehow," I said before ending the call.

Later, I spent a couple hours milling through e-mails, looking at the attachments of penises that were locking up my in-box. One e-mail in particular caught my eye. Anaconda said he needed someone to suck the venom from his huge snake, and he sent over a picture of himself sucking his own. That's when I realized that I was dealing with some real freaks. I didn't want that anymore. I'd been talking on the phone to Lester all summer. The only thing that prevented me from meeting with him was when he told me he wanted to be choked. But I'd rather choke a man out of play than watch a man choke on himself for pleasure, so I called Lester and finally arranged a face-to-face meeting.

We arranged to meet at Sambuca's, a jazz club in uptown Dallas. I went and waited for a while, but when it appeared that I'd been stood up, I left with a different man, whom I'd met that evening, and the two of us went to a hotel. I thought he was a complete stranger, only to discover that he was Lester, the man I'd been chatting with, doing what he said he did best—playing games. But things went terribly wrong that night. I'd finally gotten what I wanted—almost. At the height of his climax, it was time for me to strangle him, even though I hadn't come yet. I strapped the belt around his neck, but maybe I did it a little too firmly and held on longer than I should have. It was an accident, I kept trying to convince myself.

"Melony, where are you?" I whispered through my cell phone.

"I'm at work. Where do you think I am? You finally decided to answer your phone."

"Melony, I need your help. I got burned . . . badly. I can't say too much over the phone."

"Is it serious?"

"Very. Things got out of hand."

"Don't say any more. Just tell me where you are and I'll be there."

The Black Widow Strikes Again

I was in tears when I opened the door. Melony was standing there dressed all in black and wearing a pair of leather gloves.

She stepped inside the hotel room. "What happened?"

"I've been playing with fire and I got burned, just like you told me I would."

"Well, maybe you'll listen to me from now on." She walked around the room. "What did you touch?"

"Nothing," I said.

"You had to touch something," she said as she walked across the room and looked down at the dead body. "You touched the doorknob when you let me in. I'll have to remove it before I leave. There's too much of your DNA in this room. We're going to have to burn it."

"Cause a fire? I've already killed one person. I don't want to kill any more."

"You won't kill any more. These hotels have sprinklers. I just need a little fire to get rid of the DNA and to make it look like this is the workings of the Black Widow."

She removed a tube of red lipstick from her bag and wrote across the mirror:

The Widow Black has struck again
XXX

"You write just like her," I said with concern. "I watched the news special. Her writing is very distinctive."

"Okay, well, I'm a detective and I've worked the case so I've seen a lot of the evidence."

"Are you sure that's all it is?"

"Who killed this man, me or you? There's a party going on in the second floor ballroom. It's a public party. I need you to take the elevator to the second floor, pay whatever they're charging. Don't sign a guest book, just walk around and be seen—that way, if someone remembers you from this evening, you can always say you were there for the party. When I'm getting ready to set the fire, I'll call you. Don't answer. That's when I want you to leave and go to my house. I'll meet you there."

It took nearly an hour for Melony to call me. I wondered what she'd been doing up there for all that time, but as soon as my cell phone rang and I saw her name on my caller ID, I did as she instructed. I didn't answer, but I did leave the hotel and headed to her house. I had the key she'd given me weeks earlier and so I let myself in. I wanted to look around. See if there was any evidence that could link Melony to the Black Widow, but then there was that part of me that didn't really want to know. Perhaps it was just a coincidence that her writing matched exactly, or maybe it wasn't exact. The only thing I did remember the news special saying was that the Black Widow most likely used the Internet to meet her victims, which put me at ease because Melony didn't even own a computer.

I curled up in her bed and went to sleep.

In the morning, I woke up to the smell of pancakes and bacon. Melony had come home and cooked me breakfast.

"Good morning," she said, as she set the tray of food on the bed. "I took care of everything. You don't have anything at all to worry about. They linked the murder to the Black Widow. There's no DNA and they're just as baffled by this case as they are by all the rest."

"I'm so drained."

She started rubbing her fingers through my hair. "Well, you probably just need to get some more rest. You had a crazy night. I won't disturb you."

"You just got off work. Don't you want to take a nap?" I asked.

"No, not now. I'm kind of wired up."

"But I want you to take one with me. Are you going to turn me in?"

She shook her head. "I'm an accessory so I can't turn you in, but even if I wasn't, I still wouldn't turn you in, because I'm in love with you."

"You're still in love with me even though I killed someone?"

"We all make mistakes," she said as she walked to the closet and pulled out a black bag.

"What's in the bag?"

"My lap top. I have some work to do."

"You have a lap top? I didn't know that. I've never seen you use it before. Is it new?"

"No, I've had this for a little while. I just don't use it that often."

"So why are you using it now?"

"Like I said, I have some work to do. Go to sleep, baby. I'll join you soon enough."

When she left the room, I sprung up from the bed, but I was too afraid to leave the room. I didn't want her thinking that I suspected her, but now it was starting to come together. Now I could link her to a computer, which was a means for the Black Widow to meet her victims. Why had Melony been in the hotel room so long? Was she recreating the crime scene to make it look even more like the work of the Black Widow? Or was I just tripping because I'd killed someone and I didn't want to be the only murderer in the household. I climbed back in the bed, under the sheets, and closed my eyes trying to put the past well behind me. My entire summer vacation was a waste, not just of time, but also of a life. I'd come here because everything was supposed to be bigger in Texas, and I was hoping the same held true when it came to the men. But the only person I was able to find who was truly strapped and could satisfy me was a woman—a woman who had to strap one on—a woman who just might be the Black Widow serial killer.

I couldn't get back to sleep, but I did manage to eat some of the food Melony had brought. After a few hours she joined me in the bed, but turned her back toward me while she lay there. I asked if something was wrong and she said nothing so I left it alone.

"When are you going back to Detroit?" she asked a few minutes later.

"Next week. Why, are you going to miss me?"

"Well, honestly, I was thinking about going back with you."

"But what about your job? You're going to quit it? And what about your house?"

"I'm sure I can get on with the Detroit Police Department. Just like I'm sure I can sell this house. But I'll only come if you want me to. Do you?" I hesitated. I mean, did I? That was a good question. Even if I was stretching my imagination and she wasn't the Black Widow, would I want her to follow me home? In Dallas, I could act out a few fantasies and no one would be the wiser. But in Detroit, I'd have to answer to some folks who would be all in my business. Like Nancy, for one.

"I guess you don't," Melony said, waiting on my answer. "I guess I was just your summer fling."

"The summer isn't over yet," I said as I snuggled up next to her to initiate our lovemaking. She wasn't expecting that, but I felt that I at least owed her that much. She'd gotten me out of a jam, and since sex was a stress reliever, we had might as well relieve some.

"Do you feel bad about what you did to that man?" she asked as I was playing in her long locks.

"Not really." I kissed her soft lips.

"I can tell. So why don't you?"

"I'm not sure. The way I look at it, if he had a choking fetish, he was probably going to get killed sooner or later. The only thing I'm upset about is that the sex wasn't even worth it. I didn't even have an orgasm."

"Do you realize that less than twenty-four hours ago you killed a man, and now you're still thinking about sex?"

"It was an accident. I mean, I wasn't the one playing with fire . . . he was. In fact, in some ways, I wish that I really was the Black Widow," I said, hoping to bait her in, but it didn't work. She didn't say a word, except to tell me she wasn't in the mood for sex that evening.

The First Day of School

"Did you hear my story, Miss Cartwright?" one of my students asked, snapping me from my thoughts of the summer I'd had; a summer that I couldn't share with my students the way they were doing with me and the rest of the class on their first day of school. While some of my students could boast of a trip to Disney World or a summer they spent out of state with relatives, many others remained in Detroit the entire summer highlighting a concert they attended at the Fox Theatre of a famous urban or hip hop artist like Kanye West, or a day at the State Fair.

I sat behind my desk and pretended to be interested in what Kenya, one of my students, said about her weekend spent at the Indianapolis Black Expo, when in actuality my mind was hundreds of miles away back in Dallas, where I'd unintentionally left a deadly mark. It was easier for me not to think about what I'd done while I was there. Even though it was an accident, I'd still killed someone. And the part that concerned me more was whether I'd be caught for running away from the scene of the crime.

Knowing that Melony was going to join me permanently made me wonder if I'd ran at all. We had arrived in Detroit a week before school started, but she was going back to Dallas in a few days to take care of some business. I was purposely avoiding my best friend Nancy, who'd left dozens of messages on my answering machine in a one week period, demanding to know how my summer went.

"Welcome back, Miss Cartwright," Scottie, one of my students from last year, said as he passed by my classroom, snapping me from my daze. I turned and gestured and then watched as he stopped dead in his tracks.

"Dang, Miss Cartwright, what happened to you?" The classroom fell out in laughter as if it were an inside joke. Had I changed that much in two and a half months? I guessed so. Gone were the glasses and down went my hair. I'd turned in the flats for some stilettos and my buttoned-up blouse for plunging necklines.

"I wish I could tell you, Scottie," I said with a wink, "but you're just a little too young."

"A summer fling . . . a summer fling. I got you," he said as he disappeared down the hallway.

If I were to write my own paper about my most memorable event of the summer, I doubt if I could pen it down to just one. And first I'd have to start with the moment that changed my life, which wasn't the murder but my encounter with Black Exotica. This past summer was a wild ride from the last day of the school year to the first day back. And what happened in between was simply unforgettable.

I stood from my desk. "Well, it's been a great first day and I'm excited about the upcoming school year. No homework today but come prepared because you'll have plenty tomorrow."

The last bell for the day rang and all of my students scattered out of the classroom. I gathered my belongings and stood at the window, watching the school kids rushing to their buses or the cars that waited.

I walked down the hall to the teacher's lounge to spend the last hour doing my lesson plans for the week. When I entered, all eyes were on the television screen mounted to the wall and blasting the twelve o'clock news.

"Girl," LaShandra, one of the teachers, said, "did you bring that serial killer back with you?"

"What are you talking about?"

"The Black Widow . . . they think she's in Detroit. They found a dead man in a motel room and there were those markings left on the mirror. The room was set on fire. They say it's the work of the Black Widow, the same serial killer that was murdering those men in Texas."

"It's probably just a copycat," I said.

"I doubt that," LaShandra said, "I really doubt that. You're not the Black Widow, are you?"

"Me?" I said, shaking under my skin. "I couldn't kill a fly." I took a seat by the window and stared out at the rain that had just started to fall.

"That's strange, though, isn't it?" LaShandra asked.

The door creaked open and in walked Jamal, the gorgeous math teacher I'd fantasized about last school year. He was carrying a Pizza Hut box. He was my type of man; well-groomed, cleanly shaven, with a bald head and a clear chocolate brown complexion. I could tell he worked out regularly by the way his clothes hugged his body.

"Would you like some, Mrs. Cartwright?" Jamal asked.

"I do, but not pizza," I mumbled.

"What was that?" he asked as he sat beside me.

"Well, my little break is over," LaShandra said, then stood and walked out of the door, the rest of the room following behind her, with the exception of Jamal.

He opened the pizza box and pulled apart a slice. "Do you want some?" he asked again.

"Yes," I said, looking directly into his eyes, "I do want some . . . just not some pizza."

"Well, what do you want, Mrs. Cartwright?"

"Just call me Alexis. And I'm not a Mrs." I moved my chair closer to his. "I have a lot on my mind and I need to do something that will reduce my stress level. Any suggestions?"

"Working out usually helps me."

"Really?" I said, leaning into him. "I've been telling myself that I needed to start working out, but I hate to do it alone. Would you mind training me?" I rested my hand on his thigh and rubbed my way up and over until I had his belt buckle in my hand. "We don't need to go to a gym. We can do it all right here."

We both scrambled—I for the door and he for the window shade. The lights stayed on, so I could see just what I'd be working with. And as he stripped down to his birthday suit, I stood in awe of not only his perfectly sculpted body, varnished with tattoos and fraternity brands, but also the biggest muscle of them all—his ten-inch weight. "I had no idea you were that muscular," I said, eyeing the weight between his legs. "I better change into my workout clothes." I dropped my dress, removed my bra, and stepped out of my panties.

"Before you begin any exercise, you should start off stretching the muscles you plan to work," he said, tugging on his big muscle.

"I need to stretch my pelvic muscles, and I want you to use your big muscle that you're tugging on to help me." I sat on the table on the open lid of his pizza box, spread my legs apart as far as they could go and started to Kegel. He walked over to me and without saying one word rammed his ten inch muscle inside of me. My muscles quickly tightened around his hard as steel dumbbell.

"We're going to do three sets of ten. Make sure you inhale and exhale," he said between the heavy breathing.

Within minutes I'd come. And to think I went all the way to Dallas to find something I had right here at home.

He kissed me on the forehead. "How was that for a stress reliever?"

"It helped," I said as I stood from the table and got dressed. "Now we just need to establish a regular workout schedule—three days a week."

"I'll see you again on Wednesday, then. I got something you can work your lip muscles on."

I walked out of the teacher's lounge with a big smile plastered to my face and fresh thoughts of the best first day of school I'd ever had. The news report wasn't far from my mind either. LaShandra called the news strange, but it was more than strange. It was obvious. Now I had a dilemma. The first man I killed was by accident. The second man I killed was on purpose. And even though I wasn't the original black widow, I was trained by the best. Now that Jamal had sex with me, as good as it was, he had just become my next target.

Native Detroiter **CHERYL ROBINSON** is the author of three novels: *If It Ain't One Thing*, *It's Like That*, and *When I Get Free*. She is a graduate of Wayne State University with a degree in Marketing. She resides in central. Florida and is working on her fourth novel, which will be published in late 2007. To learn more, please visit www.cherylrobinson.com.

Divas Need Love Too

Méta Smith

Acknowledgments

I'd like to thank my muse for inspiring me to write this story. You know who you are, Spock, and you know I love you.

Thanks to my family and friends, especially my girls Angela Allen, Tracey Smith, and Dinora Lozano, for being there when I needed you. I swear I'd be in the loony bin without you. Or in jail! And once again, thanks Linda Duggins for keeping me sane, even when it's not in your job description. I love you guys.

Thanks to Marc Gerald for hooking this up, a million thanks to May Chen for your flexibility and patience while I worked on this project, and many thanks to HarperCollins for the opportunity. I've loved every minute of it.

And of course I'd like to acknowledge the talented and beautiful women who join me in this anthology: Electa Rome Parks, Cheryl Robinson, and my girl Joy King.

Prelude

A musky, exotic scent and the sound of soft music wafted through the air. I sipped my glass of Opus One and crossed my legs demurely, but I was feeling anything but demure. I repositioned myself in order to appear more alluring. There was no need to beat around the bush or pretend that I wanted anything besides an intense, passion-filled, uninhibited, buck-wild fuck session. My lover sipped a little more of his wine, allowed me to do the same, and then gently removed the glass from my hand and put it on the cocktail table. I lowered my lids and leaned forward, exposing maximum cleavage while parting my lips in expectation of a kiss. My lover allowed me to get inches away from his lips before running his hand through my hair, then slowly but firmly tightened his grip until he was almost painfully pulling my hair. I gasped in pain and delight.

"You are so fucking beautiful," he said, turning my head to face him and looking at me as if I were the sexiest woman alive.

A soft moan escaped my lips. I licked them and tried to kiss him. He firmed his grip on my hair and yanked a little.

"We have all night," he told me. "There's no reason to rush this." His tongue darted across my lips and I strained to kiss him again.

"But I want you so bad," I begged.

"Good, Songbird. Good."

He licked and nipped and nibbled at my lips, at times kissing me, at others allowing only his breath to tickle my lips as he hovered above me. I flicked my tongue outward in an attempt to taste any part of him. I caught the softly scented area beneath his chin and licked down to his Adam's apple. He felt scratchy, where the coarse hairs of his beard where growing in. I inhaled his smell; just a whiff of his cologne made me wet. He released his hold on my hair, gave me a little shove onto the couch and stood in front of me.

"Don't move," he ordered. I did what he wished.

He slowly unbuttoned his shirt and peeled it from his body. Then he unbuckled his belt and let his trousers fall to the floor before stepping out of them. I could see his hard-on bulging through the fabric of his boxer briefs, and I reached out to touch it.

"Not yet," my lover commanded. He approached me and stroked my cheek before letting his hardness brush against my face. His underwear was a little wet where drops of lubrication must have been oozing from the tip of his penis.

"I want to suck it," I told him. I needed to feel him inside of every part of me.

"I want you to suck it," he replied. I reached for him but he stopped me. He took both my slender wrists into one of his large hands.

"I want you to suck it," he repeated, "but you can't touch it. Put your hands behind your back."

Kinky, I thought, and did what I was told.

He lowered his briefs, a centimeter at a time, until his rock hard cock sprung forth and was throbbing right before my lips. I opened my mouth and leaned forward, growing excited as I tasted the faint saltiness of his pre-come. I looked up at him, and he was staring right back at me. I sucked the tip a little harder, using gentle suction to draw him farther into my mouth.

"That's right," he said. "I want you to get it wet."

I slurped and sucked away, gradually engulfing more of his dick, until I was nearly gagging and saliva was dripping from the corners of my mouth and onto my breasts. I could tell my lover was growing more excited, which turned me on a great deal. He told me that I couldn't touch him and ordered my hands behind my back, but I was going to break the rules. As he thrust himself in and out of my mouth, I caressed my breast and pinched my nipple with one hand, while slowly stroking between my legs with the other. Very soon my fingers were covered with my own juices as they slid in and out of me.

"You're cheating," he said.

I would have answered him, but my mouth was full. He pushed me away from his body.

"You're a naughty girl," he said. "I'm going to have to punish you."

"I'd like to see you try," I said, full of bravado. "Are you going to spank me?" I asked provocatively.

"I could just keep this dick to myself," he said.

Damn, I hadn't thought of that form of punishment.

"Don't do that," I said quickly.

"I won't," he replied. "I have something more devious in mind."

My lover's hands moved slowly and deliberately as he let his fingertips dance lightly over my skin. I wanted him to grab me, embrace me, fuck my brains out. I couldn't take the anguish of his slow seduction. I writhed and wiggled, arching my back and thrusting my pelvis, trying to increase our body contact, but he continued to take his time.

My desire burned hotter as my lover's hands caressed every inch of me. Articles of clothing fell from my body like a snake shedding its skin until I lay naked, shivering beneath his touch. He allowed me to touch him now, and my hands roamed over his taut, muscular shoulders. God, he had the perfect body, and I told him so. His skin was smooth and perfect, and he wasn't too big or too small. As he gently sucked my nipples, his hands never ceased kneading my flesh between his strong fingertips, causing me to tingle.

"Please," I begged him. "You're driving me crazy. I need you."

"Not yet," he replied.

He began to move lower across my torso, kissing a trail down my chest and over my abdomen until I felt his hot breath and the hairs of his goatee tickle the sensitive skin between my thighs. I sighed in anticipation, parted my legs and closed my eyes. I felt his fingertips as they spread my lips apart, and moaned when he began to taste me, flicking his tongue around my clitoris. And just as I was about to explode, he stopped. I thought he was giving me a break in an attempt to prolong my climax and that he would continue and eventually finish what he started, but he was gone.

I sat up and looked around, searching for him through the dim light of the scented candles that illuminated the room.

"That is so not fair," I pouted.

He reappeared, his erection standing out from his body in an intimidating arch. I hummed in approval.

"I wanted to be ready," he said. He'd put on a condom. Responsible . . . I can never hate that.

He dropped back to his knees and began to lick me again. I threw my head back and began to sing in ecstasy, grinding my hips eagerly against his face. As my body tensed and I felt a wave of pleasure radiate from the inside out, he stopped eating me and entered me. I throbbed around him as he plunged inside me. I hit high notes that Minnie Ripperton and Mariah Carey could never achieve.

"That's right, Songbird," he said, "sing for me," he breathed into my ear, intensifying my climax.

I moaned and sighed and screamed until my voice began to sound harsh and shrill. Then things got weird. I shut my mouth but I could still hear the shrill sound getting louder and louder. My body felt lighter and lighter, until finally I slipped from unconsciousness into the land of the living.

Damn it! Another wet dream. Literally. I ran my hand over the four-hundred-thread count sheets that were now wrinkled and damp.

I really, really need to get laid. I am hornier than a twelve-year-old boy who just discovered his father's stash of skin mags. Maybe if I get laid, I'll stop dreaming about *him*. My dream lover and I are over, and have been for some time, and moreover, there is absolutely no good reason for me to be wasting time thinking about him, my *ex*-boyfriend. He was the one who lost out on a good thing, not me! He should be in bed dreaming about me!

I'm everything a man could want and then some. A few years ago I was a thirty-year-old college grad who was waiting tables and struggling to make ends meet, chasing the dream of being a star long after what most folks said was an appropriate age to make it big. Friends and family, though they may have meant well, totally discouraged my aspirations to sing, even though there was no question that I could not just sing, but *blow*, plus I write songs that stir the soul. But they thought that because I was "smart" and had a degree, I should get serious and get a "real job" and stop pining after my "childhood fantasies." But I couldn't give up on myself like that.

I couldn't take the easy road out just because things got tough. I've known since the first day I opened my mouth in the choir of the First Chicago Missionary Baptist Church that I was born to be a singer. I knew there was no expiration date on my talent. Now I live in a mansion in Miami and have a platinum album and a trio of number one hits to my songwriting credits because of my hard work, perseverance, and uncanny ability to say "Fuck the world, I'm going for mine." Now I have everything that I ever dreamed of . . . except someone to share it all with.

God, I know that sounds pathetic! But trust me, I'm not one of those women who simply because I'm a member of the "Dirty 30 Club" feels so desperate that I'm willing to jump on anything that shows an interest. And I certainly don't subscribe to the bullshit theory that my life isn't complete without a man. But a man would be nice! Lately I've been spending more time in the studio than out looking for Mr. Right or in the bedroom getting my freak on, and the lack of action is starting to take its toll on my peace of mind and my vibrators!

It seems like the more successful I get, the harder dating becomes. I never thought that Waiting to Exhale stuff would happen to me, but here I am, thirty-something and still no better at relationships than when I was twenty-something. I'm simply no good at affairs of the heart. Either my judgment sucks or I think with the wrong part of my body or a little bit of both, but that just seems so . . . stupid. And I'm pretty sure I'm not stupid; I mean, would I have gotten this far if I was?

Maybe there's some kind of crazy generational love curse on me. None of my sisters are married, and my mother and aunts—and there are nine of them—never could stay married for long or are married to the wrong-ass men. My mom and aunts are smart; all of them have good careers and are making a decent living, and they're all fine. Nine dimes. They should have it all together. But they don't. My grandmother is the big dime. She was a straight-up fox back in the day: big legs, nice figure, with beautiful skin and hair, and a sweet disposition that hid an evil streak that struck fear in the boldest and most courageous of men. She married five times, but each of her husbands died strange and mysterious deaths at a young age. Needless to say, she's the subject of many rumors, and there has even been some speculation that Tyler Perry's character Madea's penchant for killing men with sweet potato pies was inspired by my nana!

But curse or no curse, I just can't seem to get the hang of what almost everyone else acts as if it's so simple: finding the man, hooking the man, and keeping the man until you die or kill each other. The real irony here, though, is that my name is Lucky. Straight up, it's my real name, and yes, my mother named me that. She said it was because she loves to read those books by that chick Jackie Collins, about some ballsy mafia daughter named Lucky. But those books came out *after* I was born. My aunt told me the real deal—that my mom used to date a dude in high school named Lucky—but he's not my dad, at least not to my knowledge. But with my crazy ass family, nothing would surprise me.

I've come to respect love, not just desire it, I really and truly have. I've remained open to all the possibilities of finding that special someone, staying optimistic and not becoming bitter, but now my patience is starting to wear thin. I'm not old by any means, and I know I've got some time left before I become a spinster with no one but her cats to show her love. But I'm not getting any younger. In the meantime, I keep on believing, hoping that one day, as far as my love life is concerned, I'll live up to my name.

Verse 1

I curled up under the fat, goose-down comforter and tried to go back to sleep. Despite the fact that my alarm clock had gone off, I could get in another thirty minutes before I had to get up and officially start my day, but nothing doing; the phone rang and destroyed any hope of catching more z's.

"Hey Lucky girl, are you up?" It was my publicist, Leslie. In my line of work you really need someone around that cares about what happens to you, and not just because your paycheck pays the note on their snappy little Jag, but because they have a conscience and ethics and integrity and a heart. Leslie is that someone in my life. She isn't just my publicist, she's my friend, and she helps keep me sane. She was also keeping me from the possibility of getting some extra sleep.

"I'm up," I told her.

"Are you sure?"

"I'm up."

"I'm on my way and I'm going to use my key. If I come up there and your butt is still in the bed, I'm going to drag you out by your hair extensions," she warned me.

"I'm not in bed, I'm up!" I lied.

"Good. See you in a minute," she said, and hung up.

I peeked at the alarm clock at my side, which read 3:30 A.M. Time to make the doughnuts. I reluctantly got out of the luxurious bed at my suite at the Peninsula Hotel in downtown Chicago, threw the curtains back, and took in the most magnificent skyline in the world. Sweet home, Chicago, my kind of town! I was the prodigal daughter who returned home a big success, and I planned on reveling in the glory of my accomplishments. I wanted all the naysayers and nonbelievers who thought I'd never make it to bow down and recognize the diva. I also wanted my ex-boyfriends to eat their collective hearts out.

True to her word, Leslie breezed into my suite looking totally pulled together and chic in a cropped denim jacket, capris, and a funky T-shirt. She greeted me with a hug and got right down to business. Her curly hair bounced as she pushed back her glasses and spoke to me a mile a minute in her mellow voice tinged with a New York accent.

"You ready to do this?" she asked, full of enthusiasm. I looked at her with wonder. Her copper skin was practically glowing and she seemed so organized. How she managed to be so fucking chipper, so focused, and look so good so early in the morning, was beyond me.

"Yeah, I'm ready," I said, looking longingly at the bed. Those Egyptian cotton sheets were calling my name.

"Well move, girl, like your ass is on fire. We've got a schedule to keep!" Leslie clapped her hands at me. Any minute, the "glam squad"—the hair stylist and makeup artist dedicated to making me fly—would arrive. It was going to take them at least an hour to get me appearance ready, and my itinerary was crammed full of appointments, interviews, and the like.

"Are you rested? You've got a busy day ahead of you, and tomorrow's the big night, your CD's platinum party!"

"I slept all right, I guess," I told her, thinking about my erotic dream. "But you know I'm a night owl. It's too early to be waking up. I should be just now going to bed!"

"Sleep is for the weak, so get moving. Take a shower."

I didn't move.

"What's wrong with you?" she asked, putting her hands on her hips. We spent so much time together that Leslie could easily read my moods, even when I tried to disguise them.

"I'm a little nervous," I admitted. I was a tad bit worried about how my homecoming was going to go over. Hometown artists have it hard in the Windy City. Talented cats like Common and Twista still don't get the love they deserve at the crib. I was afraid that I wouldn't be respected by my hometown, afraid that the haters would take over. *She's not all that . . . I remember when she was a nobody . . . I hope she doesn't think she's special now.* I could just hear the envious people saying all that about me.

"You've got nothing to be worried about," Leslie reassured me, grabbing my hand and leading me into the bathroom.

"What if nobody comes?" I asked in an uncharacteristic moment of self-doubt.

"Stop tripping. People are going to come. Your friends will come." She turned on the shower.

"I don't have any friends," I told her.

"Well, your enemies are going to come too," Leslie said.

"I don't have any enemies."

Leslie rolled her eyes at me and laughed. "Yes you do!" she kidded.

"Haters but not enemies," I corrected her, punching her lightly on the arm.

"Whatever," she said. "People are going to be curious. You're already a big star. And the buzz around you is phenomenal. You have nothing to worry about. When you see me worry, then you should worry."

"Okay," I said, hesitantly. "You're from New York. Chicago is not like New York. Chicago never supports its own people. This is the city of hate. Folks might not come just so they can see me fall on my face."

"Well, if they don't come, they can't see you fall, now can they?" Leslie quipped.

"Shut up," I said dryly.

"Get naked, get in, get clean, and get out," she ordered like a drill sergeant. "You've got fifteen minutes."

I saluted her, and she left me in peace. I took off my clothes, looking at my body in the mirror as I did so. My full breasts were still firm, my waistline was still tiny, and my hips hadn't spread to the point of no return. I was holding up very well. No, fuck that! I'm sexier than a motherfucker! I turned around to look at my ass and the back of my thighs for signs of cottage cheese. Not a ripple! My body was definitely tight. My finances were tight. I was talented and a nice person. There was no reason I could think of as to why I hadn't found the man I'd spend the rest of my life with or why he hadn't found me.

I stepped into the shower and closed my eyes as I let the water run over my face in an effort to wake up and get energized. I tried to get focused on business, but found my thoughts drifting back to the ex-boyfriend who haunted my dreams. I wished that things had worked out with him. It was his fault I was alone. No one could compare to him. Dating other men after him seemed like a step down.

The warm water rained down on my skin, and I began to soap my body absentmindedly with a bath pouf, imagining how my former lover's hands felt. When the sponge glided across my nipples, they hardened, and I shivered as bubbles of cucumber-melon soap dripped around my areolas. I dropped the sponge and replaced it with my hands, touching my nipples, squeezing and caressing my breasts, not thinking about how long I'd been in the shower or who might come in and catch me. I wasn't going to be able to do anything—I'd think of my ex all day—unless I released my sexual frustration.

My hands traveled lower, across my stomach, until I reached my mound, and I slipped the tip of my index finger between the lips of my vagina. I wiggled my finger around until I found what I was looking for. My knees buckled slightly as my fingertip brushed across the hood of my clitoris, and I held onto a rail in the shower for balance. I rubbed my finger in slow circles, imagining that it was my lover's tongue. I threw my head back and opened my legs a little wider as the water pelted my body, continuing to stroke myself, increasing the speed and intensity.

I was on the brink of an orgasm when I stopped touching myself and detached the removable shower head from its base. I changed the setting on it so the water gushed forth in one powerful stream and directed the spray toward my clit. Then I inserted two fingers inside my vagina and felt the muscles contract as my fingers looked for and found my G-spot. I stroked it, slowly increasing the pressure, while pretending that my fingers were my ex's hard cock.

The heat from the water pounding on my clitoris, coupled with the stimulation of my sweet spot and my fantasy, sent me over the edge, and I bit my lip to keep from crying out. Wave after wave of pleasure shook my body in violent spasms as I came once and then again as the water mixed with my juices and flowed down my leg. I debated whether to go for a third orgasm but realized that my fifteen minutes were probably almost up. Deciding against it, I gasped for breath, composed myself, and hurriedly finished my shower.

When I emerged from the bathroom, ensconced in a fluffy terry robe with a towel wrapped around my hair, the glam squad had arrived and lined up what had to be a thousand little jars, bottles, containers, and tubes of war paint, pomade, gel, and hair spray to prep me for the day's activities. Leslie and I chatted as I sat in a chair and the glam squad pulled and tugged at my hair and face from every direction.

"You feeling better?" she asked. "Refreshed?"

"Yeah," I said. She had no idea how much better I felt.

"Good," she said.

"Girl, all of Chi-town is talking about your party tomorrow night," the hairstylist Karl told me as he pulled sections of my hair through a ceramic flat iron.

"For real?" I asked.

"Oh hell yeah," the makeup artist, Bonita, chimed in.

"This girl was worried that no one would come," Leslie informed them.

"That won't happen," Karl said. "You know any guy you gave the time of day to is going to show up professing his love, trying to find a way to get back in."

"What would make you say that?" I asked him, hoping it was true, at least in the case of the ex from my dream.

"I've seen it a million times," he said. "Anytime a young entertainer comes up—especially a fine one, but hell, the ugly ones too—every time a woman blows up, all the men that fucked up and missed the boat start crawling out the woodwork!"

"Well I hope not. I went out with some crazy motherfuckers," I said jokingly. "I hope they stay well within the woodwork!"

"Do I need to get extra security?" Leslie asked me, arching her eyebrow. I'm sure she was only half kidding.

"Nah. There was nobody dangerous. A little touched, yes, but nothing the bouncers can't handle."

"Sounds juicy," Bonita said, digging for details.

"Your nosy ass," Karl said, teasing her.

"Hell, I'm nosy too," Leslie said with a giggle. "What kind of men should we be expecting to show up at your soiree?"

"Well, if your theory is right and some of the guys I used to date are going to show up, then you'll be expecting all kinds," I said, rolling my eyes and sighing. The faces of the men I'd dated shuffled through my mind. "I've got more exes than the Nation of Islam! You wouldn't know from the state of my love life now, but once upon a time, I dated so much that the chicks on *Sex and the City* looked like nuns in comparison."

"Yeah, well, that well's run dry," Leslie teased me.

"Yeah, but when it was full, it was full. And I dated some fine-ass men. But most of them were just a little off," I told them, traveling down memory lane. "Like there was this hotboy named Harley I used to kick it with. He was tall, a smooth almond complexion, and had muscles on top of muscles," I said with a shiver.

"He had a bangin' body, but his fashion sense was wack. He used to wear sleeveless shirts and leather pants and motorcycle jackets and sunglasses all the time. No matter how hot, no matter how cold. He wanted everybody to know he rode a bike. But despite all that he was a good fuck, so you know we kicked it a minute.

But outside of bed, his ass bored me to death. All he ever said was, 'And stuff, you know, whatever.' That was his way of answering damn near every question you asked." I wrinkled up my nose and shuddered.

"The men a woman will put up with just for some good dick!" Karl said with a smirk.

I laughed and thought about another nut job I kicked it with.

"It's not always even about the dick, though. There was this guy Jeffery," I said. "I met him at an art gallery and he was sprung. He sent me flowers and poetry; he e-mailed me, called me, you name it."

"You must have put it on him," Bonita said, giggling.

"Nope, not at all. We hadn't even been on a date, he was just chasing it."

"Sounds like a stalker to me," Karl said with a laugh.

"No, that's not what was wrong with him, but I'm getting to that. It wasn't creepy or anything, I just thought he was really, really sweet. He was a gentleman, you know? It was cool he wasn't pressuring me for some ass because I just wasn't feeling him that much. He was a little on the short side, and he was too old for me, but I began to develop a kind of soft spot for him. Eventually, I let him take me for coffee, and we went to museums and stuff like that. Finally he stepped up his game and asked me out for dinner and dancing.

"We went to Gibson's and had filet mignon and champagne and talked and laughed, and I was feeling so relaxed and comfortable that I was thinking that I might even give him some. Then we went club-hopping after dinner, and I thought we were having a good time but I drank too much that evening,"

"Please tell me you did not throw up on the man," Leslie said.

"No, I did not throw up on him. I wasn't drunk, but I would have gotten drunk if I knew what I was in for. I'm going to the bathroom constantly, and after my third trip, the mood of the date shifted. Jeffery started bugging the fuck out and accused me of trying to 'escape.' He said that I was using the bathroom breaks as an opportunity to flirt with other guys. Then he started crying, right there in the middle of the dance floor. I mean bawling. Dude had rolled up in a ball on the floor!"

"Oh my God, what did you do?" Leslie asked.

"I hope you left his ass right there on that floor," Karl said.

"At first I didn't know what to do. I asked him to get up off the floor. I told him to get ahold of himself. That just made things worse. He went into this rant about why he didn't date in America anymore and preferred the brothels of Thailand, because at least then you knew what you were getting."

"All that fool was getting in Thailand was a transsexual and a trip to the STD clinic!" Karl hooted.

We all cackled with laughter as they put the finishing touches on and I squeezed into a dress that was illegally tight. Leslie pulled out a black velvet bag and smiled as she unveiled the contents; a local jeweler was letting me borrow a couple of fabulous pieces from his pink diamond collection. Oh, the perks of showbiz! We oohed and aahed at the carats upon carats of pastel-colored ice set in platinum. Diamonds truly are a girl's best friend, and I switched into diva mode the instant the jewels touched my body.

The glam squad was rolling with us to make sure I looked my best during the long day ahead of us, and the four of us piled into a Hummer limo and headed off to my media appearances. I munched on a blueberry muffin and drank juice as we headed out toward the Dan Ryan Expressway, everyone still laughing at my crybaby ex.

"If you think Jeffery sounds like a piece of work, let me tell you about this other cat I kicked it with named Jodeci," I told them. They started cracking up again.

"You gotta be fucking kidding me," Leslie said.

"I wish I was. This fool had his name legally changed because he loved them so much."

"And you went out with him knowing this?" Karl asked me. "What the hell was wrong with you?"

"Look, he was fine as hell, okay! And he had a dick down to his knees. I was blinded by the dick; I'm not going to even front. He used to roll off Ecstasy, and that shit made him a big time freak who would do anything, and I mean anything that I asked him to do in bed, so hell, it was kind of working for me. But I got over that shit real quick when this fool stood outside my building unsolicited and uninvited in the pouring rain, singing 'Cry for U' by who else, Jodeci. I'm serious! He was howling at the top of his lungs! 'Laaaaadddy, I-I-I-I, will cryyyy for youuuu, tooniiiiight!' He may have been crying for real, but it was raining, so I couldn't really tell. Plus I was slumped down on the floor in embarrassment with the lights out, praying he would take his crazy ass home. I guess he was high or something, but that didn't explain the sweatshirt with my picture on the front and him holding a huge, neon pink sign that said he loved me. Don't worry about him, though. It was easy to get a restraining order for him."

"Now I know I'm calling for extra security," Leslie said, and we laughed until we arrived in Hammond, Indiana, an industrial suburb about thirty minutes south of downtown Chicago.

I visited the radio stations Power 92 and Soul 106.3, then we headed back into the city to my alma mater, where I did a concert and gave away CDs and posters and things. Finally, we headed back downtown, where I received the key to the city. All of this was accomplished by early afternoon. It's like that army commercial: I do more by 9:00 A.M. than most folks do all day.

We took a well deserved food and champagne break at Tavern

on Rush, gorging ourselves on platters of food that would take weeks to work off, and drinking more than our share of Veuve Cliquot Rosé.

"Did you have any boyfriends that weren't crazy?" Leslie asked me.

I wanted to mention the ex I'd dreamt about, but I didn't. In every woman's life there is at least one man that she just can't shake. He gets so deep down into her soul that no matter what, she'll always use him as the guide by which she measures every other man she meets. He's the man a woman will play herself for over and over again, leading her friends and family to think that she's on drugs or lost her mind. He's the man who can get you to get out of bed at two in the morning and drive across town in the pouring rain just to get a little loving. He's the one who causes aftershocks to rumble through your body at the mere memory of his bedroom antics. My dream lover was that man.

But instead of telling them about him, I went for shock value and gave them one last tale.

"Yeah, sure," I told them. "I dated some normal guys. But most of them were crazy. One almost drove me crazy too. My college sweetheart gone sour, Cali stressed me so much I almost had a nervous breakdown. We met in Spanish class and fell in love and dated for three years, but they were not a good three years. He was possessive and jealous and had a very short temper. People used to call us Ike and Tina because we argued so much, and because he thought he was a producer who was going to make me famous. It was a trip. But what folks didn't realize was how close to the truth they were. On top of all his obvious problems, he had a drinking problem, and he used to yell at me a lot. A couple of times he got violent and we fought. It was . . . ugly. I stayed in it because I loved him and I thought that I could help him. He basically kept treating me like shit in return, finally cheating on me with a stripper, getting her pregnant, and marrying her."

"Dayum," was the collective response at the table.

Then I changed the subject. Thinking about Cali put a damper on my mood that I hadn't expected; I thought I'd look back at my experiences with him and laugh, but I didn't. Whoever said that when you're a success you look back on the painful parts of your life and laugh, didn't know what the hell they were talking about. I'd had enough of talking about my pathetic love life, so I talked about the part of my life that didn't suck: my career. I chattered away about how I wanted my hair, nails, and makeup at my platinum party, and we argued over what I was going to wear until the table fell silent and I felt a tap on my shoulder. Everyone was staring at the person I felt standing behind me.

"Songbird, is that you?" a baritone voice boomed. I didn't have to turn around to see the face in order to recognize the voice. Only one man called me Songbird. It was *him*, the lover from my dreams, my ex-boyfriend, Spock. I was taken aback and clearly shaken, and I almost knocked the bottle of champagne over. *Get it together*, I scolded myself.

"Well, well, well, Spock. Imagine running into you here," I said coolly, extending my hand for him to kiss. I was the definition of a diva.

There was crazy chemistry between the two of us, and it was obvious to anyone by my feigned indifference and the grin on his face that we had history. Everyone was staring at me now and looked like they wanted to explode with questions. Spock smiled and played along, gallantly lifting my hand to his lips and kissing it, maintaining a steady gaze directly in my eyes. He has amazing, soft, light brown eyes that aren't quite hazel, and long lashes, a fact a lot of people miss because he always wears his glasses.

"You look beautiful as usual," he said, still grinning.

"Yes," I replied, turning away from him.

"Aren't you going to introduce us to your gentleman friend?" Leslie asked.

"This is no gentleman," I said with a little attitude, then laughed to cover any trace of bitterness. As much as I loved him, he'd hurt me, and I wasn't really over it. Everyone laughed with me. "I'm sorry. Leslie, Karl, Bonita, this is Spock." He shook hands with them and stood beside the table awkwardly. They looked him over from head to toe, eyes scrutinizing every inch. He looked immaculate in his Hugo Boss suit, shiny dress shoes, and crisp dress shirt with monogrammed French cuffs fastened with gold cuff links, but I could tell he felt uncomfortable.

"Well, it was good seeing you," he finally said, clearing his throat and straightening his tie. He placed his business card on the table in front of me. "In case you forgot," he said, and excused himself.

I pretended not to, but I watched him walk out of the restaurant and down the street, growing smaller and smaller until he disappeared. Back in the limo, I acted like the exchange didn't happen, but of course my crew wasn't going to let it die.

"That sure was a handsome brother back at the restaurant," Leslie said. I could tell she was waiting for me to elaborate.

"He's all right."

"So what's the deal with him?" Karl asked.

"An ex," I said casually.

"We figured as much," Bonita said knowingly. "But what's the *deal*?"

"He's a liar and a cheater and he's too wrapped up in his work. Nuff said." I dug into my purse, found my iPod, slipped the headphones into my ears, and stared blankly out the window all the way back to the hotel.

I was tripping off the fact that I literally dreamed Spock up. I wasn't expecting to see him, at least not until the party if at all. I was full of mixed emotions. Spock was a brother who took my body to heaven and my mind through hell. Things were great for us in the beginning, as they almost always are in any relationship. We were set up by mutual friends, and it seemed that we had everything in common. He loved music like I loved music, maybe even more, but he was an engineer by trade, and a very successful one at that. He had a big muckety-muck job with the city, a great loft in the West Loop, and a convertible BMW, not to mention he was very, very well-endowed.

He was also a University of Chicago graduate, was in a fraternity, and he was a gentleman. He was pretty cute too. He looked good in person and on paper, and I really cared about him. I did everything I could think of to please him, including cleaning his house and cooking for him and leaving meals in his freezer to be reheated later so he wouldn't spend so much money on junk food and eating out. Things were perfect. Too perfect.

Of course, Spock wasn't perfect, he was a cheater. I found out that he had another girlfriend, some lawyer chick, whom he neglected to tell me about. That's when his ugly side reared its head. His punk ass wasn't even man enough to face the music. He pulled a straight up bitch move and wouldn't answer my calls or texts when I wanted to get to the bottom of things. That instantly turned me off. And when we broke up, that was when I got the idea to leave Chicago, because if he was the best that Chicago had to offer, I was better off somewhere else.

I moved to Miami and didn't look back. Everything fell into place once I moved. I got a job bartending at this restaurant called Mango's on South Beach, where the staff all did sexy dances on top of the bar. We weren't strippers but wore these skimpy little

animal print catsuits and bodysuits and shook our maracas and
poom-pooms to salsa, reggeaton, reggae, you name it. I learned
a gang of Latin dances plus I met all the movers and shakers in
Miami and high-profile tourists, including plenty of people in the
music biz. I scored gigs singing and dancing backup for Latin artists, which paid the rent and bills and led to writing songs in both
English and Spanish, which led to my getting a record deal of my
own. I guess I should thank Spock for being a man-whore. If I
hadn't found out what a lying dog he was, I might have still been
in Chicago chasing dreams and him.

Leslie tapped me on the shoulder, and I removed my earplugs.

"One last question. Why do you call him Spock?" she asked. "I
know that isn't his given name."

"Because he's a nerdy know-it-all that is only half human. The
other half is a cold, emotionless Vulcan, just like Spock on *Star
Trek*. Remember how women used to dig him but he'd remain detached and aloof? That's Spock for you. He's great with facts and
figures, and his mind and body go through the motions of life, but
I'm not sure if he has a heart."

I replaced the earplugs and stared out the window. The undis-
putable truth that stared back at me in the darkly tinted glass was
that I was still in love with Spock, even if he was heartless and ma-
nipulative. It disgusted me to want someone who had hurt me so,
and disgusted me more that not only did I want him, but my body
craved him and I dreamt of him. I felt a pull in my midsection every time he was near, and I know that he felt it too. I might sound
delusional to you, but I know what I know. We just had it like that.
And it wasn't just because we had amazing sex. It was something
more. The fact that he cheated on me didn't change that.

I felt my purse vibrating from the ringing phone inside. I pulled
out my Treo and saw that there was a text message.

Great running into u. I know ur busy, but think u can
meet me 4 a drink 2nite? I'd luv 2 show u my nu crib.

I stared at the phone until the display faded to black and then
pushed a few buttons to look at it some more.

"Just go," Leslie said. She'd peeped the message over my
shoulder.

I furrowed my brow and pursed my lips crossly. I sighed and
thought about it. What did I have to lose? I had the upper hand. I
was rich and famous. Yes, he'd broken my heart, but he still wanted
me. I saw it in his eyes. Then a more sinister thought crossed my
mind. I'd finally have the chance to pay him back for breaking my
heart. What could be better than dangling myself like a carrot in
front of his nose and letting him chase me? I would tease him, drive
him crazy with lust, and then I would reject him cold. He'd be left
with the angst of seeing my image every time he turned on the
television, and the torture of hearing my voice every time he turned
on the radio, but he wouldn't have me. And I'd finally have a sense
of satisfaction and closure and be able to move on with my life.

I texted back:

Let's meet at Ruth's Chris. Maybe I'll go see your crib
later.

I thought about my dream, the reality that inspired it, and the
effect he had on me then and now. He was the best lover I'd ever
had. The things he made me feel, both physical and mental, were
dangerous. He pushed me to the limit and challenged me in every
aspect, and I had an insatiable appetite when it came to him. He
had me so twisted out of shape when we dated; I went through a
ton of ups and downs because of him.

Willpower, girl, I told myself. I had to have willpower. And I had to remember that I had the upper hand. *I'm the star! He's just a groupie.* We arranged to meet at nine.

Once we reached the hotel, Leslie and I let the glam squad use the limo to go shopping, and we went upstairs to my room. The smell of flowers hit us as soon as we opened the door to the suite.

"Right on cue," Leslie said. "I told you this was going to happen, didn't I?"

"What the hell?" I asked, looking around at the forest that had been transported into the room.

"Someone's making their move," Leslie said, nudging me with her elbow.

"These are not from Spock," I told her.

"Well no, not all of them, silly. But I bet he had an arrangement sent."

"What makes you think that?" I asked her.

"He seems like such a classy guy."

"He is classy, but flowers aren't his style. Vulcans think flowers are a frivolous gift. To buy something that will undoubtedly die is illogical," I said, doing my best Leonard Nimoy imitation, which wasn't that good. "Besides, they couldn't have gotten here that quickly."

"Only one way to find out," Leslie said. I could tell her curiosity was getting the best of her.

"I don't care. You look," I said, and nodded my approval. She ran about, collecting the cards from the various bouquets placed around the room. She rifled through them, scanning each one.

Wondering what to wear on my date with Spock, I began to sift through outfits, trying to decide if I should roll with something I already owned or wait to see what the glam squad brought me back from their shopping trip.

"Ah ha!" Leslie said with excitement. "I knew it!"

"Knew what?" I asked. Could it be? Could Spock have found a true romantic bone in his body and sent me a bouquet?

"Oh, I was just looking at this card for these flowers, but you don't care, do you?"

I rolled my eyes. "Who are they from?" I tried to conceal it, but I was a little eager to know who'd sent them.

"They're from . . . the label," she said, laughing. "Gotcha!"

"Good Lord!" I said, rolling my eyes. "I'm going to take a shower. Are we done here?" I asked her.

Leslie was staring at a card with a concerned expression on her face.

"Who's that one from?" I asked.

"Huh?" she said, looking up, then smiling a tight-lipped smile.

"You were staring at that card kind of hard. Who were the flowers from?" I asked her.

"Oh, girl, just the hotel. I couldn't understand the handwriting," she explained, then tore the card into little pieces.

Chorus

This may sound a little vain, but I had Karl and Bonita ride in the limo with me on the way to my date with Spock. I wanted to make sure I looked devastatingly beautiful when I saw him so that I'd be impossible to resist, but I planned on resisting the hell out of him. After what he did to me and how he hurt me, there was no way in hell any woman with any self-worth would give up the goodies. Right? Naturally! Still, I knew that I was going to be very, very tempted.

I was working my bright red wrap dress as I strolled into the restaurant, aware of how the silky fabric hugged every curve and moving my body in a way that would ensure that everyone else was aware of it too. I looked like I stepped off a magazine cover, with my perfectly applied makeup and not a hair out of place. I looked around to locate Spock, but he was nowhere to be seen. I took a seat at the bar and looked at my Rolex. I was giving him fifteen minutes, the same amount of time it would take for me to down a glass of single-barrel Jack on the rocks with just a splash of tonic and a twist of lime and not look like a total lush.

I felt a little conspicuous. My grand entrance was wasted on Spock, but not on the patrons who, upon recognizing me, began to murmur and point and ask for autographs. I was definitely starting to get pissed off, but kept a fake smile plastered across my face. It was nearing the fifteen minute mark and Spock was nowhere to be found. I couldn't be rude and just get up abruptly and walk out the door and leave people hanging, but I didn't want to be there if he arrived a half hour late, or worse, if he never showed up.

Finally, I excused myself from my fans to go to the ladies' room. I was going to reapply my lipstick and then hot-tail it out of there. I had to stop myself from looking at my cell phone to see if he'd called. What did it matter if he had some excuse? I was Lucky! I didn't have to wait for any man. He should have been early, if anything! I checked myself out in the mirror, and with my fake smile still in place and my head held high, walked confidently out the bathroom and toward the front door.

"Going somewhere?" Spock asked. He was standing at the hostess station, arms folded across his chest and smiling.

"You better know it, buddy. You're late! I'm outta here!" I said, moving to the side to step around him. He reached out and grabbed me, pulling me into an embrace.

"I wasn't late, Songbird," he breathed into my ear. "I just didn't want to disturb your groove. You were surrounded by fans."

"Yeah right," I said doubtfully, pulling away from him.

"I'm serious. I was here early. I stepped into the men's room. I had to make sure I looked my best, you know," he said, still grinning.

"Mmm-hmm," I replied. I wasn't buying it for a minute.

"Honestly, you can ask the hostess," he said. I pursed my lips and rolled my eyes.

"How much did you pay her to lie?" I asked.

"What? You don't believe me?" He shook his head in disbelief.

"We all know how you lie," I said sourly.

"Don't be that way," he said.

"I'm not being any way," I said quickly. I hadn't been with him for five minutes and already I was playing myself. I couldn't let him know how much our past relationship had hurt me. That would be giving him the upper hand.

Conveniently, the hostess interrupted us. "Your table is ready," she said.

"I thought we were having cocktails," I said to Spock.

"You're not hungry?" he asked. "Don't tell me you've gone all Hollywood and stopped eating. The Lucky I know will eat anything at any given hour."

"I haven't changed," I said with a laugh as we were ushered to our seats in the private dining room. I nodded approvingly and told him, "You know I want a filet Oscar, and a bunch of appetizers."

"I know, that's why I took the liberty of calling ahead to make sure they could prepare it for you," he said. "Songbird, you don't even have to look at the menu. Anything you could want is already on its way." Damn, he was as debonair as ever. That was a classic Spock move, not something he was doing just because I got famous and he was kissing up. He always took care of the smallest details and made sure that each and every single time we were together he did something small but big to show me that I was special and appreciated. Spock's only flaw was that I couldn't trust him, and that's a pretty big flaw.

I honestly don't know how he could have had two girlfriends. I know I wore his ass out, and I got plenty of his time and money. We had to have truly drained him, though I suspect that she wasn't putting it down in any department, especially not the bedroom, and he had been with her for the business connections and appearance of being with a lawyer. It damn sure wasn't for her personal appearance, because I saw her picture once, and she certainly wasn't cute. She was downright matronly.

Just thinking about it made me heated all over again. What had been so wrong with me that I didn't look good enough on paper? I had a degree and I was smart, plus I had talent and was fine and a freak. I just wasn't pulling in the big dollars nor was I well known. But I made sure he was satisfied in every way that I could. I could never understand what she gave him that I didn't. Especially since I knew that his "side counsel" was getting sloppy seconds; there's no way in hell they could have had the kind of physical connection we did. I couldn't help but wonder if she was still in his life, but I wasn't going to ask. What did it matter anyway? We were just two old friends sharing a meal.

We talked about music, one of great shared loves, and the industry. As his lips moved, I fantasized about how they would feel, nipping at my neck, licking my clavicle, and sucking my nipples. I shifted uneasily in my chair and felt my La Perlas getting moist. And I know the sexual attraction was mutual. Spock found reasons to touch my hand, rub my shoulder, and he even brushed a stray lock of hair from my eyes. I know it sounds innocent, but it was suggestive as hell. He wanted me too.

Dinner was perfect, and we finished up with key lime pie for dessert and coffee. It wasn't the coffee that had me feeling warm, though, it was Spock. I was burning up inside with uncontrollable desire, although I maintained the illusion of composure. I excused myself to go the ladies' room while Spock settled the tab. My hands shook lightly as I reapplied my lipstick, dusted my face with a sweep of powder, and washed my hands. The moment of truth was coming. The games were about to advance to the next round.

The time had come for us to decide if I would go back to see his new house. I knew that if I went, the only room I would see was his bedroom. I wanted so badly to go, but I knew that would destroy my entire plan. I wanted to tease him, torture him, and make him want me. But the plan was backfiring. I wanted to jump his bones. I didn't want to tease or beat around the bush, I wanted to fuck.

"I'm sure you have a long day ahead of you," he told me as he looked at his watch. It was around midnight.

"Yeah, I do," I said, and it was true.

"Did your car wait, or can I do the honor of escorting you back to your hotel?" he asked. I was glad he didn't ask if I wanted to see his house, because I didn't want to be tempted, but I was disappointed at not having the chance to turn him down.

"You still got that big, pretty quarter-to-eight?" I asked, referring to his BMW 745.

"Yeah. I've got a Porsche Cayenne too."

"Big baller," I teased.

"Nah, that's you."

"Yeah, it is me," I said with a laugh. He laughed too.

I don't know what came over the both of us once we got in his car. I don't know if it was the music from the smooth jazz and R&B station that was playing, or the wine we drank at dinner, but something overwhelmed us. At the first red light, we caught each other's eye, fell into each other's arms and started kissing. Not a simple, chaste peck either. I'm talking about straight-up busting slob. It was like we were two high school kids getting in last minute gropes while trying to make curfew; we were all over each other, touching every body part within reach. A horn blared from behind us and Spock reluctantly broke our embrace and drove through the intersection, but that didn't break the mood.

As soon as we pulled into a space in the hotel parking garage, we picked up where we'd left off. We kissed and touched each other urgently, pulling at each other's clothes. I unbuttoned his shirt and ran my hands across his chest. He reached inside my dress and squeezed my breasts, stroking my nipples until I was moaning and squirming.

Spock must have paid the programming director at the radio station, because every song that played seemed like it was meant just for us. I looked into his soft brown eyes as Mint Condition sang "Pretty Brown Eyes," and felt the lyrics deep down inside when the lead singer Stokely begged, "Quit breaking my heart." The next song hit me just as hard when Kem asked, "How did you find your way back in my life?" Tina Marie's "Out on a Limb" told just what was in my heart: "I've never felt so sure and yet I feel so insecure, what am I gonna do?"

"You still want me, don't you, Songbird?" Spock asked me in between kisses.

"Yes," I gasped, grabbing his crotch. "And you want me too."

His hands found his way under my dress and beneath my panties. He began to explore me, his fingers expertly stroking all the spots that made me purr.

"You're so wet," he said, plunging his fingers inside of me. He knew exactly what buttons to push and how I would respond. He teased my clit, bringing my body higher and higher, until I was about to explode. He ran his fingers along my inner lips, causing me to arch my back and spread my legs. It wasn't the most comfortable position, sitting in the front seat with the console between us, so I suggested that we move to the back seat. He ignored me, instead using the controls by his side to maneuver my seat until it lay flush against the back seat. He crawled over the console and got on top of me, kissing me deeply. Our tongues danced and intertwined and we moaned, pulling at each other's bodies in an effort to get even closer.

"You want me to fuck you, don't you?" he asked.

"Yes!"

"Say it!"

"I want you to fuck me," I moaned. "Please fuck me, baby."

He inserted his fingers into my pussy again and wriggled them around a bit while circling my clit with his thumb.

"I've got to feel that dick. Please give it to me." I was begging now. Fuck pride; I had none left. My plans for stringing him along were aborted. All I had left was desire. He prolonged the torture, continuing to finger fuck me. Finally, he pulled his fingers out, brought them to his lips, and then licked them.

"You taste so good," he told me. Then he dipped back into my pussy, this time bringing his fingers to my lips.

"Taste," he ordered. I sucked his fingertips into my mouth slowly, imitating fellatio.

"Is that how you want to suck my dick?" he asked.

"Yes," I gasped, then flipped him over like a Sumo wrestler and straddled him. Our eyes locked as I pulled his jacket off and grabbed his shirt by the collar. I kissed him deeply before pulling the fabric of his shirt until I could feel the buttons pop off and knew his chest was exposed. I licked my way down his body before yanking off his belt and opening his pants. I didn't bother to take them all the way off; I couldn't in the cramped space, so I just pushed them down around his ankles.

His throbbing dick greeted me, erect and at least ten inches long. I slid it into my mouth, savoring the taste of him. Flicking my tongue along the shaft, I looked up at him to gauge his reaction. He was definitely enjoying it. I moved my mouth up and down slowly, caressing his balls with one hand and stroking his hardness up and down with the other.

"Damn, woman," he muttered. "I missed you."

My hand pumped like a piston as I sucked harder and harder. He was on the brink of losing control and pulled me away from him by my hair, looked at me with animalistic passion and growled, "I need to feel you."

The windows of the Cayenne were all fogged up, and it wasn't the most comfortable situation, but none of that was on my mind. I needed to feel him the way he needed to feel me. I dug in my purse for a condom, rolled it on, and then lowered myself onto his monster cock. We rocked together in perfect rhythm, looking into each other's eyes, moaning, grunting, and sighing, making a melody all our own.

I rode him with all my might, thrashing and winding my hips in ecstasy. He made me feel so good, but at the same time, I started to feel so bad. The pain of the memories of how badly he'd hurt me mingled with the pleasure of him inside me, and tears started to roll down my cheeks.

"It's okay, baby," he said. "Let it out."

I didn't break down and cry, though. I gritted my teeth, grabbed him by the throat and squeezed. I was choking him, riding him furiously, and before I could stop myself, I slapped him. I thought he was going to freak out, or worse, slap me back, but he didn't. It excited him, and he thrust himself hard against my body in an attempt to match my maniacal pace. I slapped him again and again until he grabbed my hands. But he didn't stop fucking me. Instead he pulled my body against his and told me he was about to come.

"Come with me baby," he whispered in my ear, and I did.

Afterward, I felt weak in every sense of the word. He held me in his arms and stroked my hair, kissing my forehead and cheeks. He sang softly to me and told me all the little things a woman loves to hear. You're so beautiful. Your skin is so soft. Your hair is so pretty. You make me feel so good. I could feel my emotions getting caught up; the love I used to have for him had come rushing back. I was doomed.

Verse 2

I was just about to turn in and go to sleep when my cell phone rang. I almost broke my neck running to get it, and it was exactly who I'd hoped it would be.

"Hey," he said. It was Spock.

"Hey," I replied, trying to disguise the fact that I'd been anxious to answer.

"I was just calling to tell you good night. Or good morning. You know what I mean."

"Thanks. I had a good time this evening, or this morning. You know what I mean," I said. We laughed a little.

"Good . . . me too," he said, sounding a bit distracted.

There was an awkward silence.

"Can I see you again before you leave town?" he asked suddenly.

I thought about it. Was he asking me if we could fuck again before I left? That's what would happen if we saw each other again. But I wanted to fuck him again, so it didn't really matter.

"That would be nice," I told him. "Will you come to my party tomorrow night?"

"Are you sure that I won't be in the way? I saw how many fans you had tonight at dinner. You're going to be mobbed."

"I wouldn't ask if you would be in the way."

"And I wouldn't miss your party for anything in the world. I'm flattered that you invited me."

"Cool. I guess I'll see you tomorrow night. You know where it is?"

"Everyone knows where it is," he said. "It's all the city is talking about. Lucky is back in town with her platinum album and her golden voice. You did it, girl. I'm proud of you."

"Thank you, baby," I told him.

"I'm serious. Your CD is hot. You did a good job."

"It means a lot, coming from you. I guess all my hard work paid off."

We sat there a second holding the phone until he cleared his throat.

"That was good tonight, wasn't it?" He went ahead and brought up what we'd both been thinking about and pretending not to.

"Mmm-hmm. Better than good."

"I can't stop thinking about being inside of you," he said. My pussy started to juice up again from his statement. The richness of his voice was always enough to get me going, and the mere thought of how we felt together made me horny. I was satisfied, but my sexual appetite wasn't satiated. I needed to feel him, but in the meantime I'd feel myself.

"I can't stop thinking about it either," I confessed. I slid my hand beneath my panties.

"I don't want you to think that it's just about sex with you and me. You know it isn't like that," he explained.

"I know," I told him. But none of that mattered at that moment. The sex is what mattered to me.

"But the sex is so good," he said.

"I agree," I whispered.

More silence before he asked, "Are you thinking about it now? And are you doing what I think you're doing?"

"Yes. You know me so well." I wasn't just thinking about it, and he knew it. As I lay there in my bed, my free hand was stroking my pubic hair and massaging the lips of my vagina.

"What are you thinking about?" he asked.

"I'm thinking about how thick your dick is, and how good it feels inside of me," I told him.

"Mmm. And what are you doing?"

"I'm touching my clit. I wish you were here to do it for me. What are you doing, now that you know what I'm doing here?"

"I've got my dick in my hand."

"Good. I want you to stroke it for me. I want you to remember how good my pussy felt this evening, how wet it was, how tight it was. Can you do that for me?"

"I'm doing it. I'm stroking it. And I'm pretending that my hand is your pussy. It feels so tight when I first stick it in. It feels so good that I want to come right then. But I could never be that selfish. I need to make you feel good too. And I need you to stick your fingers in your pussy and rub your clit with your thumb at the same time, the way I did to you earlier tonight. Imagine that I'm there."

"Ooh, I'm doing it. You're here with me, baby, and I'm so wet for you. You don't know what you do to me, baby, you just don't know."

"I know, Songbird, I know," he told me as I whimpered and moaned. "That's right, girl, do it," he encouraged me. "Take it there."

I cut loose like I was all alone, my fingers exploring every part of me. I moaned and panted and grunted and squealed with delight. His sexy baritone voice encouraging me, telling me what to do.

"I want you to lick your fingers," he told me. "Lick them like you licked mine tonight. I want to hear it," he instructed, and I was an attentive and obedient student. I sucked the juices of my fingertips noisily and hungrily. I began to rub my clit again.

"You're gonna make me come," I told him.

"Come, girl, and keep on making yourself come. I know you can do it. I know that pussy. You know I know that pussy."

He knew my pussy, all right. It was no problem for me to reach as many orgasms as I wanted, provided I had the right mental stimulation and the right stimulation of my G-spot. It was a gift he fully appreciated and took advantage of in the past. I shook and screamed as the first orgasm hit me.

"Work that spot, girl. You remember how I used to love to watch you masturbate? You were such a showoff. I used to get so hard, just looking at you. Remember how I used to stroke my dick in front of you while you made yourself come over and over?"

"I remember. You know I remember. Do you remember how much I used to love it when you came all over me? Do you remember—" I screamed as my second orgasm washed over me. I wondered if anyone could hear me; I have a naturally loud and powerful singing voice, and even when I don't try, it carries pretty far. I kept on screaming, though. I didn't care who heard me as long as my guy was getting an earful.

"I love to hear you moan, girl. Nobody but me knows the kind of music you can make. Sing for me, baby. One more, girl, make yourself come, girl, and I'm going to come with you," he told me. That was all I needed to hear.

"I'm coming again, baby," I told him. "I need you so bad. I'm going to fuck the hell out of you tomorrow."

"I'm there, Songbird, I'm coming," he told me. I heard him shout and could imagine the look on his face. For a moment I felt as if our souls met on some other plane, some parallel universe, because our connection was so strong. I felt him inside of me, inside my heart, my body, and my mind all at once as our heavy breathing carried across the telephone line.

"I guess I ought to let you get some rest," he finally said.

"Yeah. I've got a big day ahead of me. But, uh, that was nice too," I said.

He laughed, and I could tell he felt just as silly as I did for having phone sex, but hell, we both enjoyed it, and we'd both sleep well and have pleasant dreams.

The next day, Spock was all I could think about. He didn't call, but I didn't really expect him to; we'd been on the phone half the night. And it wasn't like I could have talked to him if he had because I was so busy getting ready for my special night. I did a couple of radio satellite interviews and an online Internet chat for my fans. I love doing stuff like that, so I was on a high. Leslie was on her BlackBerry nonstop, handling last minute details and cursing anyone out who didn't meet her standards. I promised her I'd take her to the Turks and Caicos for a week when this was all over.

"Brazil, baby, you've got to take me to Brazil. You owe me big-time!" she said, and I agreed.

"We can go wherever you want. I need a vacation!" I told her.

"Well, maybe your boy Spock can take you somewhere romantic."

"Nothing happened. We're just friends, you know. We had a good time," I lied.

"Yeah right," Leslie said. She wasn't buying it. I started giggling. I couldn't help it.

"Okay, I fucked him," I admitted. "And it was good."

"You go, girl," she said, giving me a high-five.

"But this was not supposed to happen," I explained. "He hurt me. I was supposed tease him and leave him hanging."

"But you needed to get laid."

"Yeah, but now what?"

"I don't know. That's up to you guys."

"I want some more dick. It's like he's all I can think about," I admitted.

"Then get some more, girl! Who knows when you'll get the chance again?"

"That's just it. I think I kind of want to get back with him. You know, be a couple again, but I'm not sure."

"Well, I can't tell you what to do about that. Only the two of you know if that's a chapter of your lives worth revisiting. But remember, no matter what happens with this guy, you're fabulous," Leslie said. I smiled and was going to say something, but her phone started ringing again and things shifted back to business.

More flowers came to the suite. Not a lot of them, but enough to seem a little strange. I let Leslie do the honors again of collecting all the cards and seeing who they were from. None were from Spock, but I didn't care. I generally like flowers, but there is such a thing as overkill, and my allergies were starting to act up. It was also starting to feel like a damn funeral. I donated most of them to the cleaning staff and hotel employees and didn't bother to ask who they were from. Leslie didn't tell me either, she just kept her BlackBerry plastered to her ear.

The glam squad arrived, and after the obligatory hours of primping and preening, the big moment had finally arrived. It was time to head to the party. Leslie radioed the security guards she hired for the night, who were stationed outside my door. Three burly guys came lumbering into the suite, facial expressions gruff and mean.

"What's with all the bodyguard stuff?" I asked her. Usually one guy was enough.

"I just want to make sure that you're safe. You're a lot more famous than you seem to realize sometimes. It's part of your life now," she explained.

"I don't think all this is necessary. It feels weird," I said.

"Get used to it," she told me.

I went along with it even though it seemed like the bodyguards were a bit much. It made me seem like I was trying too hard to look like I was a star, but Leslie was steadfast in her decision. The bodyguards escorted us into a private elevator and then into a waiting Bentley. Two of them rode in the car with us and another rode in a separate car that trailed behind us. I felt like the President or something, and the whole thing was making me nervous.

"You're going to knock them dead," Leslie assured me, rubbing me on the back. I took a deep breath and poured myself a glass of champagne.

"To me!" I exclaimed.

"To you!" Leslie said, toasting me.

"And to you too," I said, leaning over and hugging her. "You're the best publicist a diva could have."

"I am, aren't I?" she said, laughing, as we drank our bubbly.

Spotlights flooded the sky and Hummers painted with my image and CD cover patrolled the streets around the club. There were traffic cops out making sure things went as smoothly as possible. There was a line around the corner of the club. People were dying to get inside to kick it with me. I was dripping in diamonds and looking flawless, and thanks to about two hours of preparation, it looked as if it were natural and effortless. My makeup and my hair were perfect, and my dress by Chicago designer Barbara Bates fit me like a second skin.

I tore that red carpet up. The photographers were already clicking away at the celebs who came to celebrate my success and were in the house, but they really went crazy when I showed up, pushing and shoving each other and calling my name. I posed and twirled and showed off my dress and body, knowing precisely what angles to position my limbs and hips in order to accentuate my hourglass shape. And when I stepped inside, everything was exactly as I imagined it would be. Every detail had been attended to, the club looked amazing and everyone seemed to be having a fantastic time.

I greeted my fans and the press and my guests with enthusiasm and appreciation. Chicago had come through for me, after all, and the athletes and entertainers who showed up added to the star factor. The DJ was off the hook and had everybody dancing until they were dripping in sweat.

"I told you that you had nothing to worry about," Leslie screamed over the blaring music.

"Who was worried?" I kidded her.

"Think you can handle yourself?" she asked. "I love you, but I want to mix and mingle."

"Do your thing," I encouraged her.

"Security will roll with you," she informed me.

"I'm good," I told her.

"I insist," Leslie said. "Don't let her out of your sight," she told my bodyguards. "Not even to go to the bathroom," she added, and then disappeared into the crowd.

Leslie was being overprotective. There was nothing but love there. I surveyed the room. I saw a lot of people from high school, girls who didn't like me and guys who ignored me, and I ran into a couple of guys I used to date, and oddly enough I didn't feel like throwing my success in their faces like I thought I would. I was happy; there was no reason to make anyone else miserable.

After an hour or so of getting reacquainted with old friends and hanging out, I decided to seek refuge from the crowd in my private VIP room. It was more like an oversized booth with a huge bed in it and heavy silk curtains that could be pulled shut to shield you from the crowd. It was perfect for what I had in mind. I looked in my purse to check my phone and see if I had missed calls or texts. Of course I was checking to see if Spock had called, but he hadn't. I sent him a text.

When r u coming to my party?

A little while later I received his reply:

Already here. Where r u?

I gave him directions to my private booth and instructed one of the bodyguards to make sure he got to me with no problem and to make sure we wouldn't be disturbed once he did. I was all smiles when he slipped inside.

"Hello, Songbird," he said, hugging me and holding me tight. Even over the deafening noise of the party, I could hear the desire in his voice.

"Hello," I said. "I ordered a bottle of your favorite." I motioned to the huge bottle of Bombay Sapphire sitting on the cocktail table.

"Damn, that's a big bottle."

"Well, I want to get you pissy drunk so I can take advantage of you and make you my sex slave," I told him with a wink.

"You don't have to get me drunk in order to get that," he replied.

"Oh yeah?" I asked him.

"No doubt. Your wish is my command. You know there's nothing I wouldn't do to please you." He leaned forward and kissed me. Then he put my hand on his crotch and whispered, "I jacked my dick this morning thinking about the taste of your pussy. My dick has been hard all day thinking about you."

My body shivered.

"But I don't just want your body. I want all of you. I need all of you, Lucky. I want it to be right this time. Can we take it slow and get it right? I can't let you walk out of my life again."

I thought about how much his infidelity hurt me, and how he didn't in my opinion try hard enough to make things up to me when he got busted. He was ruining the mood.

"Why talk about this all of a sudden? You didn't want to talk to me when you got caught cheating. Let's just forget about that and enjoy each other." It didn't matter who else he was or wasn't fucking. I was horny. I hiked up my dress and spread my legs. "Don't tell me how you feel. Show me," I said.

Whatever had been on his mind before was pushed aside. He stared at me, shaking his head.

"What are you waiting for?" I asked him.

He pushed me back onto the bed and pulled the straps of my dress from my shoulders, exposing my breasts.

"I want you so much," he said.

"Don't talk," I told him. I guided his mouth to my nipples. He sucked them attentively, making sure to increase and decrease the pressure, wetness, and suction, according to my body's response.

"You were always so good at that," I whispered before pushing him away. "But you were always good at something else too." I carefully removed the dress and laid it neatly on the corner of the bed.

"Take my panties off," I requested, and he did as I wanted, slowly and deliberately.

"Now, take off my shoes." He slid each of my shoes off and cradled my feet in his hands. "Suck them," I told him, lifting my toes to his mouth. He smiled and did as I asked. His tongue glided between my toes as he sucked each one gently in his mouth. He licked my instep and kissed my ankle. Then he repeated his actions with my other foot.

"I want you to eat it." I spread my legs wide so there'd be no doubt as to what I was referring to.

He licked his way up my calf and up my inner thigh in little circles. Then he spread my lips and swirled his tongue slowly around my clitoris.

"That's right," I told him. "Like that." He licked me softly and I squeezed his head between my thighs.

"Give me more," I sighed.

He nibbled and sucked at my clit, applying more pressure, and then inserting his fingers inside me and stroking my G-spot. I came almost instantly, but still wanted more.

"Now take your clothes off. I want to look at you," I ordered breathlessly.

He hesitated. "What if someone sees me?" he asked.

"You're worried about that *now*?" I asked back. "Look, my security isn't going to let anyone in. Now get naked," I ordered. I could tell he wanted to protest, but I spread my legs and began to play with my clit and he got back on track.

The sounds of hardcore gangsta rap blared through the club's speakers as he slowly peeled off his clothes until he had nothing on. I could tell by the way he was walking toward me—like a man on a mission—that he wanted and expected me to give him head. I wasn't going to, at least not now, not because I didn't want to, but because I was getting off on the feeling of being in control. Plus I had a special treat in store for him if he could follow instructions.

"Get a condom," I said, and he did even though I could tell he was a little disappointed that he wouldn't be getting a blowjob. Once the condom was on, he mounted me, entering me slowly. We both groaned as he filled me up and began to move slowly inside of me.

"You like that pussy, don't you?" I asked him.

"You know I love that pussy, girl."

"You missed this pussy, didn't you?"

"You know I missed it. I missed it so much, I can't let you go again," he said as he pushed himself deeper and deeper and I got wetter and wetter.

"Ooh, you don't want to let me go, do you?" he asked. "I can feel you gripping my dick. I know you don't want to let me go."

I squeezed and clenched my muscles, gripping him so tightly that I could feel him throbbing inside of me. He gave a few thrusts before pulling out and flipping me over onto all fours. Inch by inch he entered me from behind, working my clit with one hand and caressing my breast with the other. Every stroke made my body shake and twitch as I threw my hips at him. I needed him deeper and deeper inside of me.

"Mmm, fuck me harder," I pleaded. "Give me all of that big ass dick."

He pounded and pounded me from behind to the rhythm of the thumping bass pulsating through the club.

"I want you to fuck me, baby," I told him again. "And when you come, I want you to come in my mouth."

This comment sent Spock into overdrive, and he fucked me harder, spanking me on the ass hard. He slapped and slapped until my skin was sore and I begged him to stop and to come in my mouth. Finally he pulled out of me, yanked the rubber off, and shot a forceful load of semen into my awaiting mouth. I swallowed every drop.

"I want more," I said, smiling at him.

"Oh my God," he said, out of breath. "You're a nympho!"

"Yep," I agreed with him. I reached for his penis and he pulled away.

"I think we should continue this in another venue," he suggested, and began pulling his clothes back on. "I've got some things I want to do to you." I pouted and reluctantly pulled my clothes back on. I was so horny I could have fucked him all night in that VIP booth. And I wanted him so bad that I couldn't wait the time it would take to get to his house; my hotel was closer. Besides, we'd already wasted an opportunity to utilize my gorgeous suite with our tryst in the parking lot. I wasn't going to let another one go by the wayside.

"I've got a great suite. You didn't get a chance to see it the other night. Let's go," I suggested.

We caught up to Leslie and I informed her of my plans.

"Looks like you already got started," she said, smoothing my hair, which was probably standing out all over my head. "Go on and get out of here before somebody sees you looking crazy!"

"I don't look that bad," I said to her.

"You don't look that good either."

"Well I feel good," I said, raising my eyebrows at her. She laughed and gave me a hug. "I'm out."

"Take Security with you," she told me.

"We're just going to the hotel," I told her. If anyone was going to need a bodyguard, it was going to be Spock. I was going to tear his ass up.

"Have them follow you."

"I don't want to. I might want to do something freaky to him in the car. It's not that serious, Leslie, I'll be okay. Spock is with me." I grabbed his bicep. "He'll guard my body."

Leslie looked like she was debating, but there would have been no point in her doing so. I was going to do what I wanted, which was get the hell out of the crowded club and somewhere more private.

"Go straight to the car and straight to the suite. Don't sign any autographs. Got it?" she asked.

"Got it."

Spock and I made our way outside the club, holding hands as we waited for the attendant to pull his car around to the valet stand.

"Which whip are you in tonight, Mr. Big Stuff?" I asked him.

"The Cayenne," he said. "Why, you wanna repeat of last night?" He pulled me close to him, and as we were about to kiss, we were interrupted by someone calling my name.

"Lucky! Luuuuuccckkkkaaaayyyyy! Lucky, Lucky, Lucky!" the voice screamed. I tried to ignore the voice and kissed Spock. Then I heard the scream again. It was the most irritating sound ever.

"I know you hear me, Lady Luck! Hey, Ms. Singer Lady! I know you're not going to leave the party without saying 'bye to me!" I turned around with a practiced but gracious smile on my face. I'd deal with this fan quickly and then get back to the real business at hand.

In front of us stood a man who looked like stir-fried shit. He was so broke down he made Old Dirty look like a high fashion model. His hair was matted and hung down his back in unkempt, ill-formed, oddly shaped dreadlocks. A couple of his front teeth were missing, and the remaining ones were yellow, brown, or black with rot and decay. His Sean John sweatsuit was torn and dirty, and he stank with the funk of forty thousand years. A crackhead, no doubt.

"Have a good night," I said with a cheery wave and a smile. I looked him directly in the eyes because I think that it's disrespectful not to make eye contact with someone just because they're homeless or have issues. You never know who could be an angel in disguise. I studied the dirty face a little harder and recoiled in shock. It looked like my ex-boyfriend Cali. It couldn't be!

"Don't tell me you forgot your first love?" the grizzled man asked.

Holy Golden Gate Bridge, Batman! It was *Cali!*

"Did you get my flowers?" he asked.

"Fl-fl-flowers?" I stammered.

"I went through a whole lot to get you those flowers. I got your favorite: tulips. I stole a credit card to get you all those goddamned flowers." Cali's voice began to escalate.

"Thank you," I said, nervously looking around. Where was that damned valet? I tightened my grip on Spock's hand.

"Are you okay?" Spock asked me.

"Yeah, she's okay," Cali said to him. "I'm her first love. She gonna always be okay when she's with me. Ain't that right?" he asked me.

"What happened to you?" I asked. It wasn't that I cared about him so much as that I was curious. He had clearly fallen all the way off.

"As you can see, I'm a little down," he said. "I invested in a record company with these hustlers and to make a long story short I lost everything. But it can all be different now. We can get back together and pick up where we left off. I wrote some new stuff for you to sing. It's gonna be hot. So why don't you leave this clown and come on with me where you belong."

"You've got to be fucking kidding," I told him. "This ain't 'What's Love Got to Do with It?' You can't just come into my life after all this time. Not like this."

"But I need your help," he said, looking helpless. I felt a little sorry for him. I took a deep breath and thought about what I saw. I exhaled, hoping I wouldn't regret what I was about to say.

"Okay, well that's different. I can get you into rehab or something. I can help get you cleaned up and get your life back on track, but I can't be with you again, and we aren't going to work together. You need to focus on you," I said gently, walking toward him. "You deserve better than this."

"Lucky." Spock spoke my name but nothing else. He grabbed my hand to prevent me from getting any closer to Cali.

"Who is this clown?" Cali asked, hocking and spitting at the ground just short of Spock's Gucci loafers.

"I'm her man," Spock said.

"Uh, you are?" I asked Spock.

"Lucky baby. Why are you even talking to this corny motherfucker? It took a lot of hustling for me to get all the way here. You see I don't have shit. I got here all the way from Atlanta. I had to steal a car to stalk your ass to figure out where you were. I come all this way just for you baby, to show you that I love you, and you're hooked up with this guy? You's a selfish bitch!"

"That's enough," Spock said to Cali. "I believe the lady has had enough. I suggest that you move along."

Cali laughed so hard that he farted. Loud. And it stunk like four-day-old garbage that's been sitting in the sun.

"I suggest you move along," Cali said, mocking Spock. He

reached in his jacket pocket and pulled out a switchblade. He danced around, jabbing at the air with the knife in an attempt to intimidate us. It was working, as far as I was concerned, but Spock was cool and collected. I hid behind him, shaking.

"You don't want to try anything," he said to Cali. "You'll regret it."

"Oh, I'll regret it?" Cali scoffed. "Nigga, puh-lease! I'm gonna whoop your ass and then I'm gonna whoop this bitch's ass. Hmm, should I beat her ass before or after I fuck her? I know, I'll beat her ass while I fuck her!" Cali lunged at us. Spock pushed me aside, managing to remove me from harm's way but barely missing the swipe of the blade.

"Oh God!" I shrieked. I looked around and saw that my very big bodyguards from the club were headed our way, but before they got a chance to do shit, Spock regulated things. He started doing karate or jujitsu or something like his ass was Jet Li. By the time Security got to us, Cali was lying in a ball on the cement.

"What the fuck?" I asked Spock.

"Remember I told you I took tae kwon do growing up? I was a big-time nerd in the hood. I needed something to defend myself," he said.

I remember him telling me something of that nature but had written it off as him just trying to impress me.

"Are you okay?" he asked me.

"Yes, I'm fine," I told him.

Leslie came running up to me, hysterical, while my bodyguards grabbed Cali. Then Leslie, Spock, and I went back into the club's office, where we called the police and waited for them to arrive.

"Oh my God. This is too crazy!" Leslie said, shaking her head in disbelief. "I feel responsible. I should have had your security go wait with you. I just thought you'd be safe."

"I was safe. Spock didn't let anything happen to me," I told her. That didn't seem to matter. She still seemed riddled with guilt. "This isn't your fault, Leslie. Cali is crazy. That's obvious. He always has been, but nobody could have predicted this insanity."

"I knew you were too big to go without security," she said. "Not at an event like this. And then . . ." Leslie said, tears rolling down her face.

"What?" I asked her gently.

"There were a few cards that came with the flowers yesterday and today . . . they must have come from him."

"What did they say?"

"The cards said stuff like, 'Always watching. Always wanting. Always connected. It's me or no one.' It was creepy, but it just seemed like run-of-the-mill overzealous fan stuff. I was going to tell you, just after your big party. I didn't want you to worry about anything. So I hired the extra security and had them stick with you. I just figured you'd be safe with Spock and needed some privacy. It was a dumb move. What if something would have happened to you because I was slipping? Oh God, I'm so sorry." Leslie was crying and I could tell she was really shaken up. I felt like I needed to be strong for her.

"It's not your fault," I said. "You did what I wanted you to do. You wanted to see me happy. It was an honest mistake." I wrapped my arms around her and hugged her.

We ran down the whole episode to the police.

"I think that drugs are an issue," the officer filling out the report said. "We found a crack pipe and quite a few rocks in his pocket. You press charges, we'll make sure he does the maximum, and he'll be out of your hair for a long time."

"Oh, I intend to," I told him. "I'll take this as far as it needs to go."

The officer handed me some paperwork and left.

"Are you okay, Songbird?" Spock asked me.

"Hell no," I told him. "I can't believe that fool showed up here and tried to . . ." My voice cracked as I broke down. It all hit me at once. My ex-boyfriend had basically stalked me and had planned on doing who knows what.

"I am not going back to that hotel," I announced. "I know I probably have nothing to worry about, but who knows what other sickos are waiting for me. It just feels creepy. I won't feel better until I talk to the police again."

"We'll check you into another hotel," Leslie said. "I'll get right on it." She pulled out her cell phone, but her hand was shaking so much that it fell to the floor.

"You can stay with me," Spock offered. "I have more than enough room."

Leslie and I looked at each other.

"I think that would be a good idea," she said. "You don't mind if a bodyguard sits outside the house? You know, to keep an eye on things of course."

"He can wait inside. Like I said, I have more than enough room, and a state of the art alarm. He's more than welcome. In fact, I insist that you come too," he said to Leslie. "You're in no condition to be at the hotel alone."

"I'll get room service, pour a good, stiff drink, take a bubble bath and lose myself in my work," she said, attempting to compose herself. "I'll be fine. I'll have a bodyguard come with me."

"Are you sure?" Spock asked her.

"I'm sure. Tell him, kid," Leslie said.

"Leslie lives for her work. Keeping her from it for the night would drive her crazier than staying at the hotel. She's from New York, she's tough," I said, trying to lighten things up. It was the truth. Leslie was a professional, the best publicist in the biz. If anyone could handle this kind of drama, it was her.

"Queensbridge, baby," she said, smoothing her clothes and wiping her face. "No doubt."

"Make sure to let him comfort you," Leslie whispered in my ear as she gave me a hug and we parted.

Chorus

The bodyguard, Spock, and I rode in silence from downtown to Spock's new house in a recently gentrified neighborhood called Bronzeville on the south side. The area had changed so much from my childhood. Dilapidated buildings were now replaced with condos and renovated brownstones. The asking prices still seemed a little steep, though; an uneasy feeling crept over me as we rolled through the streets. The buildings might have changed, but the unsavory characters still remained. Crackheads lurked with heads down, their eyes frantically scouring the cement for a dropped rock. Transients begged on corners. It reminded me of what had transpired with Cali earlier. I just wanted to get away from it all.

"Where do you live?" I asked impatiently.

"Just around the corner, on St. Lawrence," Spock informed me. "Don't worry, Songbird, we're almost there. Besides, no one can hurt you when you've got us around looking out for you. Ain't that right, man?" he asked the bodyguard.

"No doubt," he agreed.

We pulled into Spock's garage, he deactivated the alarm with a remote, and we entered the house through the back door. It was a breathtaking, tastefully decorated, updated graystone with lots of the original finishes and trim. A woman had to have helped him with it.

"Look, we may as well get this out of the way," I blurted. "If you've got a girl, you may as well tell me. I appreciate what you're doing for me, but I don't want any drama."

"Lucky, chill. I don't have a girlfriend. My mother and sister helped me decorate. You remember my sister, the artist, right?"

"Yeah I remember," I admitted.

"That's the girl who helped me pull this all together. I know that's what you're thinking. Calm down, okay. I want you to relax. Let me take care of you."

The bodyguard looked at me and then at Spock. I'm sure he felt awkward as hell. Spock let him off the hook. He fixed me a glass of wine, told me to sit on the couch, and gave me the remote control. Then he showed the bodyguard how the alarm worked and set him up in a guest bedroom.

"Come upstairs Lucky," Spock told me, and I followed him up a winding staircase. We went into his bedroom, which was dark, but he didn't turn on the lights.

"Just relax," he said, guiding me to the bed. I kicked off my shoes and squinted to make him out. He lit candles placed around the room. I couldn't help but wonder who else he'd lit those candles for, but shooed the thought from my mind and gulped down my wine.

Spock went into the bathroom, where I heard him running water in the tub. He came out and told me to get undressed and get in. I hesitated.

"Don't get shy on me now," he teased.

"It isn't that. It's just that I'm really questioning my judgment when it comes to men. You see what happened earlier. I seem to be a really bad judge of character. I attract all the wrong men. Why are we here, Spock?" I asked. My mind was spinning from the incident outside the club with Cali. I felt like I couldn't trust myself when it came to who I loved.

"I am nothing like that man. Songbird, I still love you. Is that what you need to hear?" he asked. I could tell he was trying not to get frustrated.

"Only if you mean it," I admitted.

"I do. Lucky, this isn't about you being famous, or me just trying to get some ass or whatever you might be thinking. I love you, and everything was fine before the night went wrong, but I'm trying to change it. Will you let me do that?" he asked. I sighed and took off my clothes.

"I'll will," I said. I stepped into the warm, sudsy water, and Spock activated the jets that sent powerful and relaxing bursts of water onto my weary body.

"Want some music?" he asked.

"Sure," I told him.

"What do you want to hear?" he asked.

"You're so good at telling me what I want to hear. Why don't you choose?" I snapped. I couldn't help it. I knew I'd been though a lot, but a part of me couldn't trust why he was being so nice to me and was so frustrated that I lashed out on the person closest to me.

"I'm going to ignore that comment," he said. "I'll play you some of my stuff. But don't worry; I'm not trying to work you over to help me get a deal. And if you hate it, you can feel free to tell me. But I don't think you will." I did believe that he just wanted to share his music with me, no strings attached. That was one of the things that made our relationship in the past so special. We collaborated on lots of songs, just fooling around in his home studio, and it always seemed to just fit. To borrow a corporate term, there was a synergy between us.

He cued up a couple of tracks he'd been working on, and I hummed quietly along, freestyling and improvising lyrics here and there. My tension dissolved into the water, and soon I was totally at ease, singing softly while I lounged in the luxurious bath.

"I want to hear you better," he said. He knelt beside the tub and turned the water jets off. I smiled and sang a little louder.

"We sound good together," he commented.

"We always did," I replied.

"How's the water?" he asked. I gazed up at him, thinking about what we had done earlier, and what we were on our way to do before we were interrupted by Cali's foolishness.

"Why don't you find out for yourself?" I asked him. Spock was disrobed and in the tub with me in less than sixty seconds. We were like two little kids in the soapy water, splashing each other and putting bubble beards and hats on each other. You know I had to be feeling good to let him mess up my hair and makeup. The glam squad would be thoroughly pissed when they saw what I'd done with all their hard work.

"Come here," he said. Luckily, the tub was large enough for me to move around easily. He opened his arms and I slid in between them. We sat there, soaking, and every now and then he'd caress my body or kiss me on the cheek or neck.

"You're going to turn into a raisin," he teased me, lifting my hand and inspecting my wrinkled fingertips. "Let's get out."

I pouted, splashing my hands on the water's surface and poking out my bottom lip like an impudent toddler.

"Come on, you big baby," he said. "Lay down on the bed."

I got out of the water quickly and cocked my eyebrow at him suggestively.

"I'm going to give you a massage," he said. "Get your mind out of the gutter."

"I like my mind in the gutter, and you like it too!"

"We're getting to that," he said. "You're always in such a rush. You always try to make things happen. Calm down. Enjoy the journey," he said.

He spread a bath towel on his king-sized bed and I laid down on it. I buried my face into his down comforter, not caring if I smeared what remained of my makeup on it. Hell, I wanted to leave a reminder of myself behind in case any chicks came over. Besides, if he didn't like it, he had a good job—he could pay to get it cleaned or buy another one. I could smell a stick of incense burning as Spock squeezed some oil between his palms and rubbed them together. They were warm when he placed them on my body and began to rub and knead my shoulders.

"You have such a beautiful body," he told me as he caressed my skin with what smelled like almond oil. He took his time while working on my lower back, hips, ass, and thighs. I was weak beneath his touch, and I knew that my inner thighs were going to be particularly slippery, and not from the oil. He made his way slowly down my calves and finally to my feet, working on my strained insteps, massaging the damage from the stilettos I adore. I moaned and sighed as he worked out every bit of stress I had, and I was ready to take the rubdown to the next level. I think he was too, because he stopped rubbing my backside, flipped me over and made that face men make when what they see what looks real good to them.

But he didn't jump my bones. He poured oil directly on my

breasts and looked into my eyes as he began to rub it in, his hands gliding and sliding over my nipples. I returned his stare, biting my lip and thrusting my chest upward. I know he liked to drag things out and savor every moment, and I loved that about him, but I could rarely wait when I was near him.

"Kiss me," I whispered. He leaned down and kissed me, and I could feel the hairs on his chest sliding over my breasts. I wrapped my legs around his and kissed him deeply, hungrily sucking his tongue into my mouth as we squished and slid against each other.

He pulled away. "Not yet," he said.

"Come on, baby. Why do you torture me like this?" I asked.

"I told you, you need to appreciate the journey. You know you're going to get there . . . a bunch of times," he said, and chuckled softly. He continued his rubdown, making me squirm beneath his fingertips.

"I want to feel your cock inside of me right now," I said forcefully. I needed him to take me to the place that only he knew, and I needed it right then. He stopped touching me and just looked at me. He looked like he was going to say something, but he didn't. I couldn't wait anymore. "Please, please, I need you now," I whimpered.

"Shh," he said, putting his finger to my lips. I stuck my tongue out and licked it before quickly drawing it into my mouth and sucking. He pulled it out and I nipped it gently with my teeth. His hand drifted between my legs, and I eagerly spread them, giving him full access. His nimble fingers rubbed my clit until I was at a fever pitch.

"You're such a freak," he told me.

"Yeah," I panted. "And you love it."

"I do," he replied.

"Stop all that talking and put your mouth to work," I said. Our relationship and our lovemaking were like tug of war, a constant battle of will and strength. I always lost, but I put up a good fight.

"You always tell me that," he said.

I grabbed him by the back of the neck and pulled him down to my crotch, but instead of him diving in the way I wanted, he rained soft kisses across my mound. He gently opened me up with his thumbs and forefingers and licked slowly, teasingly, around my pearl. He brought me to three orgasms, kissing me and stroking my face, giving me a few minutes to rest after each one before beginning again.

At last he reached into the nightstand and got a condom; he put it on quickly and pulled my body to meet his. He entered me forcefully, and I could feel him grow even harder as I engulfed him in my wet sweetness. He pumped powerfully on top of me for what felt like an hour until he could barely move and we switched positions.

He lay down on the bed and I sat on top of him again and rode him, this time turning my back to him and facing the mirror that sat perched atop his dresser. We both watched our reflections illuminated by the flickering candlelight as I reached down and gently played with his scrotum, bouncing up and down his pole, my breasts bouncing up and down with me.

Spock spread my ass cheeks apart and gently wiggled a finger inside. I gasped, tensed, and then relaxed as he reached around with his other hand and massaged my clitoris. Before long he had three fingers inserted in my ass, and the sensation of the three different kinds of stimulation sent me soaring. I screamed his name over and over, not caring if I woke the whole damn neighborhood.

Soon he exploded as well, and I watched the expression on his face in the mirror with sensual satisfaction. We curled up in each other's arms and held each other tight. We didn't speak. We didn't dare break the perfect silence between us, and soon drifted off to sleep.

Bridge

The next morning, Spock treated me to breakfast in bed. He slipped pieces of fresh tropical fruit between my lips, kissing me after each bite and savoring the sweet taste of nectar on my lips.

"How do you feel?" he asked me, nibbling on my neck.

"Much better," I told him.

"Well I'm about to make you feel even better."

Spock slid beneath the sheets and began to lick and suck at my nipples, gently biting each one before going lower and lower until he was nestled between my legs. He parted his lips and sucked my clit between them before plunging his tongue in and out. I was shivering, bucking my hips upward, straining to meet his tongue.

"You taste like fruit," he said, before throwing my legs back over my shoulders and fucking my moist slit with his tongue. He gazed into my eyes with a look of pure mischief, before grinning, and then he licked the puckered opening of my anus.

"What are you doing?" I gasped.

"You know what I'm doing," he said, grinning, and continued to lick the crack of my ass, teasing me before inserting his tongue inside the tight crevice. I let out a small yelp and squirmed to change position.

"Oh no you don't," he said. "I'm going to lick it, get it nice and wet, and then I'm going to stick my cock inside of you."

My eyes widened in fear.

"I won't hurt you, baby," he promised. "I'm going to go nice and slow. And you're going to love it."

I held my breath and my body tensed, but soon I was relaxed and gave in to the sensation of him giving slow, seductive licks to my backside. Spock stopped, put on a condom, and lifted me up, flipping me on all fours. He held onto my shoulder firmly.

"I'm going to put it in now. I want you to relax. If you don't like it, we'll stop. But I know you're going to like it. I warmed you up with my fingers last night, and now I'm going to give it all to you and you're going to take it. You're going to take it and give it back to me."

Millimeter by millimeter, I felt my rectum expand. There was pain intermingled with pleasure and I felt dizzy and weak from the sensation. Spock reached around to work my clit, heightening my pleasure, and before long he was at least halfway inside me, which was good enough for both of us, because we came soon after, him clutching me and muttering my name and that I was beautiful in my ear as we did.

As we lay there in the bed, spent, I wondered what it was about Spock that made me so willing to give every part of my body to him. Was I sexually addicted to him? Was it because I loved him? And more important, did he feel the same way for me, or was this just a fling? Sure, he'd tried to verbally reassure me, but didn't all men say what they felt they had to in order to get what they wanted?

The sound of Spock's BlackBerry vibrating snapped me out of my thoughts, as he untangled his arms and legs from my body and got up to retrieve it. He frowned as he read a text message.

"Don't hate me," he said.

"Don't tell me," I told him. "You have to go to work."

"There's a massive computer outage at the mayor's office. Everything's screwed up around there."

"But can't you just delegate the work?" I asked. I wanted to spend as much time with Spock as I could before I had to leave. Who knew what would happen between us once I was out of sight? No matter what our fate, I wanted to remain in the bliss of the present for as long as possible.

"Not if I want things to be done right, and not if I don't want the mayor to tear me a new asshole." We looked at each other and cracked up laughing at the new asshole reference.

"You're a pervert," I teased him.

"So are you."

I spent most of the day lounging around, watching TV, something I never get a chance to do. Then I went into Spock's home studio and messed around with equipment and listened to the stuff he'd been working on. While I was fooling around, experimenting with making beats, the phone in the studio rang. I should have ignored it, but I couldn't. I looked at the caller ID. It read: JURIS PRESCOTT. I knew that name. It was his other ex-girlfriend, the one he had when we dated before. That motherfucker! Nothing had changed! I was going to kill him, but not until I handled one bit of important business. I did something I never did before, but that I should have done years ago when Spock's little love triangle first became apparent. I picked up the phone and pressed the Talk button.

"Hello?"

"Uh, hello? Who is this?" Juris asked, surprised.

"This is Lucky, Juris," I told her. There was silence. "Do you remember me?"

"Of course," she said. "How could I forget? I just wasn't expecting to hear your voice."

An awkward silence.

"Can I speak to him?" she asked.

"No, you can't," I said.

Another silence.

"Why are you calling him, Juris?" I asked.

"Why are you there?" she asked back. She didn't say it with a funky attitude; in fact, she seemed amused, which just pissed me off even more.

"You know what?" I asked. I was about to read her from A to Z when I realized that it wouldn't solve anything. "Never mind," I said and hung up.

This was stupid. I didn't need to ask her why she was calling. I already knew why. He was still playing the both of us. I was getting the fuck out of there. If I didn't by the time Spock came home, there would be a bloodbath. I had way too much going for me to ruin my life over some jerk. I'd just pulled on my clothes when my cell phone rang. It was Spock, of course.

"What do you want?" I barked into my cell phone.

"I just spoke to Juris."

"So did I," I said.

"Oh good," he said, sounding relieved. "So then you know that nothing is going on."

"No, I don't know that," I told him. "In fact, I'd say the opposite is true. I should have known better. You're still the same lying motherfucker you were before. Nothing's changed."

"Songbird—" he said. I cut him off.

"Don't Songbird me! Don't call me that stupid name! Don't say shit to me!" I screamed.

"Lucky, damn it, listen. I don't want you to leave. Promise me that you won't leave before I get there. I can't make it home just yet, but I'll be there around eight." I looked at the clock. It was six. "Lucky, please? I hope you're still there when I get there. We need to talk about this because it really isn't what you think."

I hung up my cell. Damn it! Was I going to stick around to hear whatever lame excuse he was going to offer? I was. But I wasn't going to let him know that. I was going to make him wonder until he brought his ass home. But I knew that I was going to stay, even though I tried to convince myself a million ways that I shouldn't. There was one thing that overruled all my arguments: I loved him. There was no escaping it. And it was because I loved him that I told myself that maybe there was a reasonable explanation for her call.

My bodyguard must have heard me screaming because he came busting into the room. I screamed in shock.

"You okay, Lucky?" he asked, looking around. I placed my hand over my chest, where I could feel my heart racing like Seabiscuit.

"Yeah," I told him. "I was on the phone."

"Oh," he said. "Well, are you sure everything is all right?"

"Yeah," I told him.

"Do you want to stick around here?" the bodyguard asked. "We can go back to the Peninsula if you want. We can move your things, but since you're leaving tomorrow, you don't have to if you don't want. I'll make sure you have nothing to worry about."

"No, that's all right," I said. "I have some unsettled business to take care of."

I didn't have any more work-related business to do for the remainder of my stay. I just wanted to hit Michigan Avenue for some shopping. But I checked in with Leslie while I waited for Spock to return. She pressed me for details of the night, which I kept to myself. And I didn't tell her about the phone call from Juris. I just told her that I'd fill her in later, which I would undoubtedly do. I just hoped I wouldn't be weaving another tale of woe.

Spock finally made it in, and my bodyguard and I both eyeballed him with sour looks on our faces. I excused the bodyguard, and Spock and I went into the kitchen. He fixed us a couple of cocktails and then we slipped outside to sit on his deck.

"Okay," I said. "You've had enough time to come up with a good-ass story. So let's hear it."

"There's no story. Juris and I are just friends. That's all," he said.

"Why was she calling you?" I asked him.

"Do you really want to know why?" he asked.

"Hell yeah!"

"She saw on some entertainment show the story about your ex-boyfriend pulling a knife on you. She wanted to know if I'd talked to you and if you were okay."

"That's bullshit and you know it," I said.

"For real. Juris and I are over. We never belonged together in the first place. Who do you think encouraged me to go for another chance with you?"

"Damn sure not her!" I said.

"Well, it's true," he said. "I wanted to move on after you left, but I couldn't. Not with her, not really with anyone. I didn't stay at home knitting, but no one could take your place. Nothing compares to you. Juris and I stayed friends and, well, I used to talk about you to her sometimes."

"I wish I believed that."

"Well, you should. Her husband even knows how I feel about you," he said.

"Her husband?" I said, shocked.

"Yeah. She got married a few months ago. To my frat brother."

"How the hell did that happen?" I asked.

"He always liked her. And when things fell apart—"

"When you got busted," I said, correcting him.

"Whatever. He stepped to her, and she liked what he had to say. She told me she wasn't going to wait for me to make up my mind. They're expecting a baby."

I felt stupid, but not really. I was just looking out for myself and for my heart. I was glad that I stuck around, though, because if I hadn't over a misunderstanding, then I really would have felt stupid.

"I love you, Lucky. You're the one for me. No one else," he told me. I didn't know what to say, which was cool, because he kept talking. "Call her back if you want to. You didn't give her a chance to tell you. She was just surprised to hear you answer the phone. Talk to her husband. Look, I'm going to prove to you that I'm sorry I ever let you go. And I know that I wasn't the man you needed me to be. But I can be now. Don't give up on me yet. I really care about you and I need you in my life."

I took a moment to look up at the night sky for stars, as if they could guide me, but I didn't see any. The night sky was either too cloudy or maybe stars don't shine as bright in Chicago. Since I couldn't find what I was looking for, I went on ahead and said what was on my mind.

"I love you too. But I don't want you to hurt me again. I will not be your fool again."

"I'm not going to make a fool out of you."

He said those words with what appeared to be earnest sincerity, and yet I still wasn't sure.

"What am I going to do with you?" I asked.

"Just love me," he said.

"Loving you is easy," I told him. "Being in love with you is what's hard."

We sat there on the deck, holding hands, saying nothing. Although many questions lingered between us, we sat in peaceful silence. Time would be the answer.

Repeat Chorus

I can't explain why I love him, why I can't move forward without him. I guess I just like having him along for the ride, although I'm afraid that one day I'll look over on the passenger's side and it will be empty. But for now, he's there, right where I need him to be. What the future holds for us, the uncertainty of it, all scares me. I still have issues with trusting Spock. Fool me once, shame on you, fool me twice, shame on me and all that shit. Maybe one day the past will truly be buried and we can live happily ever after. But I'm happy right now, and that's what counts.

Fade Out

MÉTA SMITH was born in Philadelphia and raised on the south side of Chicago. She is a graduate of Spelman College, where she received her bachelor's degree in English. She is a DJ, a creative writing teacher, lecturer, and the author of two novels, *The Rolexxx Club* and *Queen of Miami*. She lives in Miami and Chicago with her son, Jordan.